I0780823

N
MOUNT BRENNE
FIORAN
THE KEEP
FORGOTTEN FOREST
FIORAN CASTLE
WEST MARKET SQUARE
DOVENEER
RACINE
JACKLANDS

THE KINGDOM OF ELARIA
NORTHERN PORT MORANA
KENDALL
EAST MARKET SQUARE
SOLUME
SYNAN
AGRONA SEA
MINES
ISSLOTS
T. MUNRO 2021

Other books by Emilee King

Arie's Story:

Surviving on a Whisper
Surviving through the Night
Surviving to the End
Surviving the After

Elarian Chronicles:

Pieces in the Cinders
Cracks in the Tower

THE ELARIAN CHRONICLES

CRACKS IN THE TOWER

EMILEE KING

ISBN-10: 1966173069
ISBN-13: 978-1966173069

Cover designed by MiblArt
Map designed by Tiffany Munro

For every princess still locked in a tower, thinking her story is over.

It's not.

CHAPTER 1

THE HIGHEST WALLS

She knew the monster was with her.

Rosalind's breath stuttered as she stood frozen in the inky dark, every muscle stiff
and sore from being rigid so long.

How long *had* it been? She didn't know. She never knew.

It always felt like years.

Electricity shot through the stagnant air around her, and it smelled like something had burnt. The tightly coiled dread in her stomach unfurled, spreading through her veins like slow rolling magma that scorched her from the inside out.

A sinister presence loomed behind her. The hair rose up on the back of her neck, but she forced herself to stay still, to stay facing forward. Even when the darkness lifted. Even when her eyes tracked the all too familiar scene in front of her.

She couldn't look back. That was even worse than what lay ahead.

A sharp breath slid through her teeth when the boy entered her line of vision. After all this time, she still winced when she saw him run and jump, stumbling with the intoxicating invincibility of childhood. The blissful innocence in his eyes sent a fissure through her feeble heart.

She couldn't watch him lose it again.

But, inevitably, the monster rose up and focused its sight on the young boy. Though she knew what would happen—that she couldn't stop it no matter how hard she tried—her hands clenched into fists, her nails digging into her palms. The energy behind her grew, surging, sucking the life out of her with each shaky breath.

Rosalind knew what would happen.

Again.

Still, she lurched forward, desperate to save the boy this time, but she had barely taken a step when the energy around her pulsed and crackled. The atmosphere split open for a moment. Rosalind had only a second to register the taste of burnt metal in her mouth, the roaring in her ears, before a force blew her back and she skidded across the ground.

Trembling, Rosalind jerked her head up, eyes darting around in a desperate attempt to find the boy, hoping vainly that he had somehow escaped.

A broken sound erupted from her when she saw him: twisted, bruised, in a puddle of red.

Horror shook her bones. She scrambled back, colliding with the presence behind her, and instinctively turned around.

Her scream tore her throat in half.

* * * * * * *

Rosalind shuddered awake with her hands still in fists, realization dawning before she was even fully conscious. She didn't open her eyes as reality snapped back into her, as she became aware of her clinging nightshirt damp with sweat, the dull ache in her stomach, and the slight tug of her hair on her scalp. Despite the harrowing nightmare, she huffed a sigh when she recognized it must be morning.

Her body had become accustomed to a schedule without her permission. Like clockwork, she'd just opened her eyes when a soft knock sounded on her door.

"Rosalind," a melodic voice called from the other side. "Breakfast."

The sound of footsteps padded away. Rosalind's mom had stopped expecting a response whenever she came to her sanctuary of a room. Even with so many thick walls between them, Rosalind could imagine the way her mom's honey hair shimmered as she swayed down the hallway. Genevieve Corona, with golden skin and soft curves, was all grace and warmth, as if life itself bled from her dainty fingertips.

Rosalind was nothing like her mother.

She was all angles, unruly inky hair, and harsh pale skin. A black hole that sucked everything up only to spit it back out. Always taking, but never really gaining.

Rubbing her face, Rosalind yanked enough hair out from under her pillow to push herself onto her elbows, then cracked her eyes open. The thick curtains were still drawn over her lengthy windows, keeping her room shrouded in shadows despite the sun rising behind them, and the air was warm and stuffy, too, indicating how much time had passed since she'd last opened the door.

Groaning, she fell back onto her pillow with a cushioned thud. Time lurched and dragged, swirling with the groggy darkness. By the time another knock sounded, strong and assured, Rosalind had barely moved.

"Rosalind," her father called, always chirpy at eight in the morning. His voice awakened some of Rosalind's childhood awe, how she marveled that one person could be so powerful and soft at the same time. "Are you up for a trip out today?"

Echoing the memories of yesterday, the day before, and every day before that for years, Rosalind shifted her head enough so she could say, "No, thanks."

"Okay, then." He never sounded angry or hurt, but she knew serving on the royal council had perfected his ability to keep his emotions invisible. "I'll see you tonight."

She gave a muffled, noncommittal grunt in response. They both knew he wouldn't be seeing her tonight.

Once his footsteps faded, Rosalind let out a long breath. If her father was upstairs, then breakfast was over, and if breakfast was over, then it might be safe for her to sneak into the bathroom unnoticed.

Get up, she told herself, but even the need to use the bathroom couldn't motivate her lethargic muscles into motion. *Get up.*

It's too hard, her body whined back.

She couldn't argue with that.

A few hours passed, the faint light peeking out from the curtains changing as the sun climbed higher in the sky. Rosalind had managed to flip onto her back despite the massive pile of her hair that was tangled up in her pillow. Groaning, she started to sit up.

Another knock. Quick and fleeting, like it was running out of time.

She froze.

"Rosy?"

She counted the heartbeats as they pounded in her chest. Her fingers twitched into fists, and she glanced at her nightstand. It was the perfect barricade for the little door next to her bed—he couldn't get through the secret tunnel that used to connect them if she blocked it. He probably couldn't even fit through the opening anymore.

But she glanced anyway. Just to check.

"Hey, Rosy, you there? You wanna come out and play?"

Rosalind closed her eyes, her nails biting into her palms.

"Rosy?" Even though he did this every day—sometimes multiple times a day—she still winced when she heard her younger brother's voice. "Rosy, it's so nice and warm outside. You wanna come?"

Rosalind was afraid to breathe, which was ridiculous considering Zachary *knew* she was there. But still. She was afraid to breathe, to move, to acknowledge her own existence.

"Raf says the gardens are gonna bloom soon," Zachary babbled on in his usual excited chatter. "He says there's gonna be more colors than I even know. Can you believe that Rosy? Do you wanna come see it? I was out there earlier and I let Maldo hop around. I'm pretty sure he might actually be a prince. There are stories about that, about princes being frogs but they are actually princes. Will you kiss it Rosy? If you kiss it, he might turn into a prince. He needs your help, really. Maybe he'll give you really cool shoes or something. Will you kiss him Rosy? You wanna come outside and play with me and Maldo? I'll let you guys get to know each other first. You don't actually have to if you don't want to, but I thought it would be interesting to see."

Rosalind sat in perfect silence until Zachary ran out of steam. Despite it being ages since she'd actually looked him in the eye, she knew exactly how the enthusiasm lighting up his freckled face would slowly start to dim. She could see his expression bloom into a pout like a wounded puppy dog. Years ago, Rosalind would have done anything when his face fell that way.

"Okay," Zachary finally said, deflating. "Well, you're probably busy. That's okay. Um, I'll be outside playing if you want to come. You really can. Okay."

There was another moment of quiet laced with his fragile hope so sharp and poignant that Rosalind felt it like a dagger in her side.

Then the moment passed. Zachary sighed in defeat, and the carpet audibly pressed as he made his way down the hall.

Three minutes later, Rosalind regulated her breathing. Ten minutes later, she finally pried her fingers from their fist and sunk back into her pillow.

* * * * * * *

The steps creaked underneath Gothel as he trudged down the stairs, wiping sleep from his eyes. He'd managed to get another two hours of muddled sleep after Boone's early—and vulgarly noisy—awakening. But he still felt drained. In the tiny shack they called home, you could hear every breath from everyone, whether they were upstairs or downstairs. It made Boone's obnoxious dawn rising like a horn blowing in one ear. Like Gothel, Ulf and Tor were quiet as whispers, but Calder wasn't much better than Boone.

Gothel sighed. He hated mornings.

Stifling a yawn, he paused halfway down the stairs when he heard muffled voices from the kitchen directly below him.

"Of course not!" Boone thundered, his voice as callused as a worker's palms. "We have the time. We'll figure it out."

"It's been months," Calder argued, his voice velvet in comparison. "We've waited too long. Consequences could come any day now, and we both know they aren't going to be pretty."

Boone wouldn't budge. "It won't come to that. We'll be fine." Then the door squeaked open and slammed shut, and Calder muttered a curse under his breath.

Gothel waited a second longer, then descended the rest of the stairs into the kitchen. The space was a narrow rectangle with a table running along one wall and a cracking counter and sink against the other. There was barely enough room in the middle for people to walk through single file.

Calder stood by the sink, twirling a cup in his hand. He looked absolutely ridiculous in a posh, fluffy robe he had stolen. With his styled hair and debonair smile, he resembled a young, rich nobleman who had lost his way and somehow ended up in a rotting square shack with a mice problem and barely enough space to breathe. The contrast hurt Gothel's eyes, even though he knew Calder was just as penniless and orphaned as he was.

The tiny crease of concern on Calder's forehead lifted as he smiled. "Mornin', G."

Gothel jerked his chin toward the door Boone had slammed. "What's wrong with him?"

"Does there have to be something wrong for him to be a grouch?"

Gothel shrugged. Though he'd hung around Boone's crew for a few years now—*had it really been that long?*—the man still seemed annoyed every time Gothel walked into the room. Gothel didn't take it personally; Boone wasn't one of his top five favorite people either.

Calder sighed, a rare flame of sincerity lighting in his eyes.

"He's…agitated. About the money."

Agitated? Just agitated? Gothel hadn't slept right for weeks because of that stupid money, and Boone was just 'agitated.' Perfect.

"As he should be," Gothel retorted, yanking a pitcher of juice from the lukewarm icebox and frowning at the suspicious film on top of the liquid. He nearly saw red every time he thought about the money: money that Boone had borrowed from a crime lord, money that had unwittingly marked Gothel and the rest of them as debtors.

Gothel hated debts anyway—there was no dignity in owing someone. But being indebted to Pepperjack, Elaria's king of crime and most notorious criminal, was nothing short of a death sentence.

And Boone hadn't told them. Hadn't consulted any of them about signing their souls away. He'd just done it, 'for the good of the group,' claiming they were that desperate, that they needed that money to survive.

And for what? Spoiled juice?

No, there had to be more to the story than Boone let on.

Calder just gave him a look, as though parenting a child. Gothel rolled his eyes. Calder could play any part you gave him, but his favorite around Gothel was a schooling older brother.

"Look." Calder took the juice from Gothel and poured himself a cup. "Don't start, okay?" He flashed one of his signature smiles—smiles that often won him trust, money, and women. "It's too early."

Despite having known him for years, Gothel didn't know how he could smile like that: carefree yet knowing. He acted as if life were grand and easy yet knew firsthand it was not. It seemed contrived to Gothel. Even if he didn't know Calder as one of the greatest con men in the kingdom, he'd still never trust that easy smile that always lit his face.

Nobody was *that* happy.

"Stirring up trouble, Little G?" a sweet voice sang in his ear.

Gothel forced himself not to startle. Tor prided herself on being the only one who could still sneak up on him—or anyone, for that matter.

"Just hunting breakfast," Gothel replied, casually leaning out of her touch and sitting down at the table, notably breakfast-less.

Calder gave Tor a smile—who appreciated it more than Gothel had—and plopped down next to Gothel, swinging his legs over the bench. Tor strode around the table and slid into a seat across from them. She was clearly off duty from work: she wore a simple grey shirt and dark pants with her ebony hair pulled into a ponytail, displaying the birthmark and blemishes on her face she usually hid. Even then, without trying, she was the most gorgeous woman Gothel had ever seen.

"Orange?" Calder offered Gothel a bruised fruit from the stolen basket on the table.

Gothel shook his head. Calder shrugged and started peeling it for himself.

"Nothing here up to your standards, Little G?" Tor asked with a lively smirk. Leaning forward, she rested her chin on two dainty hands, both just small enough to pick someone's pocket without them noticing, and ran her tongue along her teeth. "Maybe I can find something for you."

She winked at him. Calder grinned and winked back for him. Gothel just blinked.

He'd never understand these two.

"Not hungry," he muttered.

Irritation twitched in Tor's expression. Then she gave Gothel a brilliant smile, her white teeth glittering against her brown skin—boosted by magic, he knew. When Gothel didn't react, she rolled her eyes with a huff and Calder snickered before delving into his lumpy orange. Gothel pretended not to notice.

Suddenly, the front door swung open, barely clearing the edge of the table. Boone sauntered in with Ulf stepping lightly behind him, both of them taking up the rest of the kitchen.

The pair had founded the little group long before Gothel knew either of them, and their bond was difficult for him to figure out: the two were near opposites. Boone was a mass of a man, standing a half foot taller than all of them. His head was bald, his beard precise, and his footsteps heavy and forceful—a tread meant for making a mark on the world. Ulf, in comparison, was scrawny and gaunt, his head buzzed clumsily as though unsure whether it was supposed to grow or be shaved. While his friend stomped around the kingdom in an attempt to own it, Ulf seemed to float and encompass the space given to him without ruffling a feather. Calder once joked that Ulf was the most respectable out of all of them, but Tor had just scoffed.

"Oh, please, if he still had a tongue he'd be just as dirty as the rest of us. We *are* thieves, after all." Then she'd winked at him, and Ulf had given her one of his rare half grins.

"Nice day out today," Boone boomed when he came in, apparently already over his 'agitation.' "Royal council is holding a forum outside the palace gates this afternoon."

Calder whooped and Tor bared her teeth in a wicked smile. Rising gracefully to her feet, she leaned her head on Boone's shoulder. "Well, we should be good subjects of our beloved King Asher and attend, don't you think?"

Boone grinned and wound his arm around her. "I think so."

"Hm, then who should I be today?" She glanced around the barren room in thought and pretended not to notice Boone smelling her hair. "The pregnant bit gets the most sympathy, but the bump is a chore. A merchant's daughter, maybe? Or just a girl looking for a friend in the crowd?"

"Careful with that one, Tor." Calder aimed his easy smile at her and tilted his head like he did when he wanted something from someone. "You'll break someone's heart."

"Why?" She smirked, breaking out of Boone's hold to run her finger down Calder's cheek. "Speaking from experience there, Calder?"

Calder smirked back and pulled her onto his lap while Gothel slid just far enough away to not touch them. Everyone was too wrapped up in Tor to notice, as usual.

"I got a plan for the forum, boss," Calder said with a lazy kiss on Tor's cheek. Gothel turned to look at another spot on the wall, though the pair were still in his peripheral vision. "How about Tor and I go as lovers again? Nobody dares look at us when we're all over each other. Nothing like using discomfort to rob 'em blind."

The smile didn't leave Boone's face, but it seemed to crust over slightly. "If anyone's playing the partner game with Tor today, it'll be me."

Tor giggled at something Calder did. Gothel just wanted to leave, do the day on his own, but all the exits were blocked. Boone's smile cracked when he clenched his jaw.

"Too bad," Calder muttered.

"I'll do what I want," Tor murmured back.

Gothel looked up at the ceiling. He just wanted a plan for the day.

"If the boss needs his girl," Calder started, "then—"

Tor jerked back like she'd been slapped. "Excuse me?"

"Come on, Tor." Boone gave her a playful smirk like the one she doled out to every human within walking distance. "I need my girl."

Shoving herself off of Calder, she shot a glare at Boone, her brown eyes blazing. "I'm nobody's *girl*," she snapped, her tone sharp enough to cut through even Boone. Then, making sure to elbow Calder on her way, she turned and ducked around the corner before stomping up the stairs.

It caused Gothel physical pain to keep from rolling his eyes. Tor needed attention like a plant needs sunlight: the more she had, the more she bloomed. She'd likely shrivel up and die without it.

Calder ran a hand through his perfectly tousled hair, unperturbed by the outburst, though Tor hadn't been that angry at him since he'd tried to playfully throw her in the river. Apparently, their ferocious feline didn't like water.

"Women," Calder muttered with a shrug. "Can't live with 'em, definitely can't live without 'em."

Boone watched Tor go for a second longer than necessary, then straightened up. When he caught Gothel looking at him, he forced a casual expression, but his grey eyes were still nearly as sharp as Tor's comment.

"So," Gothel said, only because he hated the way Boone was staring at him and he was itching for a plan. For something to *do* other than watch Tor's drama and pluck at rotten fruit. "The forum?"

"Right." Boone seemed to internally shake himself off, though he didn't regain all of his previous enthusiasm. He stepped backward, nearly flattening Ulf in the process, to open one of the three cupboards. Gothel didn't know why he bothered. They hadn't had a successful raid in over a week. "The forum will—"

Boone froze. The color drained from his face, his body rigid, as he stared at something in the cupboard.

Gothel's gut dropped at the foreign behavior, and he and Ulf exchanged glances over Boone's shoulder. His nerves pulsed with anticipation, possibilities running through his mind, a dozen plans brewing in his head.

What's your play, Gothel? It had long since been the only question that mattered in his life. *What's the threat and how are you going to escape it?*

But based on Boone's expression, Gothel knew there was no escaping this one.

"C'mon, boss," Calder went on between bites, still too caught up in his orange to notice the change in atmosphere. "The forum is child's play. It's almost too easy to be fun anymore."

All three of them ignored Calder. Gothel was about ready to stand and push Boone out of the way to look for himself when the man finally broke from his trance. Slowly, he reached forward and pulled something out of the cupboard: a wheel of cheese, as big as his hand.

Gothel blinked. Ulf's eyebrows shot up. When Calder finally looked up and saw what Boone was holding, he choked on an orange slice and swore.

They had been scavenging for dinner last night. They all knew that the cupboard had been glaringly empty.

Someone had put the grave message in there while they were asleep. Someone had found their hideout and broken in without any of the master thieves knowing. Someone resourceful and determined and sinister.

Pepperjack.

A wave of dread overwhelmed Gothel with the knowledge that he was trapped, that he couldn't escape. The fear combined with his frustration and boiled over. "You know what he does to people that don't pay on time?"

"G—" Calder started.

"You want to get skinned alive, Calder?" Gothel asked. The image made Gothel cringe, and both Boone and Calder flinched. Ulf was the only constant. "If we're lucky we'll get indentured servitude for life, but even then, people don't last long."

Tor appeared out of nowhere, her practiced footsteps inaudible on the creaky stairs. The theatrics were all gone from her face. She looked younger than ever as she teetered on the edge of the last stair and leaned forward to look. When she saw the cheese, a small squeak of fear escaped her lips.

They all stood staring, the tension thick and suffocating, and for once even Calder didn't have a wisecrack to break it. Because it was *Pepperjack* they were talking about. Pepperjack, king of mobsters, leader of the underground crime circle, the walking nightmare of every citizen in Elaria. King Asher had the throne over the kingdom, but Pepperjack held his own power unmatched by all: a power built on corruption, shadows, and fear; a power that leaked into every offense imaginable and made even the strongest royal guards turn the other way, if only to save their own neck.

It was a game. Ruthless and resolute, Pepperjack played on people's desperation and kept his claws in them while he inflated interest. No hiding place couldn't be found; no one was exempt. If you turned out to be boring, useless, or unprofitable, you were discarded. With a carving knife.

Everyone knew once you got in with Pepperjack, you never got out.

Boone had practically dug their graves for them.

"How can we get the money?" Tor murmured, staring at the cheese as if in a daze.

Clenching the wheel in his hands, Boone tore his gaze from it to glare at her. "We're leaving for the forum in an hour. Everyone be ready."

"But boss," Calder said, all charm devoid from his hollow voice, "there's no way we'll even skim the surface of what we owe at a forum. It's all loose change and dangling jewelry. We won't—"

"We'll come up with something," Boone snapped. He tossed the wheel onto the table and stalked out the door. Gothel watched the cheese roll twice before toppling over, revealing the smallest spot of mold beginning to grow.

* * * * * * *

It was well into the afternoon when another knock sounded on Rosalind's door. It was soft and slow, like a hand caressing a newborn's cheek: her mom again.

"Rosalind," she called absently. "Lunch." And then she left.

Rosalind hadn't needed to worry about her mother coming inside her room for ages now. The last time she had tried, Rosalind had screamed at her and shoved her out, threatening against her coming in ever again. After she'd slammed the door between them, she'd heard her mom crying in the hallway, and that had nearly brought Rosalind to tears too. She hadn't meant to make a scene. She hadn't meant to be cruel. She had just panicked. Now an extra wall stood between them even on the rare occasion they occupied the same room.

Rosalind wiggled her toes with a sigh. They were numb and tingly from her being in bed so long. They ached for her to stand up, to get blood flowing. Zachary said that his limbs did the same thing sometimes. The thought made Rosalind bury her head under a pillow.

Maybe we should get up, her body wondered.

Why? her mind asked.

She thought and then realized she didn't have an answer.

Much later, a different knock sounded: timid yet sure at the same time. Rosalind perked up, unearthing herself from under her pillows, and glanced at the door. She hadn't heard that knock in so long.

"Rose?" a voice asked from the other side. "It's just me. Can I come in?"

Rosalind cleared her throat, but her voice was hoarse from not using it all day. Or much yesterday. "Yes. Just...just be careful."

She winced. What a ridiculous thing to say. If anyone had to be careful, it was *her.*

The door cracked open just enough for a boy to slide inside. He blinked against the darkness of the room as he softly pushed the door closed. Back when they were kids, adults used to chide Rosalind for not curtsying when he came in. She didn't understand why she should, especially since he'd asked her not to. But that was back before she understood what real responsibility was, before fear had clawed around her throat and stolen her voice, before she realized what a crown truly was and how heavy it would weigh on her best friend's shoulders.

Once he got his bearings, Prince Roman made his way through her cavernous room, expertly stepping over the piles of dirty clothes and long forgotten dishes. Servants never entered her room, so it was rarely clean, and she deserved to live in the mess she made. She tensed slightly as he approached but forced herself to breathe through it, to cling to control. Roman was the only one allowed in her room, and even that had taken a lot of convincing. He was here so much now, though, that she'd almost gotten used to it.

But Rosalind hadn't seen him in...how many weeks had it been? Two? Three? She couldn't remember. All she remembered was the two girls he'd brought to stay with them during their tour of the kingdom, and how excited Roman had been about it. His step had a bounce in it, and his eyes had glistened with anticipation, as if he were about to stumble upon something great. Now, as he got closer, Rosalind realized he looked *awful.* His skin had always been darker than hers, but it was paler than usual. His cheekbones were sunken in and wrinkles lined his forehead, highlighting the hollow shadow in his lifeless eyes.

Rosalind's thoughts went to King Asher: a man who loved his kingdom dearly but didn't manage to even tolerate his only child.

"Do you want to talk about it?" she asked quietly.

With a groan, Roman flopped onto her bed and pressed the heels of his hands into his eyes. "Not particularly."

Rosalind had to wriggle her head to free her hair enough to fully sit up and rest her chin on her hand. It hurt her to see him like this. While often miserable, he hadn't been this bad in a while.

"Where's Griffin?" she asked. The topic of Roman's best friend and adviser tended to lift his spirits no matter the situation. They were almost always together, and Rosalind had gotten over that jealousy back when she was ten. She liked Griffin. "I haven't seen him in a while."

Even buried underneath his hands, Rosalind saw Roman flinch. His shoulders curled in as he shuddered, and for a second she thought he might be crying. Rosalind's eyebrow arched. Her mind raced with possibilities, with awful scenarios, because Roman and Griffin *never* fought. Was he sick? Having a rough time? Griffin was well acquainted with sorrow, which was a big reason why Rosalind liked him so much, but surely Roman wouldn't be this upset over just a bad day.

Rosalind gasped softly. "He's...is he...he's okay, right? They didn't...they aren't..."

Roman removed his hands to meet her alarmed expression. "No. Not that."

She breathed a sigh of relief. Griffin was born a twin, which was a major taboo in the kingdom of Elaria. Many people, including his own family, wanted him dead.

"Oh." She let the word hang there, allowing him to decide whether to continue the conversation.

"Sterling's doing a forum today," Roman offered, clearly desperate to change the subject. "I heard there's going to be quite the turnout."

Rosalind nodded to be polite. Roman was usually the only reason she knew anything about her family's lives. "What's it about this time?" she asked, if only to keep him distracted.

"The ma—"

Roman cut himself off, but it was too late. He closed his eyes, horrified at his careless mistake, as Rosalind's hands clenched into fists. Harder. Tighter. She reveled in the pain of her nails piercing her palms, but it was a cool breeze in comparison to the constricting feeling in her gut, the painful fire inside threatening to overwhelm her.

Stay calm, she begged herself. *Roman is here. You have to stay calm.*

"Rose, I…" Roman trailed off with a defeated sigh—not cowering in fear like he should've been. "I'm sorry. I wasn't thinking."

Rosalind stayed rigid. If she moved, she might fall apart. She might hurt him.

Please don't hurt him. Please.

Giving a mournful glance to Rosalind's fists, Roman raised his hands up in a show of peace: a warning. Then he slowly reached behind her and untangled her hair from the mess of pillows and blankets. It nearly reached her ankles now. Roman took a few minutes to tug it all free and pull it over her left shoulder so it piled on the bed in between them. Then he leaned over and opened up the drawer on the nightstand, pulling out a golden brush with flowers etched into it. Softly, absently, he began the daunting task of brushing her hair.

Their whole lives, kids—and even some adults—had made fun of them. They'd sing childish songs about Roman and Rosalind kissing behind raspberry bushes while adults whispered too loudly that she was playing him for a crown. Somehow, the taunts had only strengthened their relationship. With her and Roman, it had never been like that, and they both knew it never would be. The chances of her kissing Roman were the same as her kissing Zachary, and the idea of either caused her to shudder with disgust.

Back when they were young, they were just best friends that loved to make up stories and play pretend—the two of them against the world. Now, their connection ran deeper. They understood each other. They suffered together, since now the world really *was* against them, and often each was the only person the other felt safe with.

But even with Roman, sometimes Rosalind felt lonely. They couldn't *really* understand each other, not with their contrasting lives. Because Rosalind's problems only plagued her, and so affected her family. They meant the world to her, but they were just a handful of people in a big, unfair world. Roman, on the other hand, had the world on his shoulders and secrets lurking within. Not only did it make him miserable and hated by his father, but it affected an entire kingdom and put the future at risk.

Rosalind had told him as much one day, years ago. She'd felt a wave of shame overtake her after she'd spent hours unloading on Roman, even when he had come running to her room in tears after a cruel fight with his father.

But instead of agreeing with her, like any other arrogant, self-important prince might, Roman had just scowled at her.

"Your problems are real too," he had told her. *"Just because I'm a prince doesn't make mine any more important than yours."*

Of course, Rosalind would never, ever, ever ask for the crown, or wish to take Roman's place—especially in that lonely castle with a mother drowning in her sorrows and a father who could barely even look at him. But if Roman and Rosalind could just trade problems somehow, rearrange the tipping balance of power...everything would be solved. For both of them.

The longer Roman brushed, the more Rosalind relaxed. Slowly, her aching shoulders sagged and her fists gradually unclenched.

"Remember when we used to play Pixies and Dragons?" he asked quietly. When in her dusky room, he never made his voice louder than hers, and hers was always barely a murmur. "You'd always help me win and let me take the credit."

A ghost of a smile nearly touched her lips. "Only to take it back again at dinner?"

Roman let out a breath that could've been a laugh if it had more life. "Yeah." She knew they'd both give anything to go back to that time.

"If you could go anywhere," she asked, "right now, where would you go?"

He hesitated a moment before blurting, "The ocean."

Rosalind shot him a quizzical side glance. Roman just shrugged without looking at her, sad eyes on her hair. He had always hated the water, and with good reason—everyone in Elaria knew how dangerous the ocean was.

But maybe that was still better. Maybe *anywhere* was better than here.

The faint sound of bristles going through her hair filled the thick silence.

"Rose?" Roman asked after a few minutes. The desperation was steadily creeping back into his tone. "Can I ask you a hard question?"

She held her breath, heart hammering in her chest. A million questions. A million answers. A million things she couldn't bear to look at, a million voices that would smash her into pieces. Which would he choose?

Roman's voice shrunk until it cracked, and she had to strain to hear it. "How do you deal with guilt?"

Something cracked in her chest. She closed her eyes against the blow. In another life, she might've even laughed at the question, gesturing around to her crypt of a room and letting it speak for itself. Instead, she felt the pressure of it all—the air, the sky, the stars—push in on her, so hard, so much, she could barely breathe.

"I don't," she whispered back. "It swallows me whole."

* * * * * * *

The forum was supposed to begin at two, so workers had the chance to come during their lunch break if they wanted to. At least, that was the formal announcement. The royal council made that the official statement, though most workers either had unrelenting task masters who wouldn't let them leave or were too overcome with chores to take a break.

But the council still looks good, Gothel thought, rolling his eyes, *and that's all that matters around here.*

Gothel hated the council. They paraded around with their fancy cloaks and unblistered palms, never seeing a day of actual work in their lives, only to preach to commoners about how they 'cared about their views' and were 'fighting for equality' and all that. Meanwhile, they sat in cool rooms all day, being

32

waited on by servants and relying on their magic—magic that was legal for them, of course, but illegal for anyone less than noble.

It was all just a game. And Gothel *hated* games.

But forums were a breeding ground for controversy, which meant the people there were highly emotional and always distracted. Boone had been bringing his group here—long before Calder took Gothel in—because of how easy it was to pickpocket.

Usually, the setting would have loosened Gothel up. He never felt truly comfortable, but he was most comfortable lost in a crowd, doing the one thing he knew how to do.

A couple passed him. Gothel bumped into the woman, sliding the bracelet off her wrist in the process, and she barely even looked at him. He didn't break his stride as he slid the bracelet into his pocket.

It was just too easy. And it wasn't enough. A fake gemstone bracelet wasn't even a drop in the ocean of how much they owed Pepperjack.

Boone was a halfwit. Borrowing money from Pepperjack wasn't just a risk—it was a lifetime deal. Even if you only asked for enough to buy half a loaf of bread, the king of crime would prey on your desperation and somehow twist it into owing him your soul. Sure, some people got away with selling their years as an indentured servant, but most met his array of skinning knives.

Gothel hadn't always been fond of himself, but he was pretty sure he'd like to keep his skin.

The sun beat down on the gathering crowd as they made their way to the podium set up in the square. There were at least fifty people here, maybe more. Gothel caught a glimpse of

Tor several yards away. Her hair was chestnut now, curled to frame her face. The patched blue dress she was wearing frayed at the edges, and the seam accentuated the fake baby bump she was showing off. With makeup dolling up her face and a handkerchief in hand, she looked younger, sweet and fragile. Gothel watched her mistakenly drop her handkerchief and bat her eyelashes at the man standing next to her. When he bent down to pick it up, she had her hand in his pocket.

Another unsuspecting middle-class man robbed by Tor's long eyelashes.

Still not *enough*.

"Excuse me, everyone," a voice announced, amplified by magic to be heard by all in attendance. "If I can have your attention, the forum will start momentarily."

The crowd quieted down quickly for how many of them were assembled. They were here for a reason, after all.

Gothel crossed his arms, standing casually in the sea of people, as the man on the stage cleared his throat and straightened up. His suit was plain but still crisp (a pathetic attempt to appeal to the poor) and lines etched his face when he offered the gathered group a friendly smile. Gothel recognized him as one of the high-ranking councilmen that served King Asher: Sterling Corona.

"Before we begin," Sterling started, "I want to thank you all for making the effort to come out today." His voice was a hybrid of assuredness and cordiality that made Gothel distrust him at once. Nobody just offered kindness. It always came with a price. "Truly, I believe Elaria has the best citizens, and I appreciate each of your help in making our kingdom the best it can be."

Sterling was losing people already. While it was relatively easy to take their watches, congregated crowds tended to offer up other valuables without any trouble at all: gossip and information.

"Did you hear what happened to his son?" one man whispered to another.

The woman behind Gothel muttered to her partner, "I heard he beats his kids and keeps them locked up so they can't talk about it. That's why you never see his family around anymore."

"His wife is a rake," the old woman to his left announced to her friend. "Didn't you know? That's why he's having an affair. Such a powerful magician, but no self control."

Sterling went on, oblivious to the quiet chatter among those he deemed lower than himself.

"Now, to the topic of the day. As you are all likely aware, it's the council's current stance—and my personal opinion— that the magical ban is necessary for safety and organization in our society. Those with a level of skill and professional training are permitted to be licensed, but for anyone else, no matter social class, it remains illegal."

An adolescent boy scoffed. "He means those rich enough to actually attend academy. I'll bet *his* kids can do whatever they want."

The farmer next to him spat on the ground. "It's still just a money grab. That's all magic and politics are these days."

One man toward the front of the podium actually spoke up to Sterling.

"That's not fair!" he called. "Just because I'm not 'noble' doesn't mean you can deny me my right to magic!" The statement received several whoops and shouted agreement.

The outcry didn't faze Sterling; he continued with fake patience on his face, his tone patronizing. Just the sound of it made Gothel's blood boil. "I hear what you're saying, sir. We aren't here to oppress you. I'm arguing that it's a matter of personal safety for everyone in Elaria, and it's my job, as well as my personal ambition, to maintain security for each and every citizen, regardless of class, financial situation, or magical capability."

Gothel rolled his eyes. Few things—if anything—made him as angry as listening to nobles lie through their teeth about the magic ban. Of course, for people like Boone and his crew, this discussion was a never-ending uphill climb with a dead end. Tor had a knack for slightly altering her appearances for a brief amount of time, but that was the extent of her capacity. Boone, Calder, and Gothel were rakes: incapable of using magic. Nobody with power cared about what they had to say.

Ulf was the only one in the group that could actually perform magic well. As a peasant unable to afford the training for licensing, his magical use was illegal despite his talent, and he got caught once years ago when attempting to help his rampion garden grow. And later, when he defended his case to a royal councilman, the monster took his land and ordered Ulf's tongue be cut out as a penalty. He hadn't used a drop of magic since.

As he stared heatedly at the podium, Gothel wondered if Sterling Corona had ever felt powerless in his entire life.

Calder appeared and went to clap Gothel on the back— which he easily dodged—breaking him out of his thoughts.

"Now there's a face for you," Calder drawled. "What's that for? You look congested or something. Moldy cheese not agreeing with you?"

Calder wasn't standing straight, his eyes slightly clouded over, and it would've been so easy to nick the cufflinks off his stolen jacket. Gothel gritted his teeth in annoyance. Calder was the closest thing Gothel had to a best friend, and yet he found it difficult to even like Calder most of the time.

"What do you mean?" Gothel asked flatly when Calder kept staring at him.

"You're kinda a closed book, G. I never really know what you're fantasizing about."

Somewhere in his mind, the comment clung to Gothel, but he shrugged it off. "I'm thinking."

Calder gave a feigned gasp of surprise. "You're *thinking*? Wow, now that's a new one, isn't it folks?"

Ulf materialized from nowhere and rolled his eyes before glancing between Sterling and Gothel, then started making fast signals with his hands. Gothel had never learned the gesture language Ulf used; he didn't even try to decipher now.

"Whoa whoa, Ulf," Calder said. Gothel started to suspect he was drunk. "Slow down there, brother. I can't read that fast."

Gothel was too impatient for this. "I have an idea."

Huffing in annoyance, Ulf pointed from Gothel to Sterling very deliberately. For once, Gothel thought they might be on the same page.

"You heard he has kids, right?" Gothel asked.

Ulf's eyes flashed with a rare blaze of emotion, the need for vengeance clear in his expression. He nodded.

Calder sobered up a little—he didn't like being on the edge of anything, especially his group of supposed pals. "What are you two talking about?"

"He's talking about kidnapping," Boone cut in. His voice came from behind Calder, who was the only one of the three that jumped. Boone nudged him out of the way to look down on Gothel, as if scolding a little kid for proposing they all go down and play in the ocean.

Gothel just shrugged under Boone's weighty scrutiny. It hadn't bothered him in a long time. "Ransom for a Corona kid? I'm thinking that'll be enough to pay Pepperjack, don't you?"

Boone glanced at Ulf, who was glowering at Sterling like he could set the man on fire through sheer willpower. Maybe Ulf *could*, with his magic, if the laws were different, if using a drop of his power wouldn't get him arrested on the spot. If they didn't live in a world where people like Sterling Corona could disfigure him just for trying to exist.

"Okay," Boone said, nodding in fierce resolve at Ulf before breaking into a wicked grin. "Kidnapping it is."

CHAPTER 2

INTO THE GARDEN

The bad news came from Zachary.

It usually did, actually. He was the one who told Rosalind whenever one of her favorite servants left, whenever he had nobody to play with, and whenever their parents got into a fight. Out of everyone's knock, out of everyone's questions and demands and attempts, his cut her in a way nobody else's could. She stopped breathing every time she heard the familiar press of the carpet in the hallway, signaling he was coming.

The knock. Fast and light, like a hummingbird's wings. "Rosy?" Rosalind honestly didn't know why he kept trying. "Rosy, you in there?"

The pen she was holding jerked across her arm, ruining the pattern she'd drawn on her wrist, and splattering ink onto her blush bed sheets. Her hands clenched into fists.

Zachary only waited a half second for her to answer these days; she couldn't decide if it hurt her more that he knew she wouldn't respond, or that he was still hopeful enough to hesitate.

"Maldo almost ran away." Rosalind might have sighed if she hadn't been holding her breath. Zachary was geared up and ready to launch without signs of slowing for a long time. "He was outside—the weather is so great outside, Rosy—and we were looking at the flowers with Raf. Some of them are starting to bloom, and he's really excited. Anyways, I got closer to look at them, and Maldo hopped right out of my lap! It was crazy!"

He went on to describe the mad chase, how he had yelled and cheered while Raf and some of the other gardeners ran around trying to capture his frog.

"I really owe Raf," Zachary finished. Rosalind silently agreed. Raf had been with them as long as she could remember and was more of a grandfather to her than her actual grandfather. "Without him, I probably would've lost Maldo, and that would've been a disaster. I mean, he's like my best friend, you know, Rosy?"

A lump formed in Rosalind's throat. She hoped she choked on it.

"Anyways," he went on, as if she had emphatically echoed his sentiments on how important the frog was. "I came to tell you something else, since you probably don't know. Guess what?" She could actually hear him bouncing in excitement. "We are having a party!"

Rosalind's stomach dropped.

No.

No.

Wildly, desperately, she glanced around her darkened room, doing a fruitless search for some way to discount what he had said. But her closed closet, dusty bookshelves, covered windows, and broken desk had nothing to help her.

"Well, it's not *really* a party. Dad says it's for publicity. He says we need to be better friends with people, to show them that we like them. Isn't that great? We *never* get to have anyone over, except a few of Dad's council people or Roman's friends for dinner or something. This'll be huge! Think of how many friends I could make, Rosy! It'll be so fun!"

The faint taste of metal touched her tongue. Panic spiked in her stomach, the familiar snake coiling around her gut and squeezing rationality out of her. She stopped listening to Zachary ramble on about the party.

The party.

At her house.

She'd be expected to go, of course. For her parents. They wouldn't make it a requirement, not after the Cerula incident, but they'd both knock once, or maybe twice, to ask. To leave it up to her. She didn't know if having the choice was worse than an ultimatum.

She'd go. She'd have to go. It was in her house. It was for her parents. If she didn't, people would wonder. People would talk. Stars knew what they already thought about their reclusive family.

How could she let her parents down again? She couldn't. She wouldn't survive it.

But how could she possibly walk into a crowd of strangers and expect to last the night without incident? She let Roman in her room after much of his intensive coaxing and her desperate need for some kind of connection. She hadn't let herself around anyone else, except for thirty minute appearances at a family dinner once a month or so when someone important was showing up. Even that was a major, dangerous stretch.

A *party*? How could she dare?

The hair on her arms rose, and a current ran over her skin as nightmares danced across her eyes, visions of dozens of party guests screaming in a puddle of red.

Don't turn around, she told herself, beginning to hyperventilate at the images some rational part of her brain knew weren't real. *Don't turn around.*

Suddenly, she realized Zachary had stopped talking. Even through the door she felt him deflating, his endless enthusiasm dissolving into sad shadows.

He rarely got like that. Zachary was as vibrant as the sun—day or night, he was always shining bright, whether you could see him or not. Somehow, despite everything, he'd remained a constant.

"Rosy?" he asked quietly, his voice nearly breaking. Rosalind heard him touch the wood of her door. "Rosy? Will you ever talk to me?"

Her shoulders caved in, as if someone had punched her, and the air whooshed out of her. It was too much. Her nails broke the skin of her palms, and she ducked underneath her blankets. Down, down, down, as far as she could go, under blankets and pillows and leftover clothes, so deep that she barely, barely, had enough air to breathe.

She stayed like that long after he was gone. It felt better to be buried.

* * * * * * *

Boone's crew *loved* the kidnapping idea. As the plan developed over the next couple days, Boone took more of it over with each formulated stage, selling it as his own, and Gothel didn't even care. It wasn't like he could do anything about the fact that Boone had signed all their names instead of just his own. That choice had been taken. Now all he could do was work to free himself from Pepperjack, using any means necessary.

The day after the forum, they'd come downstairs to scour for breakfast only to find a smaller cube of cheese next to the wheel Boone had left on the table. A corner was sprouting mold.

They were running out of time.

Gothel had led a life of evading consequences—that was the essence that made his being—but even he was smart enough to know there was no escaping Pepperjack. He was *everywhere*. He made up everything. Even if Gothel went into hiding, even if he somehow got out of Elaria and hid under a different name for the rest of his miserable life, Pepperjack would find him.

Gothel *hated* being cornered.

He felt cornered now as he stood in front of the Corona estate. His hands twitched, itching for the familiar, wanting to swipe something and disappear. He yearned for that measured thrill. For control.

But, as in many situations, being himself would only get him in trouble, and, really, the only way to control this Pepperjack situation was to get out of it. Petty thieving would have to wait.

Calder whistled quietly as he surveyed the manor. "Not quite like our hovel of a home, eh G?"

No, nothing close. The Corona house alone looked at least six times the size of their shack, and the grounds were large enough for a small, concentrated farm. Several garden areas dotted the estate, providing the perfect cover for Calder to secure jobs for him and Gothel.

The first stage of their plan began now.

A short man with dark, wrinkled skin came around the side of the house carrying a shovel. He nodded and beckoned them to come forward when he saw the pair of them standing there. Calder gave Gothel a lopsided grin—a 'here we go' type thing—and they followed.

"I'm Raf," the old man said, his sunbaked face stern but not harsh. "I'm the head gardener here. I won't waste time with orientation: it's just work. If you can use your hands, you'll pick it up eventually."

Calder smiled to show his dimples and opened his mouth, likely about to spew a smooth remark. Raf must've sensed it too, because he turned and started walking away before Calder got a word out.

Gothel followed, leaving Calder to catch up. He hated the Coronas, but he appreciated Raf's no nonsense attitude. Maybe this would be more bearable than he had thought.

Following Raf's instructions was easier than Gothel had imagined. His hands ached to snatch something, but working in the garden was a decent replacement given the circumstances. Still, he found himself plucking bits of gravel and putting them in his pocket. The action helped keep him calm while working in the enemy's refuge.

Calder continued to chat despite Raf's blatant disregard for him. Gothel tended to flower beds as he glanced around, slowly learning the layout of the grounds. He noticed about a dozen servants either working outside, coming in and out, or moving through a window of the house. They cleaned furniture, carried planters, used tools...but never once did any of them use magic. Which didn't make sense to Gothel. Why wouldn't one of the most powerful magical families in Elaria surround themselves with magical people?

To show how powerful they are, Gothel realized in disgust. *They hire people incapable of magic just to rub our noses in the dirt.*

After that, it was much harder to focus on work.

The day went faster than Gothel had anticipated and, despite the mild weather, the back of his shirt was soaked with sweat by the time Raf told them they could break for lunch. Gothel and Calder split a loaf of bread Tor had nabbed on her way home the night before. Calder was halfway through a story—Gothel had stopped pretending to listen to him years ago—when someone walked up to their spot underneath a tree toward the front of the property.

"Hello, gentlemen."

Gothel looked up at the newcomer, having to squint against the bright sun. Mouth full of crumbly bread, he raised his hand to cover his eyes, and the figure came into focus.

The bread sucked his mouth dry. It was Sterling Corona.

Up close, he looked older. His presence was commanding in a gentle way, quietly assertive, and made Gothel sit up a little straighter.

"Master Corona, sir." Calder inclined his head. "It's an honor to meet you."

Gothel bit the inside of his cheek. Hearing the words in Calder's voice, even as a lie, made his blood boil.

Sterling gave them a polite grin. "Please, call me Sterling. Raf informed me that the new recruits started today. I just wanted to introduce myself and let you know that if you need anything, you can just ask. Raf can be intimidating, but he's really sappy once you get to know him."

Calder gave a good-natured laugh before offering their fake names in introduction. Gothel clenched his teeth so hard his jaw hurt. The charade went so deep. Did Sterling even realize what a slap in the face this was?

Sterling shook both their hands, welcomed them on board, and told them to look after the sunflowers—"They're my wife's favorites," he told them—and wished them a good day before leaving.

Calder's practiced smile fell from his face the second Sterling was gone. He spat on the ground, muttering an indecent insult under his breath.

"Bye, Dad!" a young voice called from a distance.

Gothel watched as Sterling waved toward the pond before disappearing around the front of the house, then he turned to see what the kid looked like. Tor had said there were two Corona children, and they were supposed to decide which would be better for the ransom.

A boy around ten years old came over the bridge.

Calder swore quietly again. Gothel's eyebrows shot up.

The kid was in a chair that propelled itself, but that wasn't what caught the most attention: the kid inside it was severely mutilated. His legs ended at the knees, his shoulders didn't sit straight, and one arm was bent at a slightly wrong angle. Despite his patchy hair and shriveled scab for a right ear, he was beaming broadly.

"Well, there's a sight," Calder muttered. "I guess that's the son."

It took a few moments for Gothel to tear his eyes away. He shook his head to clear it and refocus. This was about the mission. Pepperjack. "There should be a girl too."

"Hopefully she looks better than *that*."

For once, Gothel agreed with him. Wiping his hands on his pants, he stood up and went back to work.

Raf watched them closely, but he watched the gardens closer—someone would've thought he was growing gold or jewels. It took a morning of carefully planned prods from Calder before they convinced Raf they were able to go grab supplies from the shed on their own (though Gothel suspected he only agreed just to get a break from Calder for a few minutes). Once out of Raf's beady stare, they slipped through the back door and went into the house.

The clamor of work and chatter melted away once they stepped inside. Gothel had always imagined noble houses were bustling with magic and splendor, the extravagance of their lives leaking out into the world so everyone knew how good they had it. But besides the occasional call of a servant or distant laugh from the disfigured son, it was largely quiet. The house was big, easily worth more than Gothel would ever make if he lived ten lives. It made Gothel feel small and dirty.

He shook the feeling off when they came upon two young ladies—obviously servants, from the plain dresses they were wearing. They saw Calder of course, who stopped to charm them and garnered giggles in record time, but they didn't see Gothel. Nobody ever saw Gothel; they saw *through* him. Like a ghost. That's what made him good.

Gothel snuck ahead, leaving Calder behind, and nearly ran into Genevieve Corona, Sterling's wife, farther down the hallway. He just kept his head down and walked by. She seemed in a daze and didn't even glance at him. She was probably used to having servants around to keep up her lifestyle for her, regarding them as nothing more than mice scurrying around her feet.

There was a different kind of stillness when he got upstairs. The air felt stiff and fragile, harder to breathe.

Gothel had come up from the back stairs he guessed were meant for servants, but now he heard a door opening down the hallway. He rounded the corner and stopped to wait. He still hadn't seen the daughter yet. Maybe she was out shopping or at some noble party, since the records Tor had snagged said she was nearly eighteen and had dropped out of academy years earlier.

As he hoped, the girl came out of what looked like the bathroom, shuffling for the door a few feet in front of Gothel. She didn't look anything like he had imagined—though, based on the boy, he should've been expecting that.

The first thing was her hair: it was inky black and fell almost to her ankles in messy ripples, nearly swallowing her up. She certainly didn't look like the daughter of a Corona, or any noble, really. Not like her naturally gorgeous mother, who seemed to pulse with magic and life, or her cordial father, who managed to keep an air of self-assured calm. The only attribute she shared was the color of her hair: it matched her father and brother's, but the similarities ended there.

The girl was plain otherwise. Angular. Somehow soft and harsh at the same time. She wore rumpled clothes, her skin was pale, and her hands stayed clenched into fists. No makeup, no jewels, and no sleep by the look of the hollow spots under her cave-like eyes. And those eyes looked right at him.

Gothel jolted with surprise. She was looking at him. Nobody ever looked at him, much less saw him.

The girl stared at him for a second, expressionless, before cracking open her door and sliding inside. The sound of it clicking closed was soft, but it echoed through the entire estate, coursing through the air as though giant cell doors had slammed shut.

After a few moments of staring at the door, Gothel decided that her eyes were so empty, she probably hadn't really seen anything in a long time. After another sweep of that side of the house, he tracked down Calder only to find him still talking with the girls rather than doing his part of the job to save their lives. Why Gothel ever bothered doing anything for him, he didn't know.

They slipped back outside, gardening tools in hand, and found Raf. The man nodded at them, and they continued working.

They snuck away every afternoon for the next week, slowly learning the layout of the house. The second time, they overheard two servant girls talking about a party the Coronas were having that weekend: apparently it had been years since they'd hosted something of the nature, and a lot of people were expected to show up.

"That'll be our window," Calder told Boone and the others the second night after they'd returned home. "The party is our best chance to slip in and out."

Tor's eyes gleamed. "I do love a good party."

"So you're sure of your choice?" Boone asked. The question was directed at Calder, but the glare fell on Gothel.

Calder nodded. "The boy might be easier to take, but the upkeep would be too difficult. He's too much of a liability. Plus, it's more likely they would notice his absence too soon. We need time to get out, and she would give it to us. She's practically a shadow in her brother's light." He curled his lip in disgust. "I don't know what Sterling's doing to her, but it's a freak show over there."

Boone nodded. "She's the one then?"

Gothel thought of the girl, hiding behind the closed door. "She'll work just fine."

* * * * * * *

One of Rosalind's earliest memories was when she was three or four years old. She'd been playing with one of her toys, a purple cat that Raf had given her, and was making up a story in which the cat was an extreme jumper. During one of its grand jumps, she'd accidentally banged it against the floor too hard. One eye had fallen off and the neck had popped so that the head hung by almost nothing while the whiskered smile had turned lopsided.

Rosalind had started crying. Her dad had scooped her into his arms, cat and all.

"What's the matter, Rosy?" he'd asked. She'd calmed a little at the sound of his voice, knowing in her small heart that her father could make anything better.

He'd held up the toy in his hand. "Oh, did your cat break?"

Rosalind shook her head. Back then, she didn't understand the meaning of the word 'broken.' In a house full of magic, it rarely happened. She didn't realize how fragile everything was, didn't know how many things in a person could shatter.

Now, standing at the top of the stairs, she felt just like her broken purple cat.

This is for Dad and Mom, she chanted to herself, the black skirt of her dress swishing around her ankles as she forced herself to take the first step. *You have to do this. Stay calm. This is for Dad and Mom.*

This is for Dad and Mom.
This is for Dad and Mom.
This is for Dad and Mom.

She stepped off the last step with a shuddering breath and glanced around the living room. The party was just beginning, and already there were too many nobles in bright suits and lavish dresses, milling around the house. Soft music played in the background—subdued yet upbeat—while chatter and laughter filled the air.

She was putting all these people in danger, and for what? A pathetic attempt to curb gossip that would come anyway? A laughable effort to somehow repay her parents for her unforgivable existence?

She clenched her skirt in her gloved fists. She just had to show up. If enough people saw her there, then word would get around that she'd attended, just like everyone expected. It would be normal. It would be fine.

Stay calm. You won't hurt anyone.

You won't.

You won't.

But what if I do?

A laugh swelled up above the others. Rosalind caught a glimpse of Zachary, his freckled face bright with happiness, as a man leaned down in front of his chair to say something funny to him.

The snake in her gut hissed. Rosalind went the other direction.

Faces blurred, but the room was sharp and full of angles that threatened to cut her to pieces. Colors shot harsh and bright across the space, bleeding in her vision like watery paint on her mother's canvas. Voices and sweat clogged the air; it was so thick and muggy. How was anyone breathing?

Rosalind's heart hammered in her chest as she forced herself to walk slowly from one end of the room to the other, then back again. She didn't stop to talk to anyone. She didn't get too close. She heard people say her name; she nodded politely at them and tried not to crumble, to quell the dangerous nervous energy that threatened to burst out of her.

The people, the noise, the expectation, the threat...it was too much. She glanced at the giant clock near the foyer. Only twelve minutes had passed.

More like twelve years.

Sweat trickled from her neck down her back. Her mouth was bone dry, but she avoided the table of refreshments and waved off the servants as they offered her drinks. Most of them she recognized and knew, but there were a few new ones milling about in purple servant attire saved for events such as these. Something sharp settled in her stomach at the knowledge that she didn't even know her own house anymore.

A commotion sounded near the front door. Those around her bowed, and she automatically fell into a curtsy, though her eyes were searching, hopeful.

Sure enough, Roman was there, giving a gracious gesture to his subjects and ushering that the party continue. It had been a while since she'd been with him in public—she'd forgotten how different his persona was. As he shook her father's hand and gave Zachary a high five, Rosalind noted the proud posture of his shoulders, the arrogant slant to his jaw, and the powerful step of his gait. Worlds different than the boy who crumbled in her room.

He had to be. He was the future king. Nobody could know the countless fault lines that ran underneath his practiced royal face.

Once Roman had said an appropriate number of hellos, his caramel eyes searched the room until he found her. They both seemed to let out a sigh of relief at the same time. The crowd parted for him as he cut through and walked up to her. She made a shaky curtsy, knowing people were watching, and heard Roman laugh under his breath. Hesitating a moment for her to prepare for contact, he shocked her by taking her hand and pulling her straight onto the dance floor in the sitting room that she'd been avoiding. She had never minded dancing with Roman, especially since she knew he loved it, but things were different now.

"What are you doing?" Rosalind hissed under her breath, trying to keep the panic from her face. Her limbs locked up, surely making their dance look extremely awkward.

Roman's lips quirked to the side. No fear showed in his dignified expression. "Dancing. I believe that's what's expected of me, and I'd rather do it with you."

"I could hurt you." Her voice cracked, and her skin heated at the nightmares she saw. The blood. The feeling of her hand in his made bile climb up her throat. "I could hurt everyone here."

"Steady, Rose," he murmured, subtly drawing her closer and swaying her back and forth, like an unspoken lullaby. "You have gloves on. You're in control. Just breathe. You came, and you're doing great."

At his words, she took a breath. In and out. One step, then another.

Stay calm.

Rosalind waited until she could breathe mostly right again, then spoke to distract herself. "You came. I didn't think you would."

"Well, I could say the same to you. Though I figured if you *did*, then you were probably about ready to evacuate and could use some support." Roman guided her around, effortlessly making her look much more graceful than she was. "I can't stay long, but I wanted to make sure you were still alive."

"It looks bad," she told him, feeling the eyes and whispers from others, "that you just came straight to me."

He actually winked at her—he was definitely the prince now. "They all probably think we're having a torrid affair."

She didn't think it was funny. "That kind of rumor could ruin you."

His eyes darkened, and she saw a hint of the fragility underneath his royal bravado. His tone dripped with contempt. "I do a good job of ruining myself."

She opened her mouth to argue, but then noted the people around her and decided it wasn't the place to discuss such sensitive things.

Roman must've come to that conclusion too. As quickly as the clouds came, they were gone, and his voice brightened again to match the fake enjoyment on his face. "While the logistics of our affair would be feasible, of course, given who we are, it's entirely too predictable and really boring. Not to mention you are like the little sister I never had, so that would just be disgusting." He tipped his head at her. "No offense."

She wrinkled her nose in agreement. "None taken."

They had kissed once, when they were...eight? Nine? After overhearing some servants gossip, they thought maybe that's what they were supposed to do. Rosalind's mom had found them later in the bathroom, both scrubbing their mouths out with soap. Afterwards they'd made a pact to never do it again.

"You're trembling," Roman commented. "Do you need to sit down? You haven't eaten, have you?"

Rosalind managed a noncommittal shrug.

"Tsk tsk, Rose," Roman said.

"Because you're one to lecture on taking care of yourself?"

He gave a curt nod. "Fair enough."

The song turned into another one. Roman didn't stop, so neither did she. He whirled them around the room, and Rosalind caught glimpses of her parents with Zachary. They introduced him to every person they came across while he beamed with excitement. She wondered how many people had already asked what happened to him. She wondered what her parents said.

"I feel like everyone knows what happened," Rosalind whispered.

"It feels like that because you live the story, every second of every day. Most people here have only heard bits and pieces—they don't really know anything."

"You don't know that."

Roman flashed her one of his grins, something she hadn't seen in a long time. "Well, I do my research."

She raised an eyebrow. "You talk to these people about me? To see what they know? That's so suspicious." For countless reasons. He was the prince, after all.

"Oh, Rose, have you lost all your faith in me? You know I'm the best at playing parts. Especially in stuffy environments like this."

That earned him half an eye roll, though her mouth actually twitched with the thought of a smile. "Thank you," she murmured.

"Anything for my favorite girl."

The song ended, and someone interrupted them. Rosalind's feet skidded to a stop, and she nearly tripped over herself before Roman's hands steadied her.

"Excuse me, Your Highness," the intruder said. Rosalind had to look up to see the woman's beautiful face, her excited eyes gleaming with a hint of mischief. "I was hoping I could ask you for a dance?"

Rosalind gulped and took a step back, suddenly aware of how close she was to too many people. It both relieved and saddened her when she let go of Roman's hand.

If Roman was annoyed at the interruption, he didn't show it. He was too good at his part for that. With a half grin, he nodded at Rosalind and she barely remembered to curtsy a little too late. The woman and Roman started dancing, and Rosalind melted back into the crowd.

Alone, she lasted four more minutes, but she couldn't take any more. Everyone had seen her, anyway. She'd done enough. As Roman said his goodbyes to her family, her dad caught her eye, and she bailed. By the time her father finished thanking Roman for coming and looked her way again, there would be a locked door between them.

Breathless, she crossed the immense room as if wading through a treacherous sea, then ducked into the hallway and went up the back stairs, desperate to get to the safety of her room. She didn't realize someone had followed her until it was much, much too late.

* * * * * * *

Gothel tracked the girl's movements all night.

After Tor had gotten the prince away from her—*she* was courting the *prince*? This girl's life did not add up—she had wandered around aimlessly with her head down, like she'd done before, nodding when she was acknowledged, but never speaking. The longer Gothel watched her, the more he realized she wasn't just wandering, she was orbiting. While she never really looked at anyone, she always seemed to know exactly where the members of her family were. And she always stayed far, far away.

The other three, by comparison, were nearly always together. Sterling and Genevieve wheeled their boy around like a trophy, using him to win favor and sympathy from their guests. If Gothel didn't know any better, he'd say the girl wasn't a part of the family at all.

What were they *doing* to her? What was so awful that she didn't dare speak, even look, and didn't fight as they kept her locked away like some kind of dog?

For a moment, Gothel wondered if the girl would end up thanking him for taking her away from this place.

"Even if this somehow doesn't work," Calder said as he fell into line beside Gothel, carrying a tray of empty glasses, "I take solace in the fact that I look exquisite in this jacket, and I plan on keeping it."

"Good for you," Gothel muttered, resisting the urge to itch his neck again. He hated the purple uniform. It was tight, scratchy, had zero pockets, and the crisp fabric crinkled with every movement.

For the duration of the unbearably long evening, Gothel and Calder had successfully managed to smuggle Boone and Tor into the party in their stolen attire while being the worst servers one of these parties had ever seen, judging by the number of dirty looks and harsh complaints they'd received. Finally, the two of them actually had to pick up trays of drinks to deliver, for the fear that someone would tell Sterling about them and they'd get kicked out. Since then, they swept from one edge of the house to the next. Calder had refilled his tray three times; Gothel had gotten rid of two glasses.

They stood at the edge of the refreshment table, watching Tor get twirled around by the crown prince himself. She was never *ever* going to let that one go—they'd be hearing that story for the rest of their miserable lives.

Their dance finally ended. Tor tried to extend it to another song, but the prince graciously declined, and she backed off after a signal from Boone. She made a face at him, but let the prince go. Gothel watched their future king, as they all did, waiting for him to leave. It was the unspoken rule that they wouldn't do anything with him here, especially since they were so close. That would be tempting fate too much.

Once he was free of Tor, the prince didn't stay long. He stopped to say goodbye to the Coronas, actually getting down on a knee to talk to the boy, whose perpetual smile nearly cracked his face in half at the sight of the prince, then headed for the door.

Calder let out a breath, like he'd been holding it for ages. Then he went rigid. "Where did she go?"

Gothel did another sweep of the place. There were more people than there had been even just a half hour ago, but the house didn't feel cramped. It took a second to glance over every head, and he got a warning glare from Boone before catching a glimpse of her thick braid ducking into the hallway. Shoving his tray at Calder, he followed.

Her shoulders slumped now that she was out of public eye. She reached a gloved hand behind her, yanked her braid to pull some of it free, and let the end bounce against her calves with every step.

Gothel furrowed his eyebrows. Gloves? It was too warm for gloves, unless she was hiding something in them. He made a mental note to check for weapons once they apprehended her.

She nearly tripped over herself lurching up the stairs, like she couldn't get away fast enough. Gothel sensed Calder following him; they reached the top just as she closed her bedroom door.

They stopped outside. Gothel held his breath for a moment, listening. Light shuffling. Rustling. A sigh. He discreetly checked the wristwatch he kept hidden underneath his sleeve and glanced at Calder. Boone and Tor should be in position by now.

It was time. This was their moment and, for better or worse (Gothel was inclined to think the second) they were going to take it.

Hopefully, they wouldn't die.

With a nod to each other, Calder soundlessly turned the knob and Gothel pushed the door open.

It was dark inside, the only light coming from an oversized illuminated clock on the wall. She had already changed. The gloves were off; her hair now flowed tangled and free. Her dress sat on top of a pile of laundry, and she was back in the simple, dark clothes she'd been wearing when Gothel had first seen her.

She jumped off the bed when the door opened and took in the servant uniforms. Something worked her jaw, as if she knew what words to say—like 'get out'—but was struggling to form them. For a Corona, she was terrible at giving orders.

Calder closed the door behind them. Her eyes widened.

"Scream," Calder said quietly, his voice friendly and threatening at the same time, "and we'll slit your throat. Understand?"

The girl stared blankly, her hands clenched into fists.

Gothel huffed. They didn't have time for a fight. They wouldn't survive one either.

What's your play, Gothel?

He shoved her thin, doll-like frame forward and kept a hand on her as Calder pushed aside the thick curtains to open the window. Cool wind stole into the room, rustling the loose papers stuck between dusty books on the shelves.

Calder poked his head out the window before nodding at Gothel. They were ready.

The girl didn't fight when they picked her up and lowered her out the window. She did give an airless shriek when they let go. There was a muffled thud from below, the sound of Boone catching her.

Calder took the rope he'd stowed inside his jacket, and they used it to scale down the side of the house. Boone's heavy hand kept the girl in place while Tor studied her like a creature she'd never seen before. Her hair in the moon made her look like a wraith, and her expression had glazed over in shock.

The grounds were empty save four couples. Keeping a casual pace, Calder and Gothel led their group to the far gate used by the servants during the day. The night air was crisp and still, faint sounds of talking and music coming from the house, as they pushed Sterling Corona's daughter through the gate and off her property.

A group of late partygoers passed them on the street. Gothel and Calder melted back, keeping the girl in between them, and Tor took Boone's arm, instantly falling into the drunken lovers ploy. The partygoers didn't even give them a second glance.

A stolen carriage was parked down the street. Calder got in first, then Gothel pushed the girl in and went after her. They sat her in between them. She was small, tinier than before, folding in on herself and starting to tremble.

Ulf was sitting across from them, waiting. He stared intently at the girl as Boone and Tor stumbled inside and shut the door.

"Get us out Ulf," Boone commanded. He regarded the girl like fresh meat he would devour raw. "Now."

Ulf made a hand motion, having lost his reservations about using magic when the stakes were this high—and, likely, the revenge this sweet. The carriage lurched forward, getting farther away from the Corona's estate with every second.

"Well, girl." Boone leaned forward, reaching his arm toward her face. "You're going to make us very rich."

She flinched away from him, her first movement since they'd barged into her room. Budding fear grew in her expression and slowly edged out her blank shock, but there was a hollowness in her cavernous eyes buried underneath the panic.

Gothel thought of the way she interacted with no one but the prince, and how people forgot about her after one glance— the way she had been locked in her room for days and appeared to be a ghost haunting her house rather than a person living in it.

He could see the reflection of the question in her eyes: how long would it be before anyone even noticed she was gone?

CHAPTER 3

A GREAT FREEZE

Rosalind's teeth rattled in her mouth as the carriage sped through the night. The old transport was practically falling apart, and every bump nearly jostled her into one of the guys sitting on either side of her. One was calm and relaxed, clearly enjoying himself and leaning closer to her just so she'd flinch and shy away. The guard on her right, in contrast, was a blank slate—maybe even a little bored.

She wasn't sure which scared her more. Her shoulders ached from trying to scrunch herself into nothing.

Strangers had taken her. She was alone.

The thoughts came sluggishly. She had to work to understand what was happening, to keep herself calm enough that the nervous energy inside her didn't break free.

Three people sat across from her: a beautiful, familiar woman who hadn't stopped smirking at Rosalind like this was all a game; a stoic man with heated eyes, buzzed hair, and a silence that seeped into the air around him; and another man, the leader by the way everyone regarded him. He only got more intimidating the longer she looked at him.

What did they *want* with her? The two guys flanking her wore servant jackets from the house—was the rest of her family in trouble? What about the party guests?

"Well, girl." The leader leaned forward with a razor-like grin, reaching his arm toward her hair. "You're going to make us very rich."

She flinched back, trying to bury herself in the worn seat.

"Skittish little mouse," the woman purred. Rosalind wasn't sure who would eat her first: the woman or her boyfriend.

"Down, kitty," the easy-going fake servant whispered, and the woman winked at him.

Their leader didn't appreciate the banter. His grin dissolved into a scowl. "Knock it off, Tor," he snapped, and the woman sat back, her eyes flashing like steel. Then he glared at the fake servant and barked, "Calder, don't antagonize her." Calder gave an easy shrug.

Not bothered. Unruffled. Like this was no big deal.

Who *were* these people?

The bald leader gestured to the silent one next to him. "Let's get this going, Ulf."

The quiet one set his intense gaze on her as he reached into his bag. Movements methodical, he pulled out a bundled cloth.

Rosalind's eyes widened. She tasted metal, and a spark ran along her fisted hands. She jerked away, and collided into the bored, fake servant to her right. He started to recoil but caught himself. His reaction to her sent a ripple in her gut, and her fists clenched tighter, as if, through sheer willpower, she could keep all of herself inside.

Ulf shoved cloth toward her face. Rosalind half screamed and turned away, but Calder held her down, giving Ulf his window. Between the two of them, they managed to press the cloth over her nose and mouth.

A heat inside her flared but the mixture was faster. The last thing she remembered was an assaulting wave of too much lavender laced with chemicals.

* * * * * * *

The dream was hazy this time. It had been years since she'd been put to sleep, and she'd forgotten how hard she had to squint through the fog.

It didn't matter. She had the nightmare memorized anyway.

A current danced across Rosalind's skin, and something skittered in her head, disrupting the dream. With a soft groan, her eyes cracked open.

A foul stench of grime and sweat assaulted her nose when she took a shaky breath. The collar of her shirt clung to her neck; her fingers ached. She raked her eyes around the unfamiliar space, but she couldn't see anything save a light in a lower corner.

Stairs. There were stairs, and the candlelight was coming from the floor below. She lay curled up on a thin mattress against the wall with something overhead. A bunk. They'd put her on the bottom bunk.

Wincing at her building headache, she turned to see another bunk bed pushed against the wall across from her. A large trunk sat by the stairs, overflowing with fabric, and someone had thoughtlessly shoved a worn mattress in the corner next to it. The whole room couldn't be any bigger than her closet back home.

Home.

Rosalind bolted upright. Her forehead would've smacked against the top bunk if she hadn't been lying on her hair. A painful whip of her neck brought her crashing back down into the mattress. She hissed, yanking her hair free from under her and petting down the wild static as she cradled her head and tried to work through her situation.

Why had they done it? Why did they need *her?* She wasn't good for anything, didn't have any special skills or talents. In all the stories she used to read, princesses were kidnapped because of jealousy or some kind of power play. She didn't have anything to be jealous of or any sway. Besides, Rosalind wasn't a princess. She was worthless.

They didn't need magic—Ulf had it. The leader must've not had much power if he didn't do the work himself, and the two fake servants, Calder and No Name, hadn't used any to apprehend her. Rosalind shivered. How did they get in her house in the first place?

Her odds didn't look good. It was five of them—at least one of them magically capable—against one little her.

What do they want from me?

A laugh sounded from downstairs. Calder. She could tell from the way he had teased her in the carriage. Even in kidnapping a girl, he was smiling and carefree. She wondered about his story. Did he take anything seriously? Or was he so used to this sort of thing that it didn't bother him? Rosalind shuddered.

"Stay focused," someone snapped. The leader. Rosalind recognized the sharpness of his voice, poised to cut and ready to watch the blood flow. "This has to be perfect."

"Easy there, Boone," Calder said. "We have some time. Ulf's already got the anti-tracking charm on her. This'll work just fine."

"I don't know," Tor said. Rosalind shuddered at the predator she sensed hiding behind that pretty face. "She didn't even look at her family all night, and they didn't interact once. Gothel's right about them not noticing, but they also might not even care."

Rosalind's stomach clenched like she might be sick. Even this random stranger knew about her place in her family.

Tor's tone turned playful and dangerous. "Although that little princeling might pay a crown or two. I wouldn't mind having *him* owe me a debt."

Roman. They were using her to get to Roman?

Boone scoffed and spit at the same time. "We aren't involving those bloodsucking egomaniacs. This is between us and the Corona house, specifically Sterling. We send the letter demanding the ransom—if they haven't noticed she's gone, they will when they get the letter. Even if they don't care about her, we just have to use her to threaten his reputation, and he'll pay. Once it's secure, we dump the girl, pay Pepperjack, and everything gets squared away. I don't care where she ends up. We just get the money and go. By the time she makes her way back home, we'll be too far for her to ID us to her royal boyfriend." There was a slap, as if he'd hit a wall or table. "It's as good as done."

It's as good as done.

Reality came at her in a rushing stampede. The odorous air was too dense, the fabric underneath her too stiff, and she couldn't breathe. Clenching her aching hands, she lurched to her feet despite her spinning head.

The floor creaked under her weight. Faster than she could blink, a shadow was there with her. She could see the glow of his burning eyes in the dark as he raised his arm.

"No!" she gasped, her soft voice hoarse. "No, please—"

But he pressed the cloth against her mouth. Lavender. She'd never be able to stand the scent again.

* * * * * * *

"She settled again?" Boone asked when Ulf came back down the stairs from putting the girl back to sleep. It sounded more like a demand—Boone was concerned. It heightened Gothel's nerves. He wasn't Boone's biggest fan, but he could still respect the man's ability to do the job, and the fact that he was coming undone proved how dire their situation was.

Ulf nodded and made a hand motion as he slid back onto the bench next to Boone. Gothel didn't know what it meant, but Boone nodded back with a grunt, so it must've been good news: the girl was still immobilized.

So far, Gothel had refused to think about the possible repercussions if they got caught. All of them were wanted for petty crimes, but kidnapping, especially a nobleman's daughter, went far past that.

"As I was saying," Boone went on, sweeping away his annoyance—and fear—about the girl's awakening, "we need to get the message written and sent. Everything will take care of itself afterward."

Gothel refrained from rolling his eyes. He wouldn't go *that* far. There were still several things that could go wrong.

Instead of voicing them, he asked, "Where's the metal?" They'd already been through it, but it was a sticky point that grated on his nerves, and the oversight could lead to so many dangerous avenues.

Calder whistled under his breath and Tor sat back, bored. Ulf settled his gaze on Gothel, unflinching even though technically it was *his* mistake, while Boone openly scowled.

"It's coming," Calder said before Boone could pounce. "Ulf already explained that the supplier was running late, but we should have it no later than tomorrow afternoon."

That was too late. Ulf had used some of his old contacts to purchase a type of metal that could render a person's magic useless. The king's fairy hunters and prison guards used it the most, and nobody else was supposed to have it, unless, of course, you knew who to ask. Ulf had asked, and they'd expected to get it before the kidnapping. Boone had ordered they continue without it since the party was a perfect opportunity. Gothel had protested. Per usual, he'd been overruled.

Of course, *he* had been the one charged with storming into her room unprotected.

"We shouldn't do anything else without it," Gothel said. "We shouldn't have even gone this far without it. It's a miracle she didn't blast us the second we put a hand on her."

"She was in shock," Tor scoffed. "Poor little mouse couldn't have done anything if she'd wanted to."

"Shock wears off," Gothel replied. "She's a *Corona*. She can probably blink us all to dust."

Boone leaned forward, resting his elbows on the old table so it creaked. His gaze was fueled, kindled, and ready to set Gothel on fire. "She won't get the chance." Each word came measured and controlled, which revealed his frustration. "Ulf will keep her unconscious until we get the metal. Maybe even after, if necessary. When she wakes up, we're gone and the ransom is paid. I don't care what happens to her after that."

They stayed locked in a stare down. Boone leaned farther forward, working his sharp jaw in an attempt to intimidate. Gothel imagined his own face remained as impassive as always, but Boone seemed to get more irritated the longer they stared at each other.

A knock sounded. The spell broke. Boone sat back and Gothel rubbed his neck as Ulf shot for the door. He didn't open it all the way as a brief transaction passed. Less than sixty seconds later, he eased into his seat again. Weighted eyes on Gothel, he dropped something on the table, and it rolled a few inches before spinning and then finally falling still. A silver ring.

Gothel raised an eyebrow. Boone set his jaw, as if inviting Gothel's skepticism so he had a reason to eat him for dinner.

"That's it?" Calder's face wrinkled with a frown, unusual for him. "It's tiny."

Ulf remained expressionless. Shocker. Boone, on the other hand, puffed his chest out defensively, as if he were the one responsible for the ring instead. "It's enough," he growled.

Tor reached forward, cat-like, and plucked the ring off the table. She managed to hold it only a few seconds before she hissed and dropped it. A resounding clink rung out as it fell back onto the table.

Calder smirked and made a show of picking it up. "Doesn't hurt me."

Tor's glare could've slit his throat. "At least I *have* magic," she spat back, then gave a wary glance at the ring. "Of course, I'm no fairy. Or Corona, for that matter."

Ulf started to sign something, but Boone waved him off. "The stronger the magic, the more metal is needed. If she's a real powerhouse, the ring just might dull the edge or make her sick, but that should be enough."

That didn't sound like enough to Gothel. Too many variables existed—Boone had to know that.

Just then, Ulf stiffened and slashed his hand violently through the air. That one, at least, Gothel knew, or could interpret: either 'stop' or 'quiet,' both of urgent nature. They fell silent, scarcely breathing as Ulf's wide eyes glanced everywhere.

Then Gothel heard it too. A scuffling sound. Outside.

Someone was here. And since they weren't knocking on the door of their hideout, that someone wasn't a friend.

Tor eased herself back to peek out their only window and swallowed hard.

"Royal guards," she whispered. "We're surrounded." She pulled back, only to be met by a band of horses neighing. They'd seen her.

A man started shouting—instructions for surrender, probably—but it was drowned out by Boone's howl of rage. Gothel barely had time to jump off the bench and get back before Boone swiped at him, effectively knocking a bowl of fruit onto the floor and shattering it. He got stuck in the bench, so his swing fell short of Gothel and caught Calder across the jaw instead.

"Traitor!" he bellowed in between a string of expletives.

"Easy, Boone," Calder said, holding his hands up as if placating a snarling wolf. "No traitor here."

Boone's face went red, his thick hands curling into deadly fists, as he snarled at Gothel. His eyes screamed murder.

He didn't show it on his face, but backed up against the kitchen sink, Gothel felt his heart pound with fear.

What's your play, Gothel?

"Our hideout is a secret protected with our lives." Boone practically foamed at the mouth with a thirst for Gothel's blood. "Someone sold us out."

Gothel opened his mouth to protest when a soft gasp sounded. He turned to see the girl stumbling down the stairs, wide eyes locked on the torchlight dancing through the window.

Tor was up and on her in less than a second. Eyes wild, Ulf jumped over the table, landing on the ground next to Gothel and yanking up the escape door on the floor by the stairs. He jumped through and vanished. Tor dragged the girl after him.

Pounding started on the door as the guards shouted at them. Gothel moved for the exit door. A solid wall of muscle went up in front of him, and he crashed into it only to get Boone's wide fist smashed in his jaw. He staggered back. Boone wound up, ready to rip Gothel apart piece by piece despite the threat of capture. He hit again. Gothel dodged. Boone snarled and went again, but Calder yanked him from behind.

"Enough!" he shouted over the pandemonium. The guards were almost through. They'd all get thrown into a tiny cell and never see light again.

Calder looked between the two of them—Calder, the boy Gothel had met in a grim orphanage, who had adopted him into Boone's crew, and knew Gothel would never sell them out—and settled his gaze on Boone.

"Come on, Boone," he said, the confidence deflating out of him as he settled with quiet resignation. He refused to look at Gothel when he pulled on Boone's shoulder and leaned down next to the exit. "Let's go."

And then he was gone. Because that was the easiest path, and Calder always took the easiest path.

Now, Gothel had a pack of royal guards behind him, and a seething Boone in front. His mind started calculating the fight, how best to get around Boone, and get out, but the brute surprised him: he jumped down the exit.

Gothel leaned down to jump—the guards were nearly through the door—but then he saw Boone blocking his path.

"You *never* belonged here," Boone snarled at him. Then he slammed the escape door shut. The heavy lock clicked as it slid into place, and the front door split apart as royal guards swarmed inside.

* * * * * * * *

Tor's grip on Rosalind's arm made her hand go numb. Rosalind would have never thought such a slight woman could be capable of so much strength, but she tugged Rosalind down the stairs effortlessly. They dropped through the escape door in the floor while Boone and No Name fought—well, Boone yelled and No Name just stood there—and Rosalind found herself with Tor in a grimy underground tunnel. Someone dropped down right after, and she recognized Ulf as he took off down the tunnel and disappeared into the blackness without so much as flinching from the drop.

With the taste of metallic dirt on her tongue, her stomach clenched with anxiety. Tor yanked her deeper into the tunnel. Rosalind hiccupped with panic and electricity surged from her gut and spread over her skin.

Tor hissed and jumped away from her, the scowl on her face a distraction from the fear glimmering in her eyes.

77

Rosalind's throat closed up, and she reached inside of herself, begging for a tendril of control. She couldn't do this here. With people. Underground.

An image flashed through her head: broken bodies and puddles of red, Tor's ebony hair singed and matted into the dirt. Tor, who thought she was the villain of this story, but had no idea the monstrosity she dragged along behind her.

Not now, please, not now. Rosalind's freedom was not worth that human sacrifice: of the kidnappers or scrap of humanity left inside her. *Just stay calm.*

Tor stared at her like she was an animal, swaying toward her and then retreating, as if she couldn't decide what to do. Then Calder was there. He didn't look at Tor, which even Rosalind had guessed wasn't like him, as he disappeared after Ulf. The door slammed so hard the sound reverberated throughout the tunnel, and then came Boone without No Name. Had he already been caught?

Boone took one look at the girls and then glowered at Tor, who scowled back despite the menace emanating from her boyfriend.

"She shocked me," Tor said, and Rosalind wished they'd just bury her in the dirt.

Boone hit Rosalind across the face so hard she crumpled to her knees. A cry of pain escaped her lips when he wrapped some of her hair around his wrist and jerked her head back so she had to look into his blazing eyes.

"You give me any more trouble," he warned through his teeth, "the slightest holdup, and I will personally make you regret ever being born. Do you understand me?"

Rosalind stayed stone still, afraid his eyes would scald her if she moved.

He rattled her head, garnering another cry from her. "Do you understand me?"

Rosalind nodded, and Boone forced her to her feet before dragging her through the tunnel with her long hair as a leash. She clenched her hands into fists and begged the stars to keep her together. For just a little longer. Until those guards found her. Then this would all be over.

The escape tunnel wound on, and Rosalind stumbled in her attempt to match Boone's pace without succumbing to the suffocating darkness. Just when she thought she'd never see the surface again, a cool breeze touched her cheek, and she breathed in the faint scent of sky and trees amid the stale dirt.

Keeping an aggressive hold on her hair, Boone led her up an incline and they emerged outside. Rosalind's eyes darted upward, and she gasped at what she saw. The sky. Inky and billowing out forever and dotted in more twinkling stars than she had ever seen. Overcome by the beauty of it, she tripped. Boone snarled in exasperation and pulled her on, and her eyes shifted to see what he was looking at.

Now a quarter mile or so away, she could see the shack they'd abandoned was overgrown with ivy and nearly falling apart. A group of six or so guards had surrounded it, and based on their shouting, she guessed more were inside. Though she had no reason to care, she tensed as the torch-fire licked the rotting wood, coming too close to setting the whole building ablaze.

It wasn't until they'd nearly cleared the dirt lot toward a grove of trees that it occurred to Rosalind she should scream and alert her rescuers.

She opened her mouth, but Boone jerked her around him and smacked her so hard she saw even more stars. "Stay *quiet*," he warned, "or I'll give you something to scream about."

Rosalind didn't have time to let the threat sink in. Something whizzed past her smarting face. Another one came at Boone, and when he ducked, the tree behind him crackled as bits of bark flew everywhere.

And then she realized something: the guards weren't there for her. They were shooting *at* her.

They didn't know she was here.

Her heart sank even as something in her head told her disappointment was ridiculous. Of course nobody was coming for her, especially not this early in the game—she'd never given anyone a reason to miss her, and they likely didn't even know she was gone yet.

She was alone. More than she'd ever been locked inside her room.

The magnitude of the thought knocked her to the ground. Suddenly, she felt the weight of the world pushing on her, and a current ran over her skin, raising the hair on her arms.

I am alone.

Boone didn't leave her time for self pity. He dragged her behind the trees where Tor and Calder ran ahead. A cacophony of angry, demanding shouts sounded behind them. Boone still had her hair.

She was running with criminals.

How did she get here?

Boone slammed to a halt, and Rosalind careened past him only to be jerked back, her scalp screaming as she skidded into the dirt. Voices argued over her, but they weren't as sharp as whatever she'd fallen onto.

Dazed, she rolled and wiped something wet off her arm, only to find it warm. The scent of mud and fire melted away, and Rosalind sucked in a sharp breath at the metallic smell that assaulted her nose.

Shaking, she looked down. Her hand was smeared red.

Blood.

The sight made her hazy, and caught her between reality and a dream. Suddenly she wasn't sure what was real. She just screamed for the young boy that frequented her nightmares, only to find him in a puddle of red.

A wave of panic crashed over her, and she fell below the surface of consciousness before she could explode at the impact.

* * * * * * *

Gothel ran for his life.

He'd barely managed to hide and then escape from the horde of royal guards descending upon their hideout, but the freedom was momentary and they quickly discovered him. The stupid horses kept sniffing and braying like bloodhounds, as though they had a personal stake in getting him caught.

After tonight, he named them his most hated animal.

The cool night air whipped against his face as he broke out of the hideout and sprinted for the trees. A zap of magic barely missed him. This wasn't the first time he'd been chased down by royal guards, but tonight was different—if Gothel got caught tonight, it would be because of Boone, and Gothel would rather his own mistakes come back to kill him than be beaten by that meathead.

For a second, Gothel wondered if, in the four years he'd spent with Boone's crew, he always knew it would end like this.

Tree branches scraped against his arms as he pushed his way through the grove of trees protecting the eastern side of their region. The grove wasn't large, but it was cover. It would work tonight.

Tonight, no matter what Boone said or did, Gothel was getting his money. No matter what came against him—betrayals and guards included—he would get that Corona girl back and get things squared with Pepperjack. Boone and the others had drawn their line in the sand, and Gothel was going to be on the living side of it without worrying about their fates. They sure hadn't worried about his.

He shook the thoughts from his scattered mind and pumped his legs faster, away from the sound of horses behind him. He barely slowed down as he launched himself into a tree. His worn leather boots found purchase in the thick bark as he scaled it, not stopping until he found a sturdy branch near the top. Then he secured himself and went still.

The night seemed to pause. Up here, nearly thirty feet off the ground, everything was sharper. Defined. Gothel tasted the ash and pine in the air as it fluttered through his hair. He could hear the distant humming of the bugs and sprites that burrowed into the trees. He could feel his palms sweating, and each beat of his pounding heart rattled against his ribcage.

Then the horses shot through the trees below him, shattering the scene and lurching it back into motion. Leaves rustled and the ground shook as the royal guards raced past him. Gothel waited until he could hear his own breath again before he nimbly descended the tree and searched for footprints.

While Ulf hardly made an imprint, and Tor and Calder had managed to practice the art of stepping without a trace, Boone was a human wrecking ball. Finding his tracks was easy, and following them was even easier considering the small footsteps that trailed behind.

Gothel was still surprised the girl hadn't put up a fight. Sure, her wide eyes bled fear everywhere, but fear only paralyzed you for so long, especially in a chaotic opportunity like this. Why hadn't she set them all on fire and made a run for it? He would chalk it up to the ring Ulf had traded for, if it weren't for the fact that the ring was in Gothel's pocket. Nobody had noticed him grab it when the guards showed up— except maybe Ulf, but he'd been too frightened at the prospect of getting caught again to do anything about it.

Fear means action, Gothel thought as he pressed on. *You might freeze at first, but then you react.* Why hadn't she reacted yet?

She would, Gothel knew. She would, and he would need to be prepared for that. The small ring in his shirt pocket thumped softly against his chest with every step. It would have to work.

Gothel slowed when he heard muffled arguing. Keeping his footsteps silent and precise, he stole through the trees until he came upon Boone, Tor, and Calder standing in a loose circle, Ulf long gone now. The girl was in a heap on the ground, scratched up. She'd taken one look at her bloody hand and passed out.

What was *wrong* with her? Maybe her family locked her up because she was defective or something.

Breaths shallow and even, Gothel stood still as a statue, nearly a part of the tree pressed to his back. He'd do this quick and easy. In and out then gone.

Gothel waited until Boone was in the thick of his argument—pushing Tor and Calder near the edge of their patience—before settling into a crouch.

One. Two. Three.

He rolled on the ground once, twice, then landed face first on the girl's limp body. Taking her in his arms and steeling every muscle in his body, he rolled with her, once, twice, out of the way. Without breaking his stride, he dragged her into a bush with him and held his breath. Then, on second thought, he put his dirty palm over her mouth, just in case she woke up too soon.

There were four beats of near silence before a muffled eruption: Tor and Calder trying to keep Boone quiet as he realized the girl was gone.

They didn't have time to hash it out, though. Gothel could hear the sound of thundering hooves getting closer as the guards circled their way back through their little grove of trees. One set of footsteps finally gave up and left—Tor's, by the sound of the graceful agility with which she got out of there. Calder was still trying to reason through Boone's string of expletives as he stomped through the brush trying to find where the girl went.

But there were no footsteps to follow—just a slight smear of dirt that could've led any direction. Gothel never left a trail, and he never got caught. It was probably the only reason Boone had tolerated him all these years.

Of course, Calder bailed once the horses got closer. Gothel heard Boone clomp around for a few more minutes, then someone must've spotted him because there was a shout, and he took off. An earthquake followed him. Gothel squinted through the branches as the royal guards sailed right past.

He waited a few minutes, just to be sure. When it seemed safe enough, he extracted himself and the girl from the bushes, pulling the rogue leaves and branches from his hair. Hers was a lost cause. Between everything caught in her ridiculous hair, the dirt and blood smudged on her skin, and the red bruises on her face, she looked worlds different from the vacant girl dressed up at Sterling's party.

The bruises, he assumed, were from Boone, not that it surprised him. Maybe that's what had scared her the most. Maybe the rumors were true and Sterling did beat her, so any violence rendered her incapacitated. It was more than believable, and if that weakness of hers helped him keep this situation under control…

Gothel's skin prickled uncomfortably at the idea of having to hit her himself. He didn't believe in hitting people outside of self-preservation—a belief instilled in him ever since he lived with Wrothen at the orphanage where he met Calder.

Calder. A spineless, pathetic excuse for a friend. Thinking of him made Gothel flare with anger: anger at Calder for his betrayal, at himself for caring when he knew he might've chosen his own survival too if the situation had been reversed.

Maybe he and Calder had never been friends at all. Maybe Gothel had never known a friend.

He'd learned from a young age that you couldn't build your foundation on people. They always crumbled, and you would always fall. He knew that, had never done it since, but for whatever reason, standing in the clearing alone and exposed, the ground felt unstable beneath his feet.

What's your play, Gothel?

With a silent sigh of exasperation, Gothel shook the distracting thoughts out of his head and looked over the girl again. Waking her up was dangerous. Leaving her unconscious was a chore. But he hadn't come this far to quit now—he'd have to carry her.

Okay little princess Corona, Gothel thought bitterly as he hauled her over his shoulder. *You'd better be worth all of this.*

And with the royal guards out for his head, his backstabbing friends out for his blood, and a kidnapped noble on his shoulder, Gothel set out into the night.

CHAPTER 4

TO OPEN
A DOOR

For the first time in years, Rosalind's dream was different: when she huddled in the dark, she sensed not one, but two monsters lurking behind her. The first she knew by heart. It had haunted her every night for what seemed like lifetimes. The other was new, but she recognized the smell of insatiable bloodlust: Boone.

He yanked on her hair, and the cavernous space echoed with Calder's mocking laugh and Tor's predatory purring. And somewhere, even in the pitch black, she felt Ulf's gaze on her, staring at her with those horrible eyes full of all he left unsaid.

Then the darkness shifted, and the young boy skipped into view. Boone smiled a greedy smile and started for him. Rosalind tasted metal and panic at the sight of such a cruel brute heading for her brother, and the air crackled with electricity, surging through her bones and knocking her flat on her face.

When she pushed herself up, she found both Boone and Zachary on the ground, her arms coated with their blood, and Calder laughed when she screamed.

Her breath hitched when she shuddered awake. Blinking against the dim lighting, she felt herself nearly gag at the queasiness in her stomach and fogginess in her head. Muscles aching and joints stiff, Rosalind started to stretch herself out when something caught on her arms and pulled at her wrists. They'd been restrained.

Her eyes flew open to a drafty, cramped room. She lay on a thin excuse for a mattress shoved in one corner, and her wrists were bound with a short rope tied to a metal notch in the wall. Her clothes were soiled and torn, and a scratch cut across her right arm. Then a glimmer caught her eye: a silver ring on her right hand. Confused, she pulled it off her finger.

Her queasiness evaporated in seconds, and her headache pittered out as some of the aching in her joints dissipated. A hole she didn't realize existed in her core filled back up. She felt lighter and more alert.

Her eyebrows furrowed as she studied the ring. What *was* it?

A subtle scratching sound captured her attention. Rosalind looked up and promptly dropped the ring, her mouth parting in a silent gasp. Huddled on the floor in the opposite corner next to the door was the one guy in Boone's crew whose name she didn't know. He had pushed his sleeves up to his elbows and was leaning over what looked like a piece of paper in his lap and a pen in his hand. His usually blank face was screwed up in concentration as he sketched or wrote or did whatever he was doing.

She only watched him for a second before he went completely rigid. Rosalind stiffened too, unsure where the first threat would come from. Where was Boone? The others? What had happened to all the guards?

Where *was* she?

No Name raised his head, body still frozen, and settled his dark eyes on her. They stared at each other. Rosalind didn't move, anticipating what he would do, what he saw. Now that it was relatively quieter and lighter, she noticed things like the watch on his wrist and that he was younger than she had first thought—maybe early twenties—and her mom would say he was about due for a haircut. She could even hear Zachary whining that he thought growing it longer gave it more 'flair.'

The snake coiled tightly in her chest. Did they know she was gone yet?

No Name watched her for a moment, his face going blank again as he subtly yanked down his sleeve to cover his watch. She saw his eyes dart to her hand, as if in routine, then on her now clenched fists. His mouth faintly twitched down.

Rosalind curled inward, her fingernails biting into her palms. Nobody ever really looked at her anymore. Even when she was outside her room, people tended not to look long, let alone stare. There was nothing to see anyway, besides her hair, which even from the corner of her eye she could tell was a disaster.

No Name seemed to be thinking about something, though it was hard to tell what. Rosalind didn't know what she should do. Ask him about his plans? Try to talk him down? Beg for her freedom? She wasn't sure how she could convince anyone—herself included—that she was worthy of freedom. She'd heard the way Boone talked about her father. No Name probably hated her family too.

A solid minute passed before No Name set aside his paper and pen and slowly got to his feet.

Rosalind tensed. She was already incapacitated, and the room was only a few feet wide—he could tell her anything from over there. A faint gasp went through her teeth when he took a step toward her.

Reality crashed into her harder than ever, pounding with every step of No Name's heavy boot against the wood floor. She was locked up with criminals, alone, in a strange place, and while they'd talked only about using her for ransom, they didn't make any promises of what they would or wouldn't do with her—or *to* her—in between. Especially No Name. He hadn't given any indication as to whether he cared about mercy, or if he was more sadistic than Boone, or if he had any personality at all.

She scrambled as far into the corner as she could, horrific images passing through her mind. What could No Name want with her all alone in this tiny room? He leaned toward her, his hand on her wrist, and she saw a flash of Boone slapping her to stay quiet.

The strong taste of metal laced her tongue as electricity surged through her. Too much to hamper. Too fast to stop. Then, when his hand clamped around her wrist, a mangled yelp escaped her and a swell shuddered through her limbs, heating her skin until something burst. The contact disappeared. She slumped face first on the mattress.

It took her a second to regain her bearings, then her blood went cold at what she saw. The mattress was ripped and singed in places, the damage rippling out from where she sat. Dings peppered the wooden walls, the slightly bent pen sat forgotten on the floor, and No Name was in a heap in the far corner, his hair a mess and part of it stuck to a small cut on his forehead.

No. Rosalind choked on nothing, unable to find air, as she looked from the destruction to her trembling hands. A distant scream echoed in her mind. *No no no no no.*

A scuffling sounded. She glanced up to see No Name now crouched on his feet, about to stand. He froze when he saw her looking at him, and slowly held up his hands in a placating gesture. There was the slightest break in his stoic expression, and she saw it, just the tiniest flash but still there: fear.

He was afraid of her.

The snake in her gut constricted around her, so tight she couldn't breathe, couldn't feel anything outside of the pain of it, outside the panic. Panic everywhere.

No Name cocked his head slightly, his eyes narrowing as he studied her, slowly lowering his hands. Rosalind wanted to warn him, to tell him to run, just in case, but she could only get out a choked apology, her voice raspy with disuse.

He seemed taken aback by that, but the surprise only flashed across his face for a moment. Movements slow, he rose to his feet and walked toward her, then settled on his knees in front of her, the mattress dipping under his weight. The ring she'd taken off rolled down the compression it made and hit his knee.

Rosalind gasped softly when he picked up the ring and took her wrist again, his actions slow and cautious now, though he tried not to show it. His face was impassive as he pried her fist open and went to put the ring on her finger.

Instead, he paused. The panic in Rosalind dried up into shame when she realized he was staring at her palm—her scarred and bruised palm ridden with dozens of fingernail marks.

When he saw her staring at him, his eyebrows furrowed with annoyance, and he shoved the ring on her finger. The second it came in contact with her skin, everything inside her recoiled. A void opened up in her core, and she felt shaky and sick again.

No Name glanced at her, as if noticing the change. "Keep it *on*," he said in a low growl. After fixing the rope around her hands so they couldn't reach each other anymore, he straightened up and retrieved his paper and pen, careful not to turn his back on her.

Rosalind flinched away from the threat in his voice, then started when the void inside her grew. Her stomach still coiled, but there was no taste of metal, no crackling in her core, no heat on her skin. Like the magic inside her had been sucked away by the ring.

That's what the metal was: magic suppressant. Only the royal guards were supposed to have it, and yet here was a thin strip around her finger, keeping her power at bay.

Immense relief echoed somewhere in her mind, but her heart went numb, overtaking any sense she'd had inside. She crumpled into the corner and set her eyes on her bound wrists, her pulse aching with the truth.

She deserved to be a prisoner.

✳ ✳ ✳ ✳ ✳ ✳ ✳

This girl was messing with Gothel's head.

He thought he knew what to expect from Sterling Corona's daughter. He had anticipated a spoiled, entitled girl that would mock his status and remind him of his place in the dirt—a girl that would be so easy to kidnap and hold ransom. A girl that would be so easy to hate.

94

This girl was nothing like he imagined.

Gothel had hauled her through the night, nervous she would wake up before he could acquire a small room at Wren's tavern. She'd stirred several times before he could secure her, and each time he'd frozen over, sure she would come to and blow him to bits. But her face just scrunched and her eyebrows furrowed and her mouth twisted around an airless groan—as if she were fighting to stay under. As if unconsciousness was safest for her.

It didn't make any sense.

He'd immediately begun to work on trying to formulate a plan, but plans weren't coming. Every idea unraveled before it came together. There were too many variables, too many issues to tackle. Especially now that he was on his own. How could he manage to keep the girl contained and hidden, send the ransom message, ensure it reached the Coronas, work out the drop off location, secure the money, get the girl back, and serve the money to Pepperjack by himself?

It was too much. Especially if one of Pepperjack's spies took their empty hideout as them running from their debt— and especially if Boone came after Gothel.

What's your play, Gothel? How could he possibly get out of this one?

Four days had passed, and he was still asking himself that question. None of his shaky ideas had panned out, and he found himself at the counter in Wren's tavern, swirling a drink in a cup he didn't actually want. The lively establishment was usually the kind of place Gothel found solace in. Drunken chaos and rowdy conversation were solid opposites to his stoic invisibility, but that was how he thrived.

Tonight, however, the roaring laughter and stench of ale only seemed to pick at his fraying nerves. With another idea falling apart, and the girl as much a ghost as ever, he'd ended up swirling a half empty cup without drinking it.

He rarely got this wound up, and he found himself nicking things off the people around him out of nervous habit, desperately seeking a way to calm his knotted stomach. Nobody suspected him.

One man finally noticed his pocket watch was gone, and threw an accusatory punch at the guy next to him. Wren kicked them out before anything got started—he had no patience for violence. He did give Gothel a hard warning look, though, as he went back behind the bar, and Gothel willed his thieving hands to relax for the night or he'd lose his room for sure.

He'd been in the room less and less, despite his earlier reservations. At first, he'd spent every moment with his eyes trained on the girl in case she made a move. But after she'd blown him into the wall, she had sunken even deeper inside herself. She didn't move. Didn't speak. Just stared at nothing, completely hollow, and was always there when he returned.

He couldn't make anything of it. That moment when he looked over and realized she was awake—and had taken the ring off—he had known he was in trouble. The moment after she'd blasted him and he'd jumped to his feet, ready to do what it took to save his life, he'd thought he was a dead man.

What's your play, Gothel? He'd thought it would be the last time he'd ever ask the question.

He had watched her, waiting for the attack, slowly realizing that she didn't have a play either. There she was, perfectly able to take the moment and leave him at her mercy, and she did nothing.

It made no *sense*.

And then, finally, she opened her mouth. He'd prepared himself for the worst. But she just stuttered and choked her first words to him without anything behind them.

She apologized.

She *apologized.* As if he wasn't the one who had stalked her house, fooled her family, and stolen her away. As if he wasn't the one who had put her in the hands of brutes, tied her up in a disreputable tavern, and refused to let her leave.

As if *she* were the villain of the story.

He could still hear the strangled words in his head, see her horrified face as she stared at her own hands—hands that were covered in scars and scabs, wounds that looked like they'd come from her own fingernails. No wonder she'd been wearing gloves at the party.

Against his better judgment, Gothel took a swig of his drink, if only to melt the images of her away. He knew her behavior shouldn't bother him: she was the perfect prisoner, after all, especially now that he'd acquired some of the sleeping concoction Ulf had used on her to keep her unconscious, which had been the plan from the beginning. The ring had been meant to be a safety net, not the main thing to rely on, but she hadn't even tried to take it off again. Why?

Wishing for anything else from her was ridiculous. He was in way over his head already. But still, it ate at him. She wasn't even trying.

And behind his infuriated irritation with her behavior, a question poked at his brain like the sharp end of a dagger: what could happen to a person to make them stop trying?

Even in his worst times, abandoned in orphanages or stealing alone on the streets, when he loathed himself most, the goal had always been to survive. That came first. No matter what.

But the more Gothel watched her, silent and docile like a broken doll, the more he realized that she didn't seem to care. He actually had to make her eat. She'd selected the crusty bread heel and glass of water he'd brought up, drinking some and nibbling less, but it seemed more out of bizarre obligation than anything.

A week ago, Gothel would've wanted to throttle her for spitting out the food and snarling that she'd never stoop low enough to eat like peasant rakes—that's what he had expected from her, after all. But now he was itching for anything, even an insult, to come from her mouth.

He thought he knew exactly how to handle a spoiled, entitled girl who had never known a hard day in her life. Now he wondered if she actually resided in a deep hole darker than anything he'd ever encountered. If he were honest with himself, he'd acknowledge that his desperate attempts to make a plan had fallen underneath his mounting obsession over the girl. Every time he tried to plan how to get a letter to her house, he plunged into compulsory brooding over what went on inside it.

What was Sterling doing to her? What had hollowed her out and turned her into this shell of a person?

Gothel thought he knew the limits of his hatred for Sterling Corona, but it had increased in the last few days. Instead of planning for his own future, he was consumed with thoughts of the silent, raven-haired girl and what went on behind the walls she had sequestered herself in.

Abandoning his drink (it wasn't that good anyway), he stood from the bar and shifted on his feet, unsure where to go. The girl upstairs pulled and repelled him like the scene of a gruesome accident.

In the end, he started heading for the door. Fresh air would clear his head—he wasn't good at being cooped up and he wouldn't go far.

"Running away again?"

The quiet voice wound its way through the commotion and breathed into Gothel's ear, slowing him to a stop. He narrowed his eyes and surveyed the tavern twice before he noticed the figure in the far corner booth.

"Well, this is a surprise." Gothel slid into the bench across from the figure.

He couldn't see much underneath the thick hood of her cloak besides her pointed chin. "I live for surprises," Irina murmured, her deep voice smooth as a melody and rough as a stone. "Though, it seems you have found yourself wormed in too many."

"Why are you here, Irina?" Not that Gothel minded. Besides Calder, Irina was the closest thing he had to a friend, but lately friendships had only brought him trouble, and Irina always showed up with heaps of it.

"I'm not supposed to be," she admitted, swirling her lithe finger around the top of her full cup. "But I caught wind of something as I was passing through."

Gothel gave half a shrug. "Probably a rumor."

Irina's head snapped up enough that he could see her bright green eyes flash. "You sold yourself to a monster."

"*I* didn't do anything."

"Really?" Irina snarled. "Then why are there three of his men roaming around this village asking for your whereabouts?"

Gothel's mouth dried up. "What?"

"Honestly, Gothel, if you were that desperate then you should've come to me."

"Boone was the one that went to Peppe—"

Irina smacked her glass on the table, and Gothel jumped despite the sound getting lost in the clamor around them. "Don't say his name!" she hissed. "Anyone here could be one of his mutts."

Gothel gritted his teeth, determined not to let it show how much her fear got to him. "I thought you don't bow to the kings of men," he said with an air of ridicule.

She scoffed. "The kings of men aren't kings at all. They're arrogant fools in denial of their own mortality."

Barely containing an eyeroll, Gothel opened his mouth to speak before she could get on a soapbox about the subject, but she moved on first.

"And Boone is a halfwit, as they all are. You should've never been involved with them in the first place. You never really liked them anyway."

"Are you actually here to help me or just read me a long list of my mistakes?"

"I came to warn you," she snapped.

Gothel sat back against the hard wood of the booth. "Warning received."

"You can't possibly hope to hide from the crime lord. He'll find you."

He hated the surety of her tone—hated that she was right. "And you want to lecture me about hiding from those chasing you?"

He could actually feel her scowl from underneath her hood. "Don't give me arrogance, *boy*." She emphasized the reminder that she had lived many more lives than he had. "Tell me you aren't as daft as those imbeciles you ran around with."

With a sigh, Gothel leaned his elbows on the table and rubbed his eyes. He could use an ally right now, and it was highly dangerous for Irina to be here with him. He told her everything: their group's desperation, Boone's deal, Pepperjack's threats, Calder's betrayal, and the royal guards discovering their hideout. He didn't have to explain that he wasn't the one who gave it up—Irina knew.

Irina sat still and quiet underneath her heavy cloak, listening intently until he mentioned the girl he had locked upstairs.

She made a *tsk* sound, a mix of chastisement and mocking scorn. Teasing always sounded strange in her perpetually grave voice. "Now, Gothel, you may not be a prince, but you're roguish enough to catch company without having to resort to this."

The tips of Gothel's ears warmed, and he clenched his jaw against the rising embarrassment. Even after living with Tor for years, Irina could still catch him off guard. "I'm serious," he muttered.

"I can imagine. You have *Sterling Corona's* daughter upstairs." She took a breath, running her finger around her glass again. "And how do you plan to pull this off yourself?"

"I can't."

"It does sound daunting."

Gothel leaned forward, scrunching his shoulders as though he could block out the rest of the patrons. "I just need you to watch her. Not for long. Just so I can get the message sent and secure the money."

Her thin lips pulled her lined chin taut, and he knew her answer.

"Come on, Irina. You hate the crown, and the Coronas are essentially the same thing."

"I will always hope for the day I watch the castle crumble," Irina responded, a sinister flame dancing in her glowing eyes. "But I will not hold an innocent girl prisoner for the sins of her fathers."

"Then deliver the message for me."

"So those monsters can eat me alive? I won't allow myself to be slaughtered like a pig and roasted for supper."

"Then arrange it for me. Surely you have methods that can take care of it."

Her voice only held cool indifference. "I'm afraid I can't offer that to you."

"Then what *can* you offer me?" Gothel asked in exasperation. "Or are you just here to watch me crash and burn?"

Irina blinked against the expression, but Gothel didn't have time to apologize for it. She cocked her head. "I want to see her."

Gothel raised an eyebrow. "Why?"

"I'm curious."

"She's a person," he shot back. "Not an exhibit."

"Oh, protective, are we? Funny, from the one holding her captive."

"It's not—"

Irina pushed her glass toward him. "Meet me at midnight." She muttered directions before rising from the booth. By the time Gothel stood and turned, she was gone.

He sat for a bit longer in the booth, swirling Irina's drink around the glass and thinking things through. Ultimately, he decided he'd meet with her—maybe he could still convince her to help.

The girl stirred and glanced at him when he opened the door to their room, but she looked glassy and unfocused, as though the action was a muscle memory she couldn't turn off. Her rumpled clothes were still dirty, her pale face still gaunt, and her mess of hair a wild animal on its own, stained with mud and blood and ridden with bits of leaves.

He checked her hand; she hadn't taken off the ring. With that safety net in mind, he sank to the ground facing her, keeping watch as he got lost in his thoughts and waited for midnight to come.

When the time came, Gothel untied her. She still flinched when he touched her, but it was more subdued now. It wasn't until he shoved her into the jacket he'd stolen on his way up that she started to come to. Her eyebrows drew together in confusion, realization dawning that this wasn't a regular trip to the bathroom.

She blinked once, twice, three times, her eyes becoming more and more focused until they settled on him. Her now free hands clenched into fists, and fear danced across her expression, the oversized jacket swallowing up her frail form and making her seem impossibly small.

"Stay close and stay quiet," was all Gothel offered her before pulling her out of the room.

Not wanting to parade her—and her crazy, memorable hair—before the tavern patrons, he led her down the stairs and through the back employee door. The night air was cool and refreshing compared to the sweaty and thick establishment. Gothel allowed himself a breath of it before checking his surroundings for possible threats, then he glanced at the girl. With the glare of the moon against her alabaster face, highlighting the shadows in her eyes, and the backdrop of the trees, she looked like a creature of the woods, rising in the night. Taking another breath, he surged on.

The girl didn't say anything during their journey, nor did she fight his grip on her arm as she struggled to keep up with his pace. She stumbled at one point, and Gothel had to slow down to help her regain her footing, but she cringed away when he turned to her.

A brief image of Boone—then Sterling—hitting her flashed in his mind. He loosened his grip on her and kept moving, a little slower than before.

* * * * * * *

Rosalind trembled as No Name pulled her from the tavern and down the road. He didn't give any indication of where they were going, or why. Did the ransom come through? Were they meeting up with his team? Her nerves prickled at both thoughts. She hadn't paid much attention to what No Name had been up to the last few days, but still, she doubted the money would've come through that fast.

An image of her parents came to mind, sitting at the dining room table with the ransom note, quietly discussing whether they could pay the amount. They had money, sure, but how much was a sullen, silent, dangerous daughter really worth? Ever since she'd overheard Boone's plan for her, she had a sinking feeling that it wouldn't go the way he wanted it to.

The streets were dark and quiet, the moonlight guiding their path. It was late and she was lost. Even if the afternoon sun shone bright, she didn't think she'd recognize whatever village this was or know how to get home.

Home. The word made her bones tremble.

They made it through the main part of the village and headed through a thicket of trees, further distancing them from the buildings. From people. Rosalind shivered at the thought, the implications. Her head was pounding, and she felt nauseated, her legs weaker and shakier than usual. She wanted nothing more than to curl into a ball in the shadows and disappear.

The feeling intensified when the trees finally broke into a clearing. A hooded figure was standing directly in the center, facing them and waiting. It was too thin to be Boone, too short to be Calder, and had a kind of grace that rivaled Ulf's. Though stone still, the figure emanated prowess that reminded Rosalind of Tor, but somehow it didn't seem to fit. Of course, Rosalind didn't know the woman, but something different was in the air here. A type of vitality pulsed from the figure that Rosalind had never encountered.

A stranger. Given the circumstances, strangers were likely not a good thing.

No Name stopped a few feet from the figure, then dropped Rosalind's arm and gestured to her. "Here she is," No Name said, keeping his voice low, though Rosalind detected a hint of annoyance in it. "Happy now?"

The hooded figure stayed frozen. Rosalind's heart hammered. She felt exposed in front of the stranger despite the huge coat No Name had stuffed her in. Was he trading her? Could he not get enough money from her parents, so he had to try a different tactic?

Nobody moved as seconds turned to minutes. What were they waiting for?

After ages had passed, the figure lifted wiry, armored arms and slid the hood from her head. Rosalind couldn't help a gasp when she saw the woman underneath.

She was taller than Rosalind and impossibly thin, but corded muscle shone underneath her tight, armor-like tunic that covered nearly her whole body. Her uneven chestnut hair had been pulled back to reveal a pointed chin and bright green eyes that seemed to glow, cat-like, in the dark. And her face, neck, and every speck of skin not protected by armor, was covered in thick, gruesome scars. The woman might've been beautiful once, even gorgeous, but now, combined with her eyes, she was grisly and fierce. Dangerous. Nearly too much for Rosalind to even look at.

No Name, on the other hand, didn't flinch. He just gave a disbelieving sigh. "Sure, just show her your face," he muttered. "There's a great idea."

She didn't take her eyes off of Rosalind, whose knees shook so hard she thought they'd buckle.

"Now, Gothel," the woman chided. Her voice sounded pained, like a beautiful song that had been chopped to bits and forced up her throat. "This is a friendly meeting. I mean the girl no harm."

No Name—or Gothel, apparently—just shook his head.

Despite the woman's claim to be friendly, Rosalind took a shaky step back when the woman stepped forward. The movement caught Gothel's eye, and he glanced back at her, the personality brought on by the woman's presence now gone, his face unreadable.

"What do you want?" Gothel asked the woman, though his eyes remained on Rosalind.

The woman ignored him. "My name is Irina. What's yours?"

Rosalind's hands clenched into fists. She felt Gothel mark the motion with his eyes, but she didn't move, didn't speak. She didn't know what to do. What kind of trap was this? Why had Gothel brought her out here? Surely it wasn't to make friends.

Irina jerked her chin toward Rosalind with distaste. "Interesting ring. I'm intimately familiar with that type of metal." She cocked her head slightly, studying her. Rosalind folded in on herself, desperate to escape the probing of those eyes. "It's small enough you can at least stand there, with some difficulty, I'm sure, but I know how much it must hurt you. The sickness. The pain. Worse, the chasm inside you, as if draining life with every breath. Gothel has not found a way to bind it to you, yet you still keep it on. Why?"

Something clicked in Rosalind's brain at the mention of the metal. This woman was powerful, she could sense it, but in a much different way than anyone she'd ever met—and coming from a noble family, she'd spent a lot of time around powerful people.

Irina was different. Irina knew the metal.

Because Irina wasn't human.

One corner of Irina's mouth twitched, as if aiming for a smile underneath her scarred flesh, and a fleeting glint of mischief passed in her eyes. "Smart girl."

Rosalind's mouth fell open. "You're…you're a…a…"

"Fairy?" Irina supplied. Gothel sighed and shook his head again.

Rosalind just stared, too afraid to move for a whole new pack of reasons. Fairies were incredibly dangerous outlaws, hunted by King Rowan after they rebelled during the Great War. And they were all supposed to be dead.

Irina took another step forward. "With a father like yours, you must have gone to an academy. Tell me, girl, what do they teach you about my kind now?"

"You rebelled." Rosalind was scared to stay quiet now, scared to make her angry. "During the Great War. Fairies all rose up against the crown, so they…so…"

"So they murdered us all?" Irina scoffed, flicking one of her long fingers clad with a dagger-like fingernail. "Rebellion.

Really?" Another step forward. "Funny, after all these years, they still teach Rowan's propaganda."

Rosalind couldn't help gaping. King Rowan, who had fought bravely and united the kingdom after the horrid rebellion, was remembered as more than royalty in Elaria. He was almost deity. Nobody spoke of him without reverence, even nearly a century after his death.

Irina gave her a wry look. "History is told by those who rule it. Those of us who lose do not get the chance to tell our story—you'd be surprised how many holes they left in your classroom education." Two more steps forward, just a few feet away from Rosalind now. It was closer than she wanted. "But enough about me. I want to hear your story, Lady Corona."

Rosalind flinched. "Rosalind," she corrected hastily.

"Interesting. Are you ashamed of your title, Rosalind? Or are you afraid it is ashamed of you?"

Another flinch. She stepped back. "I don't know…I don't know what you're talking about."

"I think you do." With the barest flick of a finger, the air around Rosalind shifted in a way she didn't like. "Come on out and show us who you *really* are, won't you?"

"Irina," Gothel muttered under his breath. A warning. It caught Rosalind's attention, distracting her from the moment the pulse in the air zeroed in on her, and the ring slipped off her finger.

Rosalind yelped when the effects of the metal dissipated, the suppressed energy now rushing through her veins. She glanced wildly across the ground, but she couldn't find the gleam of metal in the dark.

"Why do you cage yourself, Rosalind?" Irina asked, stepping forward.

Rosalind matched with a step back, her body trembling, her mouth tasting of metal. Visions blurred across her eyes: of Zachary screaming, Gothel bleeding out on the pinewood floor, her mother collapsing to her knees.

Stay calm, she begged herself, but the visions were winning and she was drowning in blood. *Stay calm, just stay calm.*

"What did you do, Rosalind?" Irina demanded.

"Irina, stop," Gothel growled.

Sensing she couldn't hold it, Rosalind turned and ran. She only made it three steps before she collided with nothing and fell to the ground. Gasping in terror, she pushed against the air in front of her, but it wouldn't let her through. A magical barrier.

The fairy had trapped her.

The snake in her gut snarled, and her skin turned hot. Electricity quivered through the air. It was too much. She couldn't take it. She just wanted to go home, but she wasn't sure where that was anymore.

Zachary covered in red. Her mother's airless shriek. Her father's face screwed up with panic.

What did you do, Rosalind? What did you do?

A shudder rocked through Rosalind's frail frame, and she doubled over on her knees. She couldn't see straight; her muscles burned with the strain of keeping herself welled up. She felt her thin control slipping through her fingers, nightmares and monsters rising up in her mind and swallowing everything else.

Gothel shouted something, but she couldn't make out the words. She only saw a sea of red and Irina's green eyes boring into Rosalind's dark, broken soul as the world pressed in from all sides. "What did you do?"

What did you do?

Rosalind snapped. A faint cry escaped her lips and power surged out, lancing across her skin, bursting harsher than usual, as if it had been fighting to get free, fighting to meet the electrifying air and dance with a force that could rival its own.

When it was all out, Rosalind found herself prostrate on the ground, cheek pressed into the cool dirt. Her pulse roared in her ears, and her heart stuttered, thumping too fast. She pushed herself to her knees, terrified to see what havoc she had brought on the clearing, and those in it.

The trees to her right and left were scorched, their blackened trunks standing in mourning over the shredded branches at their feet. Straight ahead, Irina had her hands up, but the gesture wasn't defensive or placating—it was powerful. Neither she nor Gothel had a scratch.

Irina had shielded them from the surge.

Rosalind sagged, intense relief coursing through her and making her limbs numb and limp.

She hadn't hurt anyone.

The fairy moved to come closer, her mouth open to speak, but Gothel stepped in front of Rosalind, blocking Irina's path.

"No. More." He forced the words through his teeth, sharper than anything Rosalind had heard him use before.

Irina pursed her lips into a harsh, thin line, but in the end, she turned and sauntered away.

With his back still to Rosalind, and his eyes on the fairy, he opened his palm. The ring fell, landing on the ground next to her knee. Rosalind snatched it up and shoved it on so fast, she nearly broke her finger. The void crashed on her like a wave, and she allowed the current to overtake her, to fall into the ache because as long as she was aching, everyone was safe.

Her throat beat raw and her eyes burned, but she watched Gothel, waiting for a threat or instruction from him. When a minute passed and he still hadn't moved, she gave up. Curling on the ground, she closed her eyes and let the darkness overwhelm her.

* * * * * * * *

The sun woke Rosalind up early. She wasn't used to seeing sunlight at *all*, really, and she had to blink rapidly several times before the buzzing in her eyes quieted and she could see straight again.

Rolling her shoulders, she pushed herself up to her knees and looked around. Gothel was sprawled out on the ground a few feet away, obviously not trying to hide the fact that he was acting as a barrier between her and Irina. The fairy was sitting on the other side of him. Her hood was over her head again, but Rosalind knew she was watching her. The feeling of Irina's gaze on her skin made her shiver.

"He didn't want to carry you," Irina said by way of explanation, jerking her chin out at Gothel's lazy form in the dirt. He stirred at the sound of her voice. "Evidently he did too much of it the other night to get you here."

Rosalind felt her cheeks go pink with embarrassment, and that only made her feel worse—was it wrong to feel bad about inconveniencing your kidnapper?

Gothel sat up and ran his hands through his shaggy hair, shaking himself out. While Rosalind felt groggy and lethargic, he looked wide awake in seconds. The contrast made her feel like an old woman.

She wanted to ask what the point of this was: where was Boone and the others? Were they out securing the ransom while Gothel petitioned a fairy to help with babysitting duty?

She wanted to ask, but the weight of Irina's eyes made her stay quiet. A memory of last night came—of Irina pushing her to the breaking point—and she shuddered. But she'd been so preoccupied with what the fairy wanted with her, that it hadn't crossed her mind until now what *she* could get from the fairy.

Roman had once talked about finding a fairy someday, but she had never pressed him on it, never learned his intentions, and now she wished she would have. All she knew were the stories people told: stories of powerful creatures created by demons, sent to terrorize and beguile humans. Could she trust Irina?

Irina cocked her head, as if reading her mind. "If you have a question for me, dear Rosalind, don't be afraid to spit it out."

Gothel gave Irina a wary glance. "If you're not going to help, then we're leaving."

"Ah, yes, because you have *so* many places to go." Gothel glared at her and opened his mouth, but Irina waved him off. "Let the girl speak."

Rosalind pressed a fist against her mouth, as though that could trap her irrational hopes inside, but the chance tugged at her soul—the what if. She couldn't help herself. She leaned forward, imploring, her trembling voice making her sound even more pitiful.

"Can you take it away? Please? I don't want…I can't have it anymore. I just can't."

Gothel sucked in a sharp breath, and his stare seemed to cut her, but no surprise registered on Irina's marred face. She just regarded Rosalind, her gaze going over every part of her, as if evaluating. Rosalind thought she would burst from anticipation.

Finally, the fairy spoke. "Some would kill for the raw power you have. Some *have* killed for it. Yet you want me to take it from you?"

Rosalind knew how it sounded. She knew what people would say. She didn't care.

"Yes," she murmured, her voice strung out on hope. "Please."

Irina studied her for another minute, lips pursed, then she stood. Rosalind and Gothel followed suit.

"Go sit over there, Gothel," Irina instructed in her gritty voice, gesturing to the far-off trees. "Give us some space."

Gothel shot her a look. "Space for what?"

"I don't want you in the crossfire of our training."

Rosalind's stomach dropped. Gothel's jaw nearly fell open, but he caught himself.

"Training?" he repeated. "You mean you think I'm going to sit back and let you *train* her?"

Irina made a shooing gesture. "Move along, Gothel. Unless you'd like to train too."

"I'm a rake," he replied flatly. "I have no magic. But thanks for reminding me."

"You wouldn't want magic," she told him. "It wouldn't suit you."

He started to protest further, but Rosalind beat him to it.

"I can't tr-train," she said, stuttering over the dangerous word. "It's not…it's not safe. I can't. It's not safe." She thought the spectacle last night would've been enough to convince everyone of that.

Irina nodded at her. "Child, you cannot hurt me. You must learn to control it."

"I don't *want* to." Her hands clenched into fists. "I want it gone."

"I cannot take it from you—that's not within my power." Irina's coarse voice softened slightly, as much as it could, when Rosalind deflated. "But I can help you."

To everyone's surprise, Rosalind let out a breath that sounded like a dark laugh. "You can't help me. Nobody can."

How could she make them understand? How could she get them to see?

I'm a monster! she wanted to cry, to scream, to shriek at the sky. But the words got lodged in her throat.

"Come on," Irina said, settling into a ready stance. "Take off the ring. You won't have forever."

Gothel let out a defeated sigh and stepped away.

"No," Rosalind told them, "you don't understand. I *can't*."

"Can't or won't?" Irina challenged.

Rosalind thought a moment before admitting, "Both."

The fairy continued to try coaxing her, but Rosalind sat back on the ground, covered her head with her arms, and refused to move. Thoughts of her family came, of her father's assured manner and her mother's melodic voice and Zachary's persistent knocking and Roman's unconditional love, and she found herself wanting to cry.

How had she gotten so lost?

Hours went by as the morning melted into afternoon. Rosalind still didn't move out of solidarity, out of shame, out of the fact that she didn't know what would happen to her—or maybe she just didn't care enough. Gothel and Irina spoke quietly to each other several times, but she didn't try to make out their words. She was a prisoner, a monster on their leash, and she knew it was better that she didn't try to run. Irina would stop her anyway.

When she heard the crunching of footsteps drifting away, she finally tilted her head up. To her alarm, Gothel was gone. Her hands clenched into fists as she watched Irina take a seat on the ground just a foot or so away.

"He went to find food and water," she explained.

Rosalind stayed silent, anticipating some kind of attack. Nothing came.

The sun beat down on them. Sweat dripped down Rosalind's back and plastered her scalp—she hated the heat. Irina, on the other hand, lounged back on her elbows, slid her hood off, and tilted her face toward the sun. Rosalind couldn't help but flinch. Without the shadows of the night as cover, Irina's scars were so much worse. So *monstrous*. It nearly hurt just to look at her.

Rather than stare at the horror, Rosalind dropped her gaze to the dirt.

To her humiliation, Irina caught the movement. "I have not looked in a mirror in over a decade," she said. "Though I am sure the reflection has not improved."

"I'm so-sorry," Rosalind stammered. "I didn't mean...I didn't mean to be offensive."

Irina gave a marred grin. "Darling, my *face* is offensive."

She thought of Zachary playing by himself and swallowed hard. "Still, it shouldn't reflect how people look at you. It's not fair."

"Life rarely is."

Feeling obligated to at least try, Rosalind looked up from the ground and forced herself to look at Irina the way Zachary would want to be looked at: the person before the scars. "If...if you're a fairy, can't you…I mean, aren't you powerful enough to…"

"Hide it?" Irina supplied. "On occasion. If I find myself in a difficult situation, I will to prevent being caught. But I cannot hold it indefinitely. I do not know why. My magic is still strong. Sometimes I wonder if it knows. If it wants me to live with the burden of remembering."

"Remembering what?"

Irina tipped her head back and closed her eyes. "As you said, my kind were branded traitors and put to death. Many escaped, however, and live in hiding, as I did—as I do." Something in her tone hardened and broke, making it almost painful to listen to. "Eventually, suspicions arose in my village, and a witch hunt began. I was peaceable—a girl—and I had not hurt anyone. But when they finally discovered what I was, everyone I knew, everyone I loved, turned on me. They tied me up and burned me at the stake."

Rosalind's stomach rolled, and she fought to keep the nauseating image from burying her. "And you…you survived?"

"In some ways. Though they did not intend that." The corner of her mouth pulled up faintly. "Magic, I suppose."

"I'm so sorry," Rosalind said, and she meant it.

Irina opened her eyes to look at her. "Why do you cage yourself, Rosalind?"

She felt her hands ball into fists, her shoulders slump, her head bow. She thought of Zachary. His laugh. His scream. She thought of her father and his quiet calm, and her mother and her loving heartbreak. She thought of Roman and his long road to the crown, of Boone and his malicious smile, of her own vacant eyes every time she accidentally looked in the mirror. Of everyone knocking as they desperately tried to get her to respond, not realizing that she was too far away to be reached.

After a long moment of staring in the dirt, she whispered, "I am so afraid."

Irina nodded, as if she expected that. "One would think that once a person has experienced the most amount of pain they can bear, they would no longer be afraid, but I've found it does not work like that."

Rosalind jerked her head up, gaping at this fierce woman who seemed to breathe power. "But you don't *look* afraid."

"Dear, I'm *always* afraid." She leaned forward slightly, her eyes drilling into Rosalind's soul. "But I ask you this, as I once asked myself as a scarred fairy hiding underneath fruit carts and crying herself to sleep every night while rats ran over her feet: are you going to let fear control your life?"

Rosalind's lips pursed. Her father had asked her a similar question once. It hadn't been long after Zachary's accident, but long enough that it became clear Rosalind would never be the same. He asked if she would let the incident rule her life forever. It was the last time she opened the door for him.

Now, as she did then, Rosalind remained silent. People didn't realize that it wasn't a matter of deciding whether to 'let' fear control you. Because sometimes fear *took* control, and no matter how much you yanked and pulled, you couldn't get it back.

But that didn't sound nearly as poetic, and it was a lot scarier to admit.

So nobody did.

"What are you thinking, Rosalind?" Irina asked.

"It's just..." Rosalind bit her lip, not wanting to anger the fairy.

"Just what?"

"Just...I don't believe fear works that way."

"What way?"

Rosalind looked down at the dirt again. Except Roman, she hadn't had a real conversation in ages, and those tended to either be wistfully childish or emotionally venting. She hadn't spoken, much less defended, her beliefs in a long time. Nobody had *asked* for them in a long time.

"That it's…" Rosalind found herself rubbing the ring on her finger. "That fear is a choice. Or that it doesn't consume you. We can talk of not letting it control us, but I think…I think that's us being naive. Wishful thinking. Of course it will. It's the fear of getting caught that keeps you in hiding, right?"

Now Irina pursed her lips, watching the sky as she pondered. "Yes. Also a need to survive, but, yes, the fear of capture is a dominant motivation."

Rosalind's chest felt a little lighter when the fairy didn't contradict her. "We like to say we master our emotions, but I think we just say that to make ourselves feel better."

"I agree with you," Irina said, "but I believe you are only looking at one side of the coin, so to speak. You cannot be brave if you are not afraid. Just like you cannot have light without dark, or happiness without despair. People can delude themselves into thinking they only want the pleasant side of life, but they miss the fact that peace can only be achieved in the balance of all things, good and bad. A truly happy life is not one without pain. It's one of balance."

That didn't make much sense to Rosalind. After all, her life would be so much better without the dark weights she carried and threw on everyone else. But then she thought of Zachary—a boy who cherished every star because his world had become so dark.

She watched the sky with Irina as a lone cloud rolled through. There was a moment it covered the sun, and the world around them became shadowed. Protected, in a way.

"You won't be this way forever," Irina murmured without breaking her gaze from the puffy cloud. "Right now you are saturated with misery. It feels too heavy to carry on its own, let alone with anything else. But you'll master it in time. You'll grow strong enough to carry it as well as your happiness." When Rosalind started to argue, Irina held up a finger. "Your shoulders are strong enough to carry it all. But first they must learn how."

"You're saying that…that somehow this disaster will get better?" Rosalind shook her head and rested her chin on her knees. "I don't see it."

"Not better," Irina corrected. "Just different."

Then the cloud rolled on, the sky brightened up, and Gothel returned. Instantly, the cozy and confiding atmosphere snapped in half. Irina got to her feet and sauntered to Gothel, asking if he'd noticed anyone following him and commenting he should move around for a reason Rosalind didn't catch. Again, she wondered at the mystery of Gothel's plan, of the endgame.

She drank the water and ate the apple that he brought her, then Irina announced that she had to go.

"When you're ready," she told Rosalind, "you find me." With a tip of her head at Gothel, the fairy was gone.

Gothel took her back to the room in the tavern and tied her to her spot again, though the rope wasn't nearly as tight as it had been the first night.

Heavy with the weight of Irina's words, Rosalind found herself slumping against the wall, unable to fight exhaustion.

Hours later, she awoke to a tugging on her scalp. Huffing, she wriggled her body in an effort to free the caught strand of hair from wherever it was stuck. When that didn't work, she blinked open her groggy eyes, then stifled a scream.

Leaning over her with a lock of hair in one hand, eyes gleaming with hatred in the dark, was Tor.

CHAPTER 5

LOST IN THE THORNS

Rosalind's mouth opened to scream, but Tor lunged forward to slap a hand over her lips, hitting Rosalind's head against the wall.

"Quiet, you little—"

And then Tor's weight disappeared. Rosalind flinched back from the dancing shadows, her eyes slowly adjusting through the ring's dizziness. She could barely make out the figure in front of her, which nearly obstructed her view of another lump on the floor.

"Tor," Gothel greeted curtly. Rosalind sensed the tension rolling off of him.

Across the small room, Tor rolled to her feet in one graceful movement. Moonlight seeped through the tiny—now open—window near the ceiling, the illumination glinting off Tor's eyes and something in her hand.

A knife.

Rosalind's blood went cold, and her muscles locked in terror. Was this what Gothel had kept her for? Waiting for one of his friends to come and...what?

"Come on, Little G," Tor said quietly, her usual smooth purr disrupted with something like desperation. She bounced on the balls of her feet in agitation. "Don't make this harder than it has to be."

"Tell Boone he can get his money some other way. This job is mine."

"You can't leave him out to dry like that."

"Like he left me?"

This was news to Rosalind, but Tor shrugged. "Business." Then she sighed, and her shoulders drooped with defeat. "Look, give me the girl, and I'll make sure you get a cut of the ransom. I can slide it out under Boone's nose. He never has to know."

Rosalind clenched her hands into fists, sure Gothel would consider the deal and take it. She remembered how he stood up for her against Irina and never pushed her further than she could go. If it were a choice between him and getting passed off to Tor, she'd gladly stick with Gothel.

But to her surprise, Gothel just scoffed. "Don't insult me. I've watched you do this for years. You can't play me."

"Fine," Tor snapped. Her shoulders straightened, all defeat melting into defiance. "Boone has it out for you, but I don't care. I'll get my money no matter who is holding her leash. We can do it together and cut the rest of them out."

"So Boone can chase both of us for the rest of our lives? Stop pretending to make me promises you don't actually intend to keep."

Tor hissed, taking a step forward. "Give me the girl, Gothel."

Rosalind cringed back, but Gothel didn't budge. "So, what, you can bury her out back? I don't think you'd bring a knife that big just to take some of her hair."

Realization dawned on Rosalind, and she sucked in a sharp breath. Tor was here to *kill* her. Take a lock of hair to use as proof for her family. Kill her and dispose of her body. They'd get the money and disappear, and Rosalind would never come home.

Tor snarled. "Did you really think Boone was going to let her walk away after she saw all our faces? This was always the plan. He just didn't tell you because he knew you'd be too spineless to go through with it. He didn't plan on you betraying us."

If Gothel was surprised at the revelation, he didn't show it. "Was it always the plan for you to be the one to kill her? You've pretended to be a lot of things, Tor, but I don't think even you can fake your way through murder."

"Better her than me," Tor replied coldly. "And you're lumped in now. You gave us up."

He shook his head. "You know I didn't do that."

"Boone said so, and, honestly, I'm not surprised anymore. You've never tried to be one of us. Now step aside, or I'll kill you too."

Another scream caught in Rosalind's throat when Gothel didn't move and Tor rushed forward, knife raised. She squeezed her eyes shut, unable to watch, unable to shriek, as her shaking hands clenched into fists and her nails bit at her palm.

This was it. This was how she died.

She wished she could have talked to Roman one more time. She wondered if he was looking for her. She wondered if he would ever figure out how she disappeared without a trace.

Rosalind flinched when something clattered to the floor. In a burst of courage, she opened her eyes to find the knife, forgotten in the standoff, a few feet away. Tor attacked Gothel with precision and vengeance, and though Gothel didn't reflect her grace, he managed to dodge most of her furious blows while still blocking Rosalind.

It took Rosalind four precious seconds to make the decision.

Trembling, she shifted her weight and stretched a stiff leg out. It took three tries to kick the knife within reach of her bound hands, then cut herself free.

Lurching to her feet, she barely made it two steps toward the door when Tor grabbed a fistful of her hair and yanked her to the side. Rosalind put all the weight she had into the crash, knocking both girls into the wall. Then she snatched her hair back, fighting a cry at the smarting on her scalp, and ran out the door.

She collided with someone on the stairs. A man, scruffy, burly, concerned. He asked her if she was okay, but she squeaked in fear and ducked around him, scampering the rest of the way down the stairs.

It wasn't until she got outside that she stopped. The fresh night air was silent and still, the roads around her empty. Where could she go? Where *was* she?

Rosalind didn't have long to question. Gothel was suddenly pushing her forward. She opened her mouth to protest—or ask about Tor—but as they rounded the corner, they collided with someone else.

Men again. Two of them. But they didn't ask if she was okay.

Gothel gripped her shoulder, the most contact they'd ever had, and jerked her back, closer to him.

"Gothel," the man on the right greeted, his gold teeth glinting in the moonlight as he sneered. "Where you running off to now?"

The man on the left, taller and angrier, scowled through his graying beard. "You really think you can run from Pepperjack, boy?"

Gothel's fingers dug into Rosalind's shoulder, but she barely felt it under her terror, the snake coiling viciously in her gut.

"Tell him I'm getting the money," Gothel said tightly, and, for once, Rosalind detected a hint of fear in his voice. "It's coming."

"Not fast enough," the older one growled. "Your time is nearly up."

The other stretched his grin too wide for his face, teeth gleaming—*all* of them were gold, Rosalind realized with a new wave of nausea. "Better hurry, kid. Jack's itching for some new pelts." Then he raked his gaze over Rosalind and her hair, and he smiled wider. She shuddered.

Gothel pulled on her, slowly walking them both backward and away. "He'll get his money. I'm getting it."

The men watched, one laughing, the other scowling. Once they had turned the corner of the building, Gothel yanked on her.

"Run."

She did.

The dirt road was firm under her aching feet as she ran after Gothel, fighting the urge to turn around to see if they were being followed. He ran the way they had come, passing the tavern and fleeing away from the heart of the village, closer to the trees on the outskirts.

Having lost their pursuers in the safety of the trees, Rosalind and Gothel paused to catch their breaths. Rosalind leaned on a trunk, panting against the weakness in her joints, as Gothel surveyed the space with narrowed eyes.

Through her building headache, Rosalind panicked over what to do. Boone would keep coming after her, wanting to *kill* her, and it was very possible she'd be easier to find if she stayed with Gothel. She had no idea where she was or where to go. She didn't even know how to get away from Gothel in the first place—she was tiny and frail, especially with the ring on.

Should she take it off?

A flash of an image: a pile of bodies, the dirt stained red.

An echo in her mind: Zachary's scream.

She shuddered, repulsed with herself. Of course she couldn't take it off. She had to do something else.

But what? She couldn't even remember the last time she'd *done* anything. Had she spent so much time trying not to be a monster that she'd forgotten how to be a person?

The regret hit her right in the gut, harder than ever, nearly making her collapse against the tree trunk.

When she died—tonight, by the look of it—she would die a monster.

* * * * * * *

Tor.

Tor was *here*.

Gothel had known Boone would be after him, had assumed numerous lies were told to get the crew after Gothel's head. Or maybe Boone didn't have to tell any lies. Maybe the whole group had always hated him, or at least been indifferent, and nobody had to tell them twice.

After a life of bouncing between orphanages, the sting of being unwanted should have lost its bite by now. Gothel had never really cared what Boone or any of them had thought of him anyway, but he couldn't deny the sharp lance in his chest when he woke up to find Tor in their room, knife raised over Rosalind.

Gothel wasn't stupid—he knew he was made for sneaking, hiding, and disappearing, not fighting. Tor was so incensed, it was easier to dodge her attacks, but that was the most he could do.

Then Wren showed up, having heard the scuffle, prepared to kick the violent tenants out. He stopped when he saw Gothel and had detained Tor without question while Gothel found Rosalind and made a run for it.

He owed Wren so much.

He *hated* owing people.

The threat of Pepperjack filled his lungs as Gothel panted and searched the clearing for an escape.

Boone. Pepperjack. Two sides of the coin of Gothel's potentially grisly fate. He couldn't let it come to that.

What's your play, Gothel?

Rosalind was predictably silent besides her own panting, her body shaking so hard he wondered if she'd snap in half. If she hadn't yet realized that Gothel didn't have a clue what he was doing, it was clear now. This would be the perfect time for her to run. Escape. He would if he were her. He'd wanted to, for as long as he could remember, just run, disappear, leave it all behind.

He just didn't have anything to run to.

"You heard of Pepperjack?" he asked Rosalind.

She shrugged. If he hadn't seen her plead her case to Irina, he would wonder if the girl could talk at all.

"He's…" Gothel couldn't find the right words fast enough. "…bad news. Those men that just saw us, they work for him. They're following me." He glanced away, unable to look at her pale face as he admitted what he'd dragged her into. "They've seen your face now. Your hair. They'll remember you, and they'll assume you're with me. You're their target now too."

You need to get me that money. At this point, the ransom was just as much about saving her life as it was his.

She shocked him by speaking, albeit quietly. "You mean, I can't go home if they're looking for me?"

"Not unless you want them to follow." He had an image of her sprawled out on her bed, her throat slit as hair and blood cascaded over the side of the mattress.

He blinked and shook the scene from his head.

Rosalind pursed her lips, her already ashen face paling further in the moonlight. If she had intentions of bolting, it didn't show, and that made Gothel calm and panic at the same time.

What's your play, Gothel?

Suddenly, a rustle sounded in the trees—a rustle, but no breeze.

"Go." He could barely get enough air to cough out the word. "Run."

He shoved Rosalind forward, just as the rustling burst through the trees and he caught a glimpse of the slightest shadow.

"Gothel!" Tor shouted once she realized he knew she was there. Gothel spared a second to wonder if she'd left Wren alive.

He pulled Rosalind through the trees again, the girl regaining enough composure to run as fast as her short legs would carry her despite the heavy, painful breaths that escaped her mouth.

"Gothel!" Tor shouted again, closer this time. They could only run for so long. "Stop!"

He glanced at Rosalind's pale and sweaty face. Would she be faster without the ring? Was it insane of him to even consider it?

He'd seen what she could do without it. From what he'd gathered, she was even more powerful and uncontrollable when stressed or scared. He would just have to get Tor close enough, yank off the ring, and duck. The problem would be solved.

It was such an easy plan—one Boone would love—but Gothel's stomach churned at the thought of not only orchestrating Tor's likely murder, but setting up a fragile young girl to do it for him.

No. No, there had to be something else.

What's your play, Gothel?

They ran for what seemed like seconds and hours, the ground growing rocky and uneven beneath their feet. He felt Rosalind slowing, Tor gaining. His pulse thudded in his ears as he wondered how many more heartbeats he had left.

Then he heard it, so faint he thought he was dreaming. Acting on instinct and desperation, Gothel snatched Rosalind's arm and yanked her to the left, her hair getting tangled between them as she struggled to keep up.

Hope erupted in his chest when the faint sound grew louder, into the bubbling rumble of water. A fleeting memory flashed in his mind: one of the first weeks after Calder found him again. A day out by a shallow pond, eating the spoils they'd stolen, and Calder playfully attempting to throw Tor in the water. Instead of a mischievous fight—as they'd all expected, and Calder had probably hoped for—Tor had screamed and punched until he let her go, skittering away from the water like a frightened kitten. She didn't talk to Calder for days, choosing to silently glare at him from Boone's lap while Calder sulked and Boone smirked in satisfaction.

Gothel hoped Tor hadn't gotten over her fear.

They ran toward the roar, and Tor's furious shouts drowned in it. Gothel swallowed the smell and moisture of damp earth and mossy rocks, the thick air sticking to his throat. Then Rosalind skidded to a sudden stop, halting Gothel with her. He was about to protest until his eyes adjusted, and he realized they were at the bank of the river, the water surging along somewhere below them. It was hard to tell in the night, but the drop seemed to be at least ten feet, if not more: not enough to kill, but likely enough to hurt.

Gothel turned to Rosalind. "We have to jump."

Her mouth fell open, body tensing and eyes wide. Before she could do whatever she was going to do—argue, scream, run, freeze—a shadow broke through the trees, Tor's eyes glowing with rage, knife in hand.

Gothel didn't wait. He jumped, hauling Rosalind off the edge with him.

The damp air enveloped him, tossing his hair, tearing at his clothes, pushing on his skin. The rumble of the water was deafening. He kicked his legs wildly as he fell, and fell, and fell. They should've hit by now. There was water down here, right?

Had he misjudged the sound in the dark and just thrown them off a cliff?

Then they hit, the water rising up to swallow them whole. Gothel's skin stung as he got sucked under. He lost his grip on Rosalind, and chaos surged around him. He kicked up, only to slam into dirt, and he realized he didn't know which way *was* up.

Lungs bursting, he finally broke the surface and took a big gulp of air. The freedom was momentary. Within seconds the river yanked him under again, viciously thrashing him down its path.

Gothel choked on water and air. He was dizzy. His chest hurt. His body ached. He couldn't see or move, couldn't find Rosalind, couldn't get to the bank. The current was too powerful.

He'd made a mistake.

Getting tossed around, his arm caught in some stringy moss. He tried to shake it off, but a swell came up and threw him into a rock. Under the pandemonium, he heard a whimper, and the rock shuddered beneath him.

It wasn't moss. It was *hair*.

Gothel latched his arms around the rock, his muscles straining against the current to keep from getting swept away again. Rosalind was doing the same underneath him, getting crushed between him and the stone. She'd lost her stolen jacket, her soaked clothes clinging to her frail frame, and she was trembling. Hyperventilating.

Shaking water out of his eyes, Gothel craned his head up. The slope of the bank was slick and nearly vertical—impossible to climb. He couldn't even see the top, only blackness and the spray of unforgiving water.

Another swell slammed against them. Gothel's fingers started slipping against the slick surface. A raspy scream erupted from Rosalind as a second wave hit, and they lost their grip. They tumbled back into the current, now connected by her mess of hair around his arm.

The river sucked him under again, as if eager to drown him. When he managed to find the surface, he saw a fork approaching. The right path continued on into dark oblivion. The river went past his sight on the left, but bits of water sprayed back, as if hitting against something.

Gothel didn't think it through. He yanked on the hair around his arm until Rosalind crashed into him, then he used all his strength to jerk them left. Gaining some understanding of what he was trying to do, Rosalind clung to him as she kicked against a rock, giving them the momentum to slide into the left side of the river just as it split.

Gothel nearly whooped with victory, but the sound died in his throat when they got close enough to see what lay ahead: a cave. The river threw them inside, as if a prison guard, and the darkness went from black to inky, a thick, tangible presence. The moon illuminated the entrance slightly as the waves slammed them back against the cave wall, the water levels fluctuating with the river.

They were going to drown.

Gothel struggled to swim forward, kicking off his heavy boots and using the wall behind him for momentum, but the water forced him back into the cave.

They were trapped.

* * * * * * *

134

Rosalind spluttered and coughed as her head broke the surface, gulping down the humid cave air. Her eyes burned, her limbs ached, and her hair was everywhere. The tugging on her scalp pulled harder as she finally made out Gothel's shape, urgently diving toward the cave exit. The water pushed him back. He tried again. A third time. On the fourth, the current shoved him back with extra force, as if it were a parent dealing with an unruly child.

The snake coiled tight in Rosalind's tired lungs. They were trapped.

A wave crashed in, smashing both of them against the rocky wall and dragging them under. Disoriented as she was, it took longer for her to find the surface, only to hit her head against the ceiling.

The water level was higher. Another swell, maybe two, and they would drown.

Suddenly, Gothel's shadow came closer and her hair pulled. He must've been tangled too. She squeaked in surprise when he reached for her arm, then felt his way up it, across her shoulders, and down to her other hand. Understanding came too late. She clenched her fist just after he yanked the ring off her swollen finger.

The change was instant and the relief glorious, spreading through her like a soft, contented sigh. Her limbs still ached, her head still throbbed, her stomach still knotted—she'd been wearing the ring a lot—but it was a much duller pain than before. The alleviation only brought panic because she knew exactly what came with it.

"Use your magic," Gothel barked, his carefully braided composure unravelling. "Get us out."

A creature stirred inside her, slowly waking after being put to sleep by the metal. Rosalind's skin crawled at the idea of waking it up, here, without Irina, in such a confined space, with so much at risk.

She'd kill him. She'd kill him and then she'd drown alone.

They were going to die, and she couldn't save them.

"I can't." She spit out a mouthful of water splashed in her face by Gothel or the river or maybe both. "I can't."

He gripped her arm. "You have to. Blow a new exit, stall the river, move some water out. Do *something*."

Rosalind shook her head violently. "No, no, it doesn't...I can't...it doesn't work...like that. I can't. I can't." Her chest felt like it was caving in on itself. The pressure was making it hard to breathe.

"It *does* work like that," Gothel shot back. "I've seen it. You can do it."

"I can't."

"If you don't, we will *die*."

The creature inside her growled, angry at being caged for so long. She started trembling at the heat rushing through her.

"Give it back!" She lunged at Gothel, but the water made her slow, and he caught her by both her arms.

"No! We're going to drown!"

A wave crashed in, knocking Rosalind out of his grip, and they tumbled to the side. She kicked her feet wildly, having to tilt her head back to keep her nose and mouth clear.

"Do it!" Gothel shouted.

She cringed inside herself as the sound vibrated on the walls, pressing in her, making her crack. Her teeth came down on her tongue when she tasted metal. Electricity danced on her fingertips, and she felt the water around her warm.

She gasped and tried to stop it. Turn it off. At least direct it somehow. But the water only got warmer. Warmer. Uncomfortable. Hot.

"Rosalind." Gothel quietly drew her name out with dread as he realized what was happening. "Rosalind, stop."

Steam rose from the water, pasting her already plastered hair to her face and the back of her neck. Her skin prickled with the energy emanating from it, shielding her from the rising temperature. She could smell the heat, though. It clouded up her lungs. Made her toes curl as she desperately treaded water.

A bubble broke on the surface. Gothel hissed. "Rosalind, you need to stop." He tried to keep his tone even, calm, but it wasn't working. "Turn it off."

"I can't!" she snapped back. She felt traces of anger in her system, something she hadn't aimed at anyone besides herself in years. What had he expected in taking the ring off? How many times had she said she couldn't do what he asked? "I can't!" Her voice rose, bouncing sharply off the cave walls. "I'm not enough and too much and *I can't!*"

The water erupted with her words, soaring up over their heads and dragging them down. Rosalind's head slammed back against the wall; stars danced across her vision. She barely managed to keep holding her breath as her senses came back to her, and she pushed up. Something had a hold on her hair and yanked her back. Panic shot through her as her lungs burned, and she scrambled in the dark to jerk her hair free. When it didn't come, she felt along the wall until she found the problem: there was a fist-sized hole in the wall, slowly sucking out water and, along with some tangled debris, her hair.

Zeal rushing through her, she managed to free the strands before shooting upward, desperate for oxygen. She broke the surface and her head smacked against something else. The ceiling. They only had a few inches left.

She heard Gothel spluttering as she took a giant breath, and the words exploded out of her. "There's a hole! There's a hole in the wall and—" Her exclamation was drowned out by the water surging up to the ceiling, as if it had understood her cry and was trying to silence her.

But Gothel had heard, at least enough, because she felt a hand around her wrist pushing her onward, asking her to guide him. Together, they fumbled along the rock with their hands and feet. The darkness was impossible; the water was unyielding. But despite her usual inclination to give up—this was *too hard*—she felt Gothel's desperation bleed into her, and that fueled her fight that had long since vanished.

Using her hair as a guide, Rosalind finally located the hole again. She tugged on Gothel's arm, blindly reaching both their hands forward. Once he found it, Gothel didn't hesitate. The water swished around the movement as he started digging, and Rosalind followed his example. She felt the skin on her hands tear, sensed the electricity buzzing at her fingertips, but she didn't stop, didn't question. Fear pulsed in her veins, thicker than her blood, and she forced her limbs through their instinct to freeze. She made them fight instead.

In the back of her waterlogged brain, the thought echoed: she couldn't remember the last time she had fought for anything.

Then a loud crack rippled through the water. Rosalind didn't have time to question or react before a powerful current caught her by the hair and shoved her forward. A yelp formed in her throat as she waited to be thrown into the wall, but only her shoulder hit. The rest of her wedged into their hole, the water urging her on. Likely still tangled in her hair, Gothel's body slammed into hers, and she fought her burning lungs to keep holding her breath as they tumbled into the inky unknown.

✶ ✶ ✶ ✶ ✶ ✶ ✶

The current spit her out in a stream. It was a soft, sweet lullaby compared to the brutal cacophony of the river, and her drowned mind and exhausted limbs would've succumbed to the peace if her lungs would have let her.

The second air touched Rosalind's skin, she shot upright, gasping and coughing through her hair plastered to her face. Despite the decided calm of this side of the river, she scrambled for the bank, eager to get out before it changed its mind again. She had to reach up—the edge was about a foot over her head—and her arms shook under her weight as she desperately tried to hoist herself up.

Mud slipped between her slick fingers, and she braced herself for the fall back into the stream, but a hand appeared and yanked her over the side. Then she and Gothel collapsed onto the ground, each panting and shaking, both tangled in her swamp of hair.

They had nearly drowned.

Rosalind's insides shuddered. She was never swimming again.

The fight slowly leaked out of her system, an exhausted kind of euphoria taking its place as she dug herself out of her soggy disaster of hair.

They had survived.

A laugh bubbled on her lips, though the sound had died by the time it left her grainy mouth. The easier she breathed, the more she became aware of the solid ground underneath her, the gentle night air, the dim sounds of a sleeping world. It made her want to burst and sing and run and just lay there and appreciate it all.

They were *alive*.

Rosalind pushed herself up on her elbows and dragged up into a sitting position, wanting to share the good news with Gothel. But when she looked at him she found him untangling his arm from her hair with his mouth pressed into a thin line. When he finished, he glanced up to see her looking and glared at her. The expression was so different from her feelings, so wrong for the victorious moment, that it brought her up short.

Still glaring, he sat up and tossed something at her. The object glittered in the moonlight before falling into Rosalind's lap.

She swallowed with her raw throat, and all good feelings screeched to a halt as reality came careening back.

The ring. Boone. Her magic. The ransom. Her parents. Pepperjack. Zachary.

Home.

Rosalind closed her eyes against the pain in her chest, the hopelessness in her gut. She put the ring back on, welcoming and recoiling from the ache it brought.

"We almost drowned," she whispered through her cracked lips.

"Yeah." Gothel's dark voice was just as scratchy as hers. "Thanks to you." Then he pushed himself to his feet and sauntered away from the stream, into a thick patch of trees.

Rosalind flinched at his anger as his shadow disappeared. Thanks to *her*? Her face stung like she'd been slapped.

Numbly, she got to her shaky feet and followed him—she didn't have another option, really. By the time she caught up, she found him huddled around a pile of sticks he'd assembled. Too tired to stand, Rosalind plopped on the ground, making sure she and her hair were a safe distance away in case Gothel's pile actually caught flame.

She wrung out her hair and watched him work. Crickets chirped quietly in the background of the wood rubbing together, and despite the relative peace after such a harrowing experience, Rosalind felt uneasy. Gothel had never once, in the week since he'd taken her, looked at her like that. Boone, yes, Tor, for sure, but not Gothel.

Unable to take the curiosity anymore, and too tired to care about the consequences of speaking, Rosalind cleared her throat. "We almost drowned." She still couldn't believe it: how close they'd come, how they somehow survived.

"I remember," Gothel bit back curtly.

"Do you actually know how to light a fire?"

At that, he finally looked up from his work to glare at her. "I apologize that these conditions aren't up to your standards, *Lady Corona*." He spat out the title, and Rosalind flinched.

"Don't call me that."

"It's what you are."

She curled her hands into fists and wrapped her arms around her cold legs as he got the wood to catch flame. "No, it's not. And, if you hadn't noticed, we're alive. So why are you so angry?"

Gothel jerked his chin at her. "Why didn't you save us?"

Rosalind blinked, stunned. "Why didn't I…" She shook her head. "I *did* save us. I found the hole. We got out."

"Yeah, after you nearly boiled us alive."

Rosalind heard her teeth click together as her jaw clamped shut. "I told you I couldn't do it."

"And why not?" he shot back. "You have the magic. You have the money. You have the status to do anything you want to. You have *everything*, and you waste it."

"I don't—"

"You asked Irina to take your magic away. I heard you." He shook his head again and threw another stick into the fire with too much force. "Thousands of people are oppressed every single day for their lack of power, they'd give anything to form a life like yours, and you would just throw it all away."

The accusations stung, smearing salt into all her open wounds, but Rosalind also found herself angry—twice in the same day. Because she wasn't stupid. Sheltered, maybe, but not stupid. She knew what she had. She knew to be grateful. She *was* grateful, somewhere in her soul, that she had been given what she had. But only she had the right to reprimand herself. Only she knew what burdens came with all those blessings.

When she spoke, her voice cracked with indignation—she still wasn't used to dealing with all these different emotions. It had only been emptiness and guilt and fear—so much fear— for so long, and even her voice was out of practice showing anything else.

"Do you know what it's like to live in that house?" she asked. "Do you have any idea?"

Gothel just rolled his eyes. "Yeah, in that little castle of yours, Princess Corona? It looks real hard. Forgive me if I'm not that sympathetic."

Her fists tightened and she scowled, words spilling out of her with a force she didn't know she had. "Yes, I have everything. Is that what you want to hear? I have everything from power and title to money and family. And they love me, despite everything. I know they love me. They all do, and they love each other, and I love them, but that doesn't heal my brother or fix me or keep my parents from yelling at each other when they think we can't hear. Yes, I have everything, all the love and magic in the world, and yet everything is still *so broken*." She found herself out of breath, unaccustomed to talking so much, to unearthing all these buried truths. "So what's the point?"

"The point?" Gothel repeated, his voice growing louder. "The point is, it's all a game—they've turned our lives into a game—and the sick part is, we can't win. We can't win and people like you, people like your father, win instead, every time."

Rosalind bristled at the mention of her father. "He loves this kingdom and its people. He'd do anything for them."

Gothel scoffed. "Your father is a tyrant. He uses safety as a front for oppression." When Rosalind furrowed her eyebrows, he went on to explain, as if talking to a little child that couldn't hope to understand. "The law requires everyone to get a license to practice magic, but you can only get one through training received at expensive academies. People like me are left scraping by at the bottom and threatened with brutal penalties for using the magic our society is built upon—we are left with *nothing*—as Sterling Corona stands on a podium and claims it's for our safety while his daughter chooses to drop out of her academy because 'it's too hard.'"

Rosalind's eyes narrowed, her body shaking with aggravation. "You don't know anything."

"I know that he's oppressive and greedy and will do anything to keep his standing. He'll probably use you too, if he hasn't already. It's no wonder he loves having the prince over to visit his daughter so much—how much easier would it be to keep his political agenda if he could just preach it from his daughter's royal mouth." Gothel glared at her. "Is that why you don't care? About anything? Because you'll be queen one day and never have to worry about a single thing ever again. Is that your play?"

"My play?" Rosalind repeated, unsure whether she was sickened or enraged. "What is wrong with you? I'm not playing anybody, especially not Roman."

Gothel arched an eyebrow. "First name basis? I didn't think princes allowed their subjects to do that."

"Roman's not like that. He's my best friend."

"He'll probably just grow into a tyrant like the rest of them."

Rosalind opened her mouth, prepared to hurl the awful truth about Roman at Gothel just to put him in his place, but stopped herself just in time. She hadn't spoken to anyone besides Roman in ages—she'd forgotten to remind herself to keep his secret. That secret in anyone's hands would cost the prince his reputation, but putting it in the hands of a royal-hating criminal? That could cost Roman his life.

Her sudden stop had caught Gothel's attention, though. He cocked his head and watched her, curiosity wafting off him, as he waited for her to finish.

Rosalind just shrugged and looked at the ground, settling for a small part of the truth. "His father is awful to him. He comes to me for a safe space. We have always been close friends and will never be anything more. Besides, I don't even want to be queen. The kingdom wouldn't want me either. They just like to talk."

Gothel poked his fire with a stick. "Yes, well when Sterling locks his daughter in his house until she becomes queen, it inspires talk."

She glared at him. "If you weren't so whiny I'd peg you for a noble—you have the judgmental gossiping down." Gothel scowled and opened his mouth, but she cut him off. "My father isn't a tyrant. He only cares so much about the magic restriction because of my brother."

"Your father is a monster. Just because one kid is born messed up doesn't mean you can go taking it out on the rest of us."

Rosalind heard an audible snap as the words broke something inside her, broke her control. Her fingernails punctured the skin of her palms and for a fleeting moment she tasted metal—she knew it was too faint, knew the ring kept her magic buried, but she still thought she might explode.

"He wasn't born that way!" she bit back, so fiercely Gothel's eyes widened a fraction. He leaned away from her, his eyes darting to check for the ring on her hand. "*I* did that...I did that. To him." The words shredded her throat like she was coughing up nails. "My father was trying to help me—*help me*—and I lost control and my *kid brother*, my...he was standing too close. Too close to me. To *me*. It's a miracle...he even...it's a miracle he even survived!"

She was shouting now, shouting truths she had buried for so long, but she couldn't make herself stop. It just kept coming and coming, as unrelenting as the current that had nearly taken her. "Everything changed. Zachary couldn't do anything anymore, and he was always in pain. My dad started working all the time, and he never used to fight with my mom before that, but it was too hard. He feels like he has to protect everyone, and it kills him that he can't because he was *right there* when his only son was torn to pieces. He's one of the most powerful people in the kingdom, and he didn't save him. He enforces the ban even though my mom hates it, but she takes one look at her little boy and won't argue against it either. Because of people like her daughter, people like me, who destroy everything they touch!"

Panting, she deflated, her tirade over. Gothel stared at her blankly, his lips parted in shock, and she found herself wanting to laugh for a moment.

She supposed it was rather shocking: Princess Corona wasn't a princess at all.

"People have the story wrong," she said, her voice hollow now. "I'm the monster."

And with that, she got up and stalked away, unable to look at his expression anymore, unable to face his reaction now that he knew the truth. Not that it really mattered what he thought of her—he had kidnapped her, after all. But criminal or not, he was the first person she'd told her real story to, and she couldn't face the horrified reaction that would surely come from that tale.

So Rosalind did what she did best: she ran away. Her eyes burned, but she didn't cry. She didn't even remember the last time she cried. It was like there wasn't anything left inside of her to come out.

* * * * * * *

I'm the monster.

Gothel heard her voice echo through the leaves long after she'd gone. He felt like he'd been hurled back in the river, his system shocked from the cold, and the wind knocked out of him as he was thrashed every which way.

Guilt. He hadn't felt it in a long while, but there it was, filling up his lungs and making it difficult to breathe.

He sat on the ground, still and straight, stunned and frozen, the argument rehashing in his mind. What had come over him? He couldn't remember the last time he'd lost his temper like that, and now he was annoyed at himself for letting it get the best of him. So they had almost drowned. So what? Like Rosalind said, they'd survived. That was all Gothel had cared about for years. It was all he *should* care about now.

But something had snapped inside him in that cave, drowning next to the girl that could save them with a snap of her fingers, next to the one with the power to rescue them—power he could never steal or barter for. What he would give for that power. What he would give to have strength and a place and *belong*.

Gothel frowned as he looked up at the night sky. He shouldn't have talked to her like that. There she was, actually responding and talking like a normal person for once, and he'd stomped all over her.

Admittedly, it had been exhilarating for a second. A relief to talk to someone that honestly without the fear of Calder's eyerolls or Boone's hostility or not being heard. But he'd used the relief as an outlet, and it was likely she'd never come out of her shell like that again. She actually had a *personality*.

The uncomfortable thought prickled in his brain that he only felt guilty because of her brother—if there wasn't a tragedy there, he wouldn't have cared.

No, he didn't care. Bad things happened to everyone. She wasn't special.

But he still couldn't shake the feeling that he'd been wrong. He'd never gotten so upset about being wrong before, especially when the consequences of a strange girl's hurt feelings paled in comparison to endangering his life, but he'd still been wrong

And Gothel *hated* being wrong.

Suddenly, he heard footsteps crashing through the foliage and he jumped to his feet, his jaw set. Why hadn't he gone after her?

Lurching toward the sound, he halted when Rosalind appeared, eyes wide and hair wild.

"I thought I heard someone," she gasped. "I thought...I thought it was—"

"Stay here," Gothel said tightly, then stepped around her. Going silently, he did a sweep of the area around them, once, twice, three times. They were alone.

When he was satisfied, he made his way back to the fire to find Rosalind sitting on the ground, one leg bent and the other stretched as far as it could go. She had her head tipped back and was breathing heavily.

As he approached, he noticed that the bottom of her foot was covered in blood.

"I tripped on a rock," she mumbled.

Gothel glanced at her face, which was paler than usual, if that were possible. Then he remembered when Boone had knocked her to the ground, and she'd passed out at the sight of blood from the resulting scratch.

"Stay conscious for me," he told her, kneeling in the dirt in front of her. "I don't want to have to carry you again."

She nodded rapidly and closed her eyes, her body shuddering as she edged toward hyperventilation. "Sorry, I just...I don't like blood...much."

"I don't think you're the only one." Gothel ripped off the end of her crusty shirt to wrap around her wound. The fabric was still damp and plastered with mud, but it would have to work. "Will you let me wrap it up?"

That paused her nerves for a second. Her eyebrows furrowed as she studied his face, and his skin prickled. Why was she looking at him like she could see everything?

"You would do that?" Rosalind asked. "Even after…" She trailed off, suddenly looking sicker than before.

Gothel shrugged. "If it'll keep you from passing out on me, sure."

Slowly, she nodded, as if waiting for him to change his mind. When he didn't, she murmured, "Yes, please."

"Take deeper breaths," he instructed her. As gently as he could, he took her ankle in one hand and stretched her leg out, careful not to get any blood on his pants despite them being ruined anyway. "In through your nose and out your mouth."

The cut nearly stretched across her entire foot, but it wasn't deep. As Gothel worked on wrapping the fabric securely around the wound, Rosalind's breaths slowly and surely evened out until she was mostly calm.

"Go-thel?" she asked, stuttering a little on his name. It was strange to hear it in her voice.

"Yeah?"

"Do *you* think I'm a monster?"

Gothel blinked, his hands tripping over themselves and losing their grip on the jacket piece. Without looking up, he picked up the end of the fabric and started over.

"Does it really matter what I think?" he finally replied, his voice gruff to hide his surprise.

"Shouldn't it?"

His eyebrows furrowed at her certainty. What he thought had never mattered to anyone before.

"I think..." Gothel blew out a breath to buy himself time. "I think you're nothing like I expected."

A raspy snort escaped her mouth—nearly a laugh, but not quite. He stole a glance at her face to see the corners of her mouth pulled up in a faint, sad smile, her eyes distant.

"Me too," she said. "I guess we can't pick our story, can we?"

Gothel stopped and looked up at her choice of words. He'd never heard anyone else say it like that.

When she caught him staring, he dropped his gaze again, tied off the fabric on her foot, and let her leg rest on the ground.

"Maybe not," he replied. He wasn't sure what made him say the words—words of a boy he once idolized, words that he'd long since forgotten. "But I like to think we can help write it." Rosalind watched him thoughtfully, surprise creasing her forehead, and he shrugged. "The story is still going, isn't it? We don't know how it ends, and until then, these are our pages."

A cloud passed in her expression, the life draining out of her. "We know how it ends, Gothel. The hero saves the day, the princess is rescued, and the monsters are slain. Nothing else really matters, does it?"

Gothel winced inwardly. He didn't know what to say to that, so he changed the subject.

"I'm not going to kill you. I know that was Boone's plan, but it's not mine. I wasn't lying to you earlier, about Pepperjack's men—they won't care who you are, and they won't ask questions. Until he gets that money, you're in just as much danger as I am."

Rosalind rubbed her face, suddenly looking years older despite her youthful features. "So what should we do?" She sounded defeated, but he was surprised she voiced the question at all. Two days ago, she wouldn't even speak.

"Help me send the ransom note and get the money. Once it's in, we'll be safe, and you can go back home."

She flinched at the word *home.*

Gothel thought of her locked away in her room, reminders of her mistakes all around her. He lowered his voice, afraid the words would further hurt her, though he had never cared before and didn't know why he was starting now. "Do you even want to go back?"

With a painful sigh, she brought her legs to her chest and rested her chin on her knees. "I don't know," she whispered.

"Where else could you go?"

"Does it matter? Out here, back there, no matter where I am, I'm still me." She sunk deeper into herself. "That's why I wanted Irina to take it. Magic fixes nothing. Rake or not, we all break in the end anyway."

Gothel shifted on the ground, overwhelmed by her heaviness. How she had managed to carry it for so long, he wasn't sure.

"Look," he said, "you don't have to decide now. We still have a lot to do before then anyway. Do this with me, help me get the money, and afterward I'll help you get wherever you want to go." He paused, waiting until he was sure he had her attention. "And I'll never ask you to take the ring off again."

For a second, he wondered if he should say he was sorry, if that mattered to her at all. He *was* sorry—about her brother, for what he said, that he had ripped her from her life and gotten her mixed up in this. Gothel choked on an apology, but those words had never been good at coming out of his mouth, so he just cleared his throat and asked, "Deal?"

Rosalind watched him for a few moments, a flicker of life lighting her empty eyes as she considered the proposition.

"Deal."

CHAPTER 6

THROUGH THE STORM

The sun warmed the ground as Rosalind walked, her limbs stiff from a night spent on the hard earth. Her disgusting feet were dotted in cuts and bruises, one wrapped in fabric, and both streaked with blood and dirt. Her feet hadn't seen anything but plush carpet and slick marble floors for years. She watched them as she walked, burrowed deep in her thoughts while she trudged next to Gothel.

She would've thought last night was a dream if not for the dull ache in her throat and sting in her chest. The conversation after seemed like a delusion.

It was a strange sensation: Rosalind felt like she'd taken a dagger and gutted herself. It was surprisingly relieving to walk without all that extra weight inside her, but she couldn't help feeling she'd given too much of herself away and should scramble to take the pieces back.

Even stranger, Gothel hadn't seemed to care. Sure, he'd been a little nicer and more forward since her blurted confession, even treating her like an ally. Most notably, he didn't seem concerned in the slightest to walk next to her. Despite knowing her darkest secret, he sauntered forward in his socks, mumbling about finding shoes.

Maybe, as a criminal, he was used to monsters. Maybe walking with her didn't disgust or appall or scare him at all. The thought made her feel better and worse at the same time.

They'd walked for so long, Rosalind was starting to feel lightheaded—whether from hunger, dehydration, drowning, or the ring, she wasn't sure—but thankfully Gothel stopped. With her focus no longer on her padding feet, she heard the faint sounds of people in the distance.

"This is Solume," Gothel told her. "Ever been here before?"

Her face pinched as she tried to imagine an Elarian map in her head and place the village, but it didn't matter. "No."

He nodded. "I haven't been here in a while, so nobody should recognize me. They won't recognize you either with any luck. But don't let your guard down. I don't know what kind of presence Pepperjack has here, or where Tor and the rest of them ended up. If you notice anyone watching us, don't stay quiet."

She nodded.

"Okay?" he asked with a little more force.

"Okay," she murmured.

Gothel grunted in approval. "First we have to clean ourselves up. We'll attract too much attention like this. Then we'll find the post and send the letter." He left the safety of the trees and started ahead. Rosalind wrapped her tangled hair around her forearm in an effort to keep it controlled, then trotted after him.

It was nearly midday now, and the community was bustling with life. A few merchant tents lined the center cobblestone streets, the dealers hollering out to passing people. Women scurried with loaded carts, men hauled sacks over their shoulders, as they went off to work or trade. Rosalind noted the cracks in the streets, the slant of the buildings, the ragged clothes. Most people did everything by hand—without magic— and there wasn't a carriage in sight. Children ran with bundles of coins or vegetables or fabrics to trade, already working rather than learning in school. There weren't any harsh lines to their sun-kissed faces, though. They seemed happy. Or, at least, busy.

It was a completely different world than the one Rosalind had grown up in.

"Stay close," Gothel muttered under his breath, and Rosalind obeyed. Her eyes darted from her feet to the crowds and back, marveling at how Gothel expertly weaved through the people. She noted he was aiming for the merchant tents; only now, she realized she didn't have any money.

As they approached the first tent, an enticing aroma sent a jolt through Rosalind. She stopped in her tracks as memories flooded back with just a scent: memories of snowmen and laughter and freedom.

Gothel had gone another step before realizing she'd stopped. Shoulders tensing, he turned to face her, eyes scouring for a threat. "What is it?"

"That smell…" she murmured and sniffed again. "It's cinnamon bread. Do you smell it?"

Gothel's eyebrows furrowed. He was not impressed. "Cinnamon bread?"

"Yeah, my mother used to make it. With hazelnut soup. It was my favorite." The ache for her old home—the ache for another time—seized her core, and her stomach grumbled loudly, whining for the loving memories which used to accompany that smell.

"Didn't your mother ever make it for you?" Rosalind asked. She couldn't understand his indifference. Cinnamon bread was the basis of childhood. It was the basis of *life*.

"No," he said curtly, moving to grab her wrist.

She pulled back, and he gave an irritated sigh. "Why not?"

"I don't remember."

"You don't remember why?"

"I don't remember *her*."

Rosalind deflated. "Oh."

Just as Gothel pulled her along again, someone grabbed Rosalind's shoulder and turned her around. A tiny yelp escaped her, and she felt Gothel's grip tighten on her wrist, both of them expecting the worst.

It was a lady, thirty or so, wearing a bulky work skirt and worn boots. Rosalind waited for the recognition, the threats, the attack, but the lady only had eyes for Rosalind's frizzy hair.

"Wow." She stroked one of the locks that had come loose from Rosalind's arm. "Your hair is so *long*."

Rosalind leaned backward, bumping into Gothel, who managed to be casually still. Of course, *he* wasn't the one being touched by a stranger.

"It's so beautiful," the lady went on, ignoring the debris woven into the strands. "Is it magic?"

"Th-thank you," Rosalind stammered. Gothel tipped his head at the lady, before pulling the two of them away from the merchant tent crowds.

"So much for a low profile," Gothel muttered under his breath when they were out of earshot.

Guilt prickling on her skin, Rosalind glanced over her shoulder to see if anyone else was looking. "People think because my hair is long they can just *touch* it." She shuddered in revulsion. "Aren't there basic human rules about that?"

Gothel glanced sideways at her, his mouth twitching upward ever so slightly. "You would think, Princess."

She rolled her eyes.

He led her down the street, not stopping until they were a block or so away from the merchant tents. It was much quieter here, despite the short distance.

"Stay here," Gothel ordered, using a light touch on her shoulders to plant her there. "Don't move. Don't talk. Keep your head down. I'll be right back." Then he slipped away and disappeared before she could protest.

Gothel's absence sent anxiety spilling out of her. She couldn't keep still. Her fists clenched as she paced in place and watched out for people. Several teenage girls chatting about kissing passed by. Rosalind blushed and ducked her head when she realized they were talking about Roman. Then two women discussing their children walked by as two men and a boy came the other way, talking about trading options as they headed for the merchant tents. The boy stopped to fix his shoe, and one of the men glanced at Rosalind. He did a double take, and his eyes narrowed as his friend prattled on about how another one of Elaria's trade ships had gone down at sea.

Where are you Gothel?

Doing her best to feign nonchalance, Rosalind walked quickly away. Sweat beaded down her back. Her knuckles were white. But she managed to turn the corner without incident, and the men disappeared from view.

She wandered a little farther, until she couldn't hear the men's voices anymore. Shaking with exhaustion, she collapsed onto the dying grass of a rundown building and rested her chin on her knees, willing herself to stay calm.

Eight minutes and thirty-seven seconds later, Gothel appeared down the street. His shaggy hair fluttered as he whipped his head back and forth, and Rosalind could see his shoulders relax with a sigh when he finally caught sight of her.

"I thought I told you to stay put." He plopped down next to her holding a canvas market bag. "Remember that?"

"A man was watching me." She wrapped her arms tighter around herself. "I got nervous."

"Did anyone follow you?"

She shook her head. "I don't think so." Then she eyed the full market bag. "Did some shopping?"

Gothel shrugged, rummaging through it. "More or less."

Rosalind's jaw dropped. Though, in hindsight, she shouldn't have been surprised. "You mean you stole *all* of that?"

"I didn't see you offering up any coin, Princess."

She started to protest—both the nickname and the criminal action—when he handed her a brown paper bag and a small canister that warmed her fingers. Then he pulled out the same for himself. Curious, Rosalind opened the bag only to be hit with the succulent smell from earlier. She popped the lid off the canister, and her mouth actually started watering. Cinnamon bread and hazelnut soup.

She looked at it in awe. "What's this for?"

Gothel just shrugged again, mouth already full. "Eating."

Rosalind stared at the miracle in her hands. He didn't have to do that. "No, really. You could've grabbed anything. Why this?"

"Just eat, Princess, before it gets cold."

She wrinkled her nose at the nickname that apparently wasn't going anywhere, but she forgot about it when the slightly sweet, nutty, and achingly familiar taste touched her tongue. It was as good as she remembered.

They ate in companionable silence, both of them wolfing down their food with barely a breath. Rosalind wondered how often he ate. Did he always have to steal food? How many days would he have to starve before he stumbled upon something else?

Probably not long, she reasoned as she chewed. After all, he'd come up with this meal in ten minutes. He was good; no wonder he'd been on a team.

"What happened with them?" Rosalind asked once she finished. She hadn't felt so satisfied in ages. "Tor and Boone and them. I thought you were all a group."

"We were." Gothel's voice was flat. "We aren't anymore."

"Why not?"

"They think I betrayed them."

"Did you?"

"No."

"Then why do they think that?"

Gothel balled up his paper bag in his fist. "You know, you either won't speak for days, or you won't stop talking."

Rosalind shrugged. "My dad used to say I'd sooner drown in all my questions than come up for air." The memory added to the headache pounding in her skull. Another repressed recollection coursed through her, and the contrast between the two scenes cracked all of her bones:

Her father, laughing and ruffling her hair as she sat on the counter firing off question after question, barely giving him enough time to answer between each one.

Her father, trying to break down her door as she screamed into her pillow, her room ravaged from another magic surge, his own sorrow choking him when she would not let him in.

What happened to my Rosy?

"One thing we agree on," Gothel muttered dryly, his voice snapping her back to the present.

"Thank you," she murmured as he stuffed their garbage into his bulging bag.

He cleared his throat, like the right response got stuck there, before finally responding, "Don't mention it, Princess."

"You're really calling me Princess now?"

The slightest pull of his mouth appeared for just a moment. "I think it fits you."

Rosalind rolled her eyes. "Wrong story, remember?" Even though she winced at the blurted truth, there was a freeing kind of thrill in saying the words out loud, of allowing a moment where she didn't have to hide behind the shadows in her life.

A beat of silence passed. Two. Then three. She almost regretted the slip of honesty.

Finally, Gothel muttered, "The soup was for last night." Then he wiped his hands on his pants and stood up, clearly ready to move on.

Rosalind suppressed the urge to smile, recognizing his attempt at an apology, and pushed through her aching joints to stand too. "Where are we going now?"

Gothel nodded at the building across the street and down two to the left. "Let's head in there. We can clean up and change clothes."

Rosalind took in the battered structure, with dirty windows and peeling paint, and pursed her lips. "We can go in?"

"Yeah." Gothel slung his bag on his shoulder, his voice dripping with sarcasm. "It's one of the few places I'm still welcome."

Rosalind raised an eyebrow—had he just made a joke?—and followed. "What is it?"

He took a longer breath before answering. "An orphanage."

* * * * * * *

Gothel felt too aware of himself as he opened the door of Flynnigan's: his breaths were too deep, his steps too loud, his weight too much, his body too bulky. The air pulsed around him as he remembered the first time he'd been on this step, crossed through the door. He was smaller then. Now he took up too much space.

He had always thought that once he was this big, nothing would bother him anymore, that he'd be able to stand on this step without flinching. He had thought that once he grew up, he would grow out of his fears too.

It seemed that belief—like many things from his childhood—was a disappointment.

Rosalind stepped in after him, her presence barely a breath, a breath Gothel couldn't seem to take. He'd never brought anyone here before. Coming to any one of these places always made his gut clench and his bones shake inside him. Here, no matter how much he'd grown, how much he'd seen, these walls always made him feel unbelievably small. Insignificant. Trapped.

Gothel *hated* feeling trapped.

"Miss Moorely?" he called, the door grating shut behind him. "You here?" His voice carried through the dank, empty hallway. He forced himself to walk forward. The wood floor creaked under every step, and the ceiling groaned above him. He refused to let himself be bullied by the familiar sounds. This was temporary. A visit. Not a prison sentence. "It's just me."

A figure appeared at the end of the hallway. From a distance she looked younger, barely a day over twenty. It wasn't until she approached them that Gothel could make out the spots and wrinkles that pulled on her once youthful face.

"Gothel?" she asked, her voice still warm after all these years. "Is it really you?"

It was an effort to look composed. He stuffed his hands in his pockets. "Yeah, it's me."

Donna stopped in front of him, her face screwed up in concentration as she looked over him. "My stars, you've grown so much. What has it been? A year?"

You've abandoned us for a whole year? She didn't say it, but Gothel could fill in the blanks on his own.

He noted the rims around her eyes, the silver streaks in her hair. "Where's Levi?"

"Dead." She didn't flinch at the brutal reality, but there was a slight lilt in her tone, as though her buried grief for her brother was seeping through. "Last spring."

Gothel blinked. She was doing this alone now? No wonder she'd aged so much.

"That's too bad," Gothel offered because he didn't know what else to say. Grief wasn't something he was used to. It always clung to the air and got caught in his throat.

"It is." Donna peered behind his frame. Gothel had nearly forgotten Rosalind was there. "Now who's this? You have a girl with you." Her brown eyes darkened as she took in Rosalind's pale face, wild hair, scraped skin, and clenched fists. She frowned. "A young one, at that."

Gothel spoke before she could jump to any conclusions. "She has a family she's headed back to. We just ran into some…"

"Trouble?" she finished, raising a skeptical eyebrow. Donna had a heart big enough to make a home for dozens of children that weren't her own, but she didn't put up with any nonsense, and Gothel's compulsive thieving habits had never made her approval list.

"An inconvenience," Gothel amended. "Can we clean up here?"

She pursed her lips, but gave in—she always would. "Yes. But you'll have to stop by upstairs, you know."

"I know." Gothel patted his bag. "I came prepared."

Donna nodded, allowing him to step past her, then set her gaze on Rosalind and used a tone best for speaking to a frightened animal. Fitting. "Hello, there. I'm Donna. What's your name?"

Gothel watched Rosalind's wide gaze flicker to him before settling back on Donna. "Rosalind," she finally whispered, her knuckles white.

Donna nodded in greeting. "Nice to meet you, Rosalind." She didn't offer to shake the girl's hand, as if knowing more than she let on. Donna had always been like that, though. She had a sense for knowing people. She'd only tried to hug Gothel that first day, when he'd shown up bruised and skittish, but he'd shied away from her, and she hadn't tried since. She just hugged with her expression, somehow. Her eyes. Warm and brown, like a soft blanket. A cup of hazelnut soup. A slice of cinnamon bread.

Was that what Rosalind had meant?

"Thank you, ma'am," Rosalind murmured back, as if in habit, and Gothel had to hold back a snort at her feeble attempt. The more time he spent with her, the more he realized she truly was not fit for court life.

Gothel tipped his head at her, and Rosalind lurched forward, eager to follow him. He led her into the boxy sitting area and through a door. Funny, how everything looked the same: same purple-ish paint, same scratchy couches, same painting of the night sky on the wall above the ashy fireplace. It even still smelled the same: of old wood and pumpkin and rose oil. The familiarity made him uneasy, but he couldn't decide if not recognizing the place would make him feel worse.

The door led them to a greenhouse area. A debilitated garden took up half the space, while the other half was sectioned into showers. Digging through his stolen market bag, he pulled out a bundle of fresh clothes and handed them to Rosalind, who glanced warily at the offering before accepting it.

"The water's always cold," he told her as he fished out his own new clothes. "Don't wait for it to heat up." And with that, he stepped into a shower and pulled the curtain closed behind him, careful to take off his watch and grab a bar of Donna's homemade soap.

He didn't realize how badly he smelled until he shed his nasty clothes and let the freezing water hit his skin. How long had it been since he had cleaned up? Too long. He could never go this long again.

The question was, where would he go? Even when he got Pepperjack off his back, returning to Boone's was obviously not an option, even if he wanted to. He'd never really felt *right* there. But despite the fact that he had never made it his home, that was his shelter. And his shower.

What's your play, Gothel? How long could he play his way through life? How many days would he scrape by, minute by minute, only to show back up here with so many years gone and still be as lost as he always was?

With a sigh, he set aside the scratchy soap bar and turned the water off, not bothering to shave despite Donna's predicted protests.

Get the money. Pay off Pepperjack. That was his plan. Then, like Rosalind, he'd go from there. He'd have to, so he would.

Gingerly, he put his watch back on, then slid into his fresh clothes and laced up his new boots. They were a little worn, but that tended to draw less attention than walking out in brand new attire.

Once he was dressed, he dumped his old clothes in the laundry bin—let Donna reuse them as she wanted—and shook the water out of his shaggy hair. Rosalind's shower was still going, so he wandered around to check on the plants. It seemed the tomatoes and beans were doing the best. Onions were struggling. The squash looked like the face of a very wrinkled and very sick old lady. How had Donna been doing this all alone?

He considered going out and talking to her, but he wasn't sure what to say, and he didn't want to leave Rosalind alone. So he wandered the greenhouse again, fiddled with his watch, pulled a dead leaf off a plant and ripped it up into pieces. What was taking her so long?

Finally, Rosalind came out. The navy shirt was a little billowy, but believable enough for a work day around here. The pants, however, were so long they covered her feet. She nearly tripped walking out, both hands holding a massive coil of slick black hair.

"Sorry," she muttered when she saw him there. "Dealing with all this takes some time."

"Why do you keep it so long?" The question had been bothering Gothel since he had first seen her. "What's the point?"

She shrugged. "There wasn't one, really. After things happened, I just never cut it. Hasn't been a problem until now." Stepping forward, she nearly slipped on the wet fabric again, and Gothel motioned for her to stop.

"I'm going to fix them," he told her. "Don't kick me."

A twitch of a smile flitted across her face. "No promises."

He knelt down in front of her and rolled her pant legs up, cuffing them at her ankles. Then he tied a knot in the hem of her shirt and set out a pair of shoes at her feet so she could step into them. He didn't have Tor to consult, but the outfit could likely pass for the current style.

"We have to make a stop upstairs," he told her, slinging his market bag over his shoulder. "It'll only take a minute, but they'd riot if we don't."

"What's upstairs?" she asked.

"You'll see."

Gothel led her back into the house and through the kitchen where the same wood chairs he'd helped Levi paint stood by the same yellow table Levi always told Donna didn't match.

The color had faded, the top chipped. Gothel tapped his finger against it out of habit before heading up the narrow staircase and stopping at the door.

"Brace yourself," he muttered before turning the knob and poking his head in. "Hello? Anyone here?"

Two dozen heads across the space stopped and turned to stare at him, some in confusion, their eyes hazy as they recognized him but couldn't quite remember from where. Then one kid in the back—Benji, broader and heavier than Gothel remembered—shouted, "It's Gothel!" and a sea of children descended on him.

"Where did you go?"

"Where have you been?"

"Have you met the king yet?"

"Did you sail on the ocean?"

"Did you bring me something?"

"Are you gonna climb the mountains?"

"Yeah, did you bring us something?"

Gothel stumbled backward as the kids pushed and pulled and climbed—somehow Elyse ended up on his shoulders, sticking her nose into his bag.

"Hey! No peeking."

Elyse giggled as he swung her down and set her on the floor, where she proceeded to jump up and down with all the other kids.

"Did you bring us something?" Benji crowed.

"Of course I did." Gothel rummaged in his bag and tossed things out. "Candy from the prince's storehouse, berries from the Forgotten Forest, and rocks from the palace grounds." The kids all oohed and awed over their spoils, chattering with one another about the flavors of candy or the possible magical properties of each rock. Gothel took a flower he'd grabbed from a market stall and slid it in Elyse's hair. She giggled and beamed at him.

"You'll tell us a story, right?" she asked.

"Of course he will!" Benji shouted over a mouthful of candy. "He always does." Then he gave a stern look to Gothel. "You always do, so you can't break the rules."

Gothel held up his hands in a truce. "I would *never* break the rules."

"Story time!" Risa announced, and the kids assembled themselves on the floor in front of their cots while arguing over who should get to sit where.

Rosalind peeked around Gothel's shoulder to watch them, a flame of curiosity catching in her expression. "Stories?"

Gothel sat on the floor and gestured for Rosalind to sit by him, the kids too caught up in fighting over seating arrangements to listen in. "There was an older kid when I was here—Eugene. Once a week or so, we'd all sit around him and he'd tell us stories. He started a kind of tradition, I guess."

"Are they true?" she asked, eyeing the candy Benji was gobbling that absolutely did not come from the prince's storehouse.

Gothel shrugged. "Does it matter?"

Rosalind's forehead creased, not understanding what he meant, and he searched for the best way to explain.

"You said you can't pick your story," he started, fighting to keep the competing reverence and bitterness out of his voice. "But with Eugene...for a second you could. You could be anything, anything other than just some orphan stuck in the corner of the world and forgotten. And that...well...for us..." He shrugged and cleared his throat, suddenly too aware of himself. "That was...a big deal, I guess."

He left out the part when Eugene left, breaking all his promises and all their hearts. He'd filled their heads with hopes and dreams that were viciously slaughtered once they got out into the real world. Until he'd met Rosalind, Gothel had buried all Eugene's fairy tales deep, only bringing them out when he came back to visit, which happened less and less.

Now, Gothel understood. He knew why Eugene did what he did, why he told the kids stories, and why he had to get out despite assuring them that their parents might have left them but he never would. He understood, but he still couldn't shake the resentment when he thought about it.

The resentment won. He shook his head. "But it's all—"

"I get it," Rosalind said softly, her usually lifeless eyes shining with something. "I used to read all the time. Sometimes...sometimes stories are the closest thing to magic we have."

With that, the resentment in him dried up. She *did* get it. Boone would've called him pathetic, Tor would've mocked him, and Calder would've kept a joke running for weeks despite having once felt Eugene's magic himself.

"Yeah," Gothel muttered. "Something like that."

"I wouldn't peg you for such positivity."

He shrugged, repeating the words he'd first heard here in this room. "Maybe we can't pick our story. But we can help write it."

The corner of Rosalind's mouth pulled up as she glanced at Elyse twirling like a princess in her ragged clothes. "Maybe."

* * * * * * *

Gothel had promised them one story. He was now on his sixth.

Rosalind wasn't sure where all the material came from, but he didn't hesitate once as he spewed off tales of palaces and creatures and swordfights. The children listened with rapt attention, chewing idly on the candy Gothel had stolen and only interrupting to correct a detail, which Rosalind thought was funny considering they'd supposedly never heard the fake accounts before.

The most surprising thing was Gothel's storytelling: he was really good at it. She'd never seen him so animated—she didn't know he could *be* animated. He came to life before her eyes, spinning story after story with ease. There were traces of tension she caught, brief moments when something he had buried started to shine through, but to her he was practically a whole new person.

Halfway through, she noticed the girl with the flower and several others eyeing her damp hair spread out behind her. She suddenly felt self conscious, but Gothel leaned in.

"You'll have to ask her if you want to braid it," he told the girls in a false whisper, the corner of his mouth pulling up slightly. "The princess is *really* picky about who can touch her hair."

The girls gaped. "You're a princess?" the girl with a flower murmured in awe.

"Um…" Rosalind glanced uncertainly at Gothel, who shrugged. "Kind of, I guess. I've been to the castle many times. And I'm friends with Roman."

The room went silent. A boy with puckered lips said, "You mean, you *know* the prince?"

Rosalind nodded.

"Is he nice?" Flower Girl asked.

"Yes, he's very—"

"I bet he's not," Puckered Lips cut in, digging his hand in his bag for the last bits of candy. "Princes don't care about orphans like us."

"Well of course he does!" Rosalind cried. "I know he does. In fact, I'll make sure he comes to visit you so you can see."

The kids gasped and squealed, their eyes widening. Gothel, on the other hand, shot her a dark look, as though his fake account of him climbing notorious Mount Brenne was somehow better than a real promise of a prince visit.

She held his gaze resolutely. "He'll come." Then she invited the girls to start braiding her hair.

It took them an hour to finish, and Rosalind had to admit she was impressed with the product. The damp hair was still heavy on her scalp, but the girls had woven it into an impossibly thick braid nearly as wide as her, and now it fell just past her waist. She stood and tested the weight, loving the feeling of security but also nervous she couldn't hide as much.

She thanked the giggling girls, who told her she could come back anytime.

"Nice job," Gothel told them. "She actually looks kind of like a person now, don't you think?"

Rosalind rolled her eyes, but there was truth there. Cleaned up in different clothes with a different hairstyle out in a different world, she felt things were a little sharper. Vibrant. It made her feel like her skin was stretching, and she couldn't decide how she felt about the sensation.

Eventually, time caught up with them. Trying to be discreet, Gothel moved his sleeve to glance at his watch—which Rosalind found very strange—and his eyes widened when he realized how long they'd been there. Untangling Flower Girl—Elyse, she'd learned—from his arm, he stood.

"You have to go?" Risa whined, tilting her head back dramatically. "But it's been so much *fun*."

"Don't wait so long to come back again," the boy with the puckered lips—Benji—told them.

Elyse slid up by Rosalind. "And you can come too."

"And the prince!" Marsha yelled.

"Oh yes." Elyse batted her long eyelashes dreamily. "And the prince."

It took several minutes to say all their goodbyes and sufficiently extract themselves from the room. When they went downstairs, Donna was sitting on one of the kitchen chairs, a lit candle on the table, her head back and eyes closed as if in a trance. Rosalind was afraid to step in and interrupt, but Gothel surged ahead anyway.

"Haven't been able to pray like that in a long time," Donna said. Slowly, she blinked her eyes open. "I know I can't convince you to stay."

"Then don't try," Gothel snapped back, his sudden agitation surprising Rosalind.

Donna sighed. "Stay out of trouble." She nodded at Rosalind. "And keep her safe."

Gothel grunted and headed for the door. Rosalind tipped her head at Donna. "Thank you," she murmured.

A soft grin came to her worn face. "You're welcome, dear." Then the smile faded. "He has grown so much, but he is still a very lost little boy. Help him find his way, will you? If you can. The goddesses know I've tried."

Rosalind bit her lip and nodded, if only to appease the nice lady. Then she turned to follow Gothel, finding he was already out the door and halfway down the street.

She was breathless when she caught up, her blistered feet grateful for the new shoes. The ring was making her finger throb and joints ache. She'd gotten so involved in the stories, she'd nearly forgotten about it, but now the pain was a sharp reminder of the bitter task ahead.

Solume's square had quieted a bit in the hours they were gone. As the sun was nearly starting to set, everyone there was getting in their last minute trades before heading home for the day. When did the post close? They should have at least another hour, right?

She glanced at Gothel. His expressionless facade was cracking, giving way to a pale and drawn face. Perhaps the visit had taken a harsher toll then she had thought. When he felt her watching him, he flinched and glanced at her, and she nodded at his wrist.

"Your watch," she said.

His eyes narrowed slightly. "What about it?"

"You checked the time on it."

He tensed and drew back, confirming her suspicions: he too wasn't used to being noticed. And he didn't like it either.

"You said you were a rake," she pointed out.

Gothel forced a breath through his teeth. "I am."

"Then why do you have a watch if you don't have any magic to make it work?"

The response was just a second delayed. "I stole it that way. The guy was a powerhouse that had set it to run forever."

"I don't believe you. You aren't the type to have magically induced objects, even stolen."

He rolled his eyes. "I liked you better when you were silent."

Rosalind dropped her gaze and went quiet.

They trekked across the square and down street after street, having to backtrack when Gothel led them the wrong way. By the time they found the post, the sun had dipped below the horizon and Rosalind was drooping in exhaustion. Thankfully, the post hadn't closed yet, but the line of waiting people went out the door and snaked around the side of a building. Heaving a sigh, they got in line.

It moved miserably slow. Rosalind fiddled with the knotted hem of her shirt and played with the ends of her massive braid. Finally they moved up a bit. Gothel's hands fidgeted and his eyes darted everywhere. They moved a little bit more.

They had almost rounded the corner when Rosalind noticed a man on the opposite side of the road leaning lazily back against the wall. By the slant of his jaw, she knew he was drunk, and the glint in his eyes told her he was looking for something. As a group of young people passed—two girls and a boy—the man whistled at the ladies, who turned red, and the young man cursed at him before they moved along.

The man laughed, leaning his head back. His eyes wandered across the street until he caught sight of Rosalind. He looked her up and down once, twice, then flashed her a grin. Her lungs caught and her stomach twisted. She shuffled closer to Gothel as her hands clenched into fists. When her shoulder bumped his arm—he was a full head taller—he flinched and jerked away.

"Sorry," she mumbled to the ground. Still feeling the man's gaze on her, she squeezed her eyes shut and tried to remember how to breathe.

Seconds passed, and she sensed Gothel shift. She cracked her eyes open to find him standing on the other side of her, effectively shielding her from the man's view. She relaxed a fraction and started to thank him, but closed her mouth after remembering his remark.

Gothel stood casually again, his deadpan display back on now that he knew someone was watching. He stared ahead when he spoke quietly to her. "You trust me?" It had started as a statement, but ended in a question.

Rosalind curled in on herself, realizing she *was* subconsciously gravitating toward him because she felt threatened. Strange. "I trust you not to hurt me," she admitted, feeling like she owed him some truth. "And...you're the first person to...*know* about me in...a long time."

He nodded. "Who else?"

"Just my family. And Roman." She wasn't sure who else had been told, and she didn't want to think about it. Instead, she gestured to the post building. "I used to send letters to him in the castle all the time until his friend Griffin gave me a magic notepad for my birthday."

"Magic, huh." He didn't sound particularly interested, but somehow she sensed he was looking for a distraction.

"Yeah. Whatever I wrote on it would appear on Roman's pad, no matter how far away we were from each other. I'm pretty sure Griffin has one too, though I doubt they have to use it much since Griffin's his advisor."

"Does it still work?"

"The pad?"

"Yeah."

"Oh, um, I'm sure it does, but I lost it a few years ago." Rosalind's stomach started to hurt at the realization. "I don't know why I never looked for it."

Because you were wasting away in bed while the world passed you by.

Gothel grunted, and the line moved ahead. As they rounded the corner, Rosalind glanced back across the street, but the drunk man had gone. Thank the stars.

"Why were you going to let me train with Irina?" she asked, aiming to keep him distracted. It'd been bothering her, and she felt she could breathe again with the man gone.

Gothel let out a snorted breath that could've been a laugh. "Did she really give me a choice? You try telling Irina no."

"That's not really an answer."

Gothel pursed his lips, and she assumed she wouldn't get an answer. But nearly a full minute later, he opened his mouth, his casual stance settling into something heavy.

"In Wren's tavern," he said quietly, "when you took off the ring."

Rosalind cringed against the memory. No wonder he didn't want to touch her.

"I thought you were fighting. I was ready to...I don't know what. But instead you just stared at your hands like…" He blew out a breath and shook his head. "Nobody should look at themselves like that."

The answer stunned her to silence. They moved up in line; they were almost to the door now.

"What do you see?" she whispered. "How do you look at yourself?"

His jaw ticked. "I don't."

"You don't look?"

"No, I…" He sighed. "I just don't see anything."

* * * * * * * *

I just don't see anything.

Gothel rubbed his forehead, trying to pinpoint how this

conversation had even started, how he had ended up here. How he'd gone from ignoring Calder and dodging Tor's advances to crashing at an orphanage and blurting his thoughts to someone he should hate.

He had to get away from this girl. She was making him say the most ridiculous things.

She's making you say real things, some part of him realized, but he shoved that realization down and swept it under the rug, indefinitely. He had no time for it now.

Finally, they made it through the door. The line followed a long counter, on which various parchments, pens, envelopes, and parcels sat. A young man stood at the end of the counter, his eyes drooping as he took payments from customers and tossed their letters into a large crate behind him.

Gothel grabbed a piece of parchment, an envelope, and a pen. Still unnerved from the trip to Flynnigan's, he drummed his fingers against the table and tried to focus. He'd been planning this letter for days—it would be simple and to the point. He was getting sick of the drama this ordeal had become.

They were the last in line. By the time he had finished writing the letter, there were only two people left in the place, one waiting with her parcel as the other was rung up. Stuffing the letter in the envelope, he asked Rosalind for her address.

She reached for the pen. "Let me write it." When he didn't immediately offer it, she held out her hand. "They'll recognize my handwriting. It's proof that you're telling the truth."

Gothel blinked. He hadn't thought of that. Scooting the envelope over, he handed her the pen and watched as she scrawled out her address. Her handwriting was scratchy and elegant at the same time.

After she finished, she pursed her lips and examined her work. "I never was good at penmanship," she said with a shrug. "They'll know it's me."

Gothel took the envelope and started sliding it down the counter, but a hand came down on it, blocking its path. He glanced up to see a man sneering at him—the same man that had been leering at Rosalind from across the street.

"Writing home, Gothel?" he jeered, breath rancid, and snatched the letter. "Hope you aren't trying to weasel out of your deal."

Forcing himself to appear calm, Gothel took a casual step back to bring Rosalind into his line of sight. At first glance, it would seem the other man standing behind her was a friend or relative with an amiable hand on her shoulder. But Gothel noticed her wide eyes and clenched fists, the way she leaned slightly to one side in an effort to distance herself from her captor.

A stone settled in his gut. They'd been caught.

The man with bad breath stuffed their letter in his pocket, then leaned too far forward into Gothel's space. "Your time is up. Come with us or your little mouse gets a blade through her ribs." With that, the two men sauntered out, Rosalind in tow. Gothel gritted his teeth and followed.

It was almost dark out, the last rays of sun flailing over the horizon before being shoved down for the night. The square was emptying; people were going home. Gothel dodged the few stragglers as he followed Pepperjack's men, watching Rosalind struggle to keep up with their pace. All four crossed the square and weaved through the backstreets, past Flynnigan's, and to the outskirts of the plaza.

An empty carriage waited for them. Gothel did not like where this was headed.

What's your play, Gothel?

The men stopped, the bearded one forcing Rosalind to her knees. Bad Breath winked at her before gesturing from Gothel to the carriage.

"Your chariot awaits," he said, then laughed at his own pathetic joke. Gothel could not believe he was going to lose to a man that laughed at his own jokes.

How did he get here again?

Gothel didn't move, keeping his stance indifferent. "I'm getting the money."

"It's too late for that now. If Jack says he wants to see someone, Leland brings that someone."

"I'm not going to see him until I have the money."

Leland nodded at his partner, who shifted the arm that wasn't holding Rosalind down. Only then did Gothel see the glint as he moved a knife from her side to her neck.

"Get in the carriage, Gothel," Leland said, leaning up against the door, "or Mackee, here, will slit her throat."

Mackee grinned and pressed his blade harder against her neck so she had to tilt her head up to avoid the edge. Her eyes were squeezed shut; her hands were shaking. She almost looked like she was praying.

Gothel took a precious second to analyze the scenario, to plan his play. Leaving her made the most sense. He'd lived his life looking out for himself first and he didn't have plans to change that. But that meant she would die right here, and he didn't know why he couldn't stand the thought. She deserved a better ending than that.

"Fine," Gothel said, still impassive. He often found that apathy was his best defense mechanism; it ruffled people's feathers when they couldn't get to you. "Let's go talk to your boss." Without any fanfare, he hopped into the carriage and plopped himself into one of the far seats, trying to look as bored as ever despite his racing heart and the distinct—and nauseating—stench of moldy cheese.

Leland took the seat by Gothel. A squeaky sound came from Rosalind before she appeared inside. Gothel gritted his teeth at the thought of either of them touching her, even just to lift her inside. She *hated* that.

Rosalind started to scoot down—to sit across from Gothel—but Leland stuck out an arm to block her.

"Not so fast there, girl," he drawled. "You stay right there so Leland can look at you, okay?" Gothel glared at him. Leland just raised a bushy eyebrow and smiled.

Rosalind swallowed hard and pulled her braid out from behind her so she could sit back against the seat, hugging it to her chest like a life preserver. Mackee got in on the other side, sliding across from Gothel. Rosalind stiffened at having him next to her, then jumped when Mackee made a motion with his hand and the doors slammed shut on their own.

"If you have magic," Gothel started, annoyed, "then why do it this way?"

Mackee gave a toothy smile that had Rosalind cringing away. "Because it's more fun this way, kid."

And with that, Leland gave a showy snap of his fingers, and the carriage lurched forward, stealing the wanted thief and missing girl away.

CHAPTER 7

RUNNING BLIND

Pepperjack's hideout was unlike anything Gothel had ever seen.

Even in the carriage, it took a good couple of hours to reach the Jacklands. The stretch of land rested on the outskirts of the kingdom which the crime lord had claimed for his own—land everyone knew not to cross into unless they wanted trouble. In the dark, the collapsing shacks looked ominous, the odd shadows the perfect cover for whatever brutes hid inside. He knew they were there; he could feel their eyes on his skin. It took effort not to shudder.

Leland stopped at one of the more decent shacks—not nice by any means, but not a pile of rubble either. Mackee all but shoved Rosalind outside, roughly dragging her up the path to the door with Leland ambling behind. Gothel had no choice but to follow. He forced his gaze forward, refusing to acknowledge the invisible eyes surrounding him. How many people could Pepperjack possibly have in his employ? How many were unlucky men like him and Boone who had nowhere else to turn?

Gothel forgot the question once he stepped inside. Rotting wood gave way to glittering marble floors clear enough to reflect the massive chandeliers hanging from the ceiling. He blinked against the sudden light, the air changing around him, and he had to do a double take. The foyer opened to two grand staircases that mirrored each other and spilled into countless hallways. What had seemed like a one-room shed from the outside was actually an extensive estate on the inside. A palace.

They were in a different kingdom now.

Mackee hauled Rosalind through the foyer—six times the size of Boone's hideout—and pushed her into one of three chairs set up by a gold table. A *gold table*. On top lay a heaping bowl of shiny fruit, half a loaf of light bread, and three wheels of fresh cheese.

Gothel stuffed his hands in his pockets. The urge to take something was a persistent itch he would have to force himself not to scratch.

Leland gestured to the chair next to Rosalind with a grin, but Gothel just stood by it, hyper aware of Mackee and Leland standing behind them. Rosalind was a seated statue, staring straight ahead, clearly not tempted by the food. Gothel thought he saw a drop of red peeking out from her fisted palm.

"Hello, hello!"

The voice echoed through the cavernous space, bouncing off the slick, gold-accented walls. A bright figure descended the left staircase. He would've been blinding if not for the inky fur wrapped around his shoulders and trailing behind him. Wolf fur. The only wolves that big were deadly and rumored to run around the Forgotten Forest.

Gothel glanced from the wolf pelt to the shiny fruit and crustless bread, suddenly remembering what Pepperjack was famous for.

Pepperjack liked to skin things. Peel them like a grape.

Gothel wasn't so hungry anymore.

"Well, what do we have here?" Pepperjack exclaimed as he stepped off the staircase and approached their table. Gothel heard Rosalind take a sharp breath once the crime lord came close enough to actually see without squinting.

His ivory skin didn't look ghastly like Rosalind's, but shone milky white, like one of the cheeses on the table. His head was shaved to the scalp on the sides, and the very top was a spiky mess of lavish blond hair that just added to his brightness. The ebony fur made the contrast even more apparent.

But his eyes snatched Gothel's attention: yellow irises with flecks of brilliant orange.

Gothel knew he was staring—how could he not stare?—but Rosalind dropped her head slightly. Pepperjack flashed a smile and sat across the table from them. When he gestured for Gothel to sit, he obeyed without a thought.

"Gothel Riden, I presume." Pepperjack plucked a grape from the bowl and popped it in his mouth. His teeth audibly tore into the fruit, and Gothel had to hold back a wince. "I'm curious, Gothel, as to why I find you here past deadline without my money, and why you are not with your crew but a girl. A Corona, no less."

Rosalind stiffened, her eyes flicking up. Pepperjack smirked and winked at her, as if teasing an old friend.

"Well of course I know who you are, Rosy." She flinched and turned a shade of green at the nickname. "It's an *honor* to have Sterling's daughter in my household. Tell me, how's that dear brother of yours?"

For a moment, Gothel thought Rosalind would actually vomit, but she just ducked her head and scrunched herself smaller.

Pepperjack laughed. It sounded like a braying horse. "I'd been told she was a peculiar one. No wonder Sterling keeps her locked up tight. Can't go around tarnishing dear old daddy's reputation, now can you?"

It seemed her shoulders would break under his words, and Gothel did not like the way Pepperjack smiled at her show of resignation.

He cocked his head, popping another grape, and rose to his feet. "A combination of Sterling and Genevieve must make an intoxicating child." The hair on the back of Gothel's neck stood on end when the crime lord kneeled in front of Rosalind, his fur coat sweeping the floor. Gothel could practically hear her heart pounding in time with his own. "How much power do you hold, Rosy?"

Gothel couldn't tear his eyes away, couldn't open his mouth, but he willed her to lie, begged the stars to let her sense him imploring her to make something up. Power or not, Pepperjack was a fierce wolf, and he stared at Rosalind like a long lost sheep.

This had been a huge mistake.

Rosalind ducked further. Her braid had come loose from behind her back and hung against her shoulder. She slowly twisted her fists in her lap—hiding the ring from view, he realized—then shook her head.

Pepperjack clicked his tongue. "I don't like liars, Rosalind. Now look at me."

She cringed but did not move. A second passed and something flashed in Pepperjack's face, a glint in his eyes. Rosalind gasped and her head jerked up; Pepperjack grinned when she was forced to meet his gaze.

"There we are," he said, wrapping a hand around her throat. He didn't choke her, but the hold was possessive. It made Gothel's skin crawl. She squeezed her eyes shut and clamped her mouth closed as Pepperjack leaned in to her and smelled her neck. He was *smelling* her. And he must've not liked her scent because he frowned.

"I don't sense any power in you. Strange." Mercifully, he straightened up and released her throat, tracing one finger up the side of her face and to her hair. "Good girl for not lying to me, though you don't hold quite the same possibilities anymore." He stroked her braid, his gaze fixated on it, which was when Gothel noticed his eyes: they had changed to a stormy gray at the edges with a teal ring around the center.

Gothel swallowed hard. Boone was insane for getting involved in this.

Still stroking her hair, Pepperjack nodded at his silent employee behind her—Leland—who grinned at her like the miscreant he was. "I suppose Leland could use a new friend—"

"They'll still pay for her," Gothel blurted, leaning so far off the edge of his seat that he almost fell off it. Leland scowled at him, but Pepperjack cocked his head, watching him with those creepy eyes—eyes that were turning yellow again as Gothel spoke. "Her parents. They don't care about her lack of magic. They still want her back, and they'll pay for her too. A safe return."

"Is that so?" The blue in his eyes battled with the yellow as Pepperjack stood and seated himself back in his chair, garnering a near silent sigh of relief from Rosalind. He popped another grape in his mouth. "Tell me more."

So Gothel did. Everything about Boone's financial issues, Gothel's kidnapping plan, and how he'd been betrayed and had struggled to carry out the plan himself. He hoped his desperation didn't shine through his voice, but he couldn't stop the account from rolling out of his mouth as he felt entranced by those horrid eyes.

"I had finally gotten to the post to send the ransom letter when your guys interrupted us," he finished, enjoying the slight grunt of disapproval Leland made. He hoped the guy got berated for it. "I never planned on skipping payment. I was going to get you the money."

Pepperjack's eyes shone completely turquoise now and they narrowed as he tapped his lips with one finger, over and over. The man really needed to cut his nails.

The sudden thought of those nails biting into his skin made Gothel cringe. Now that they were here, in Pepperjack's grasp, the wild situation could fall completely out of Gothel's control, and he doubted the crime lord tolerated anything that wasn't useful.

"I'll still do it." The words burst from Gothel in a spray of clear desperation that he loathed. "I can still get the money, and you won't have to do anything. I can take care of it." He cut a glance at Rosalind, like the line of eye contact would bind her to him. "We can get the money."

The crime lord arched an eyebrow. "Really? You think so?"

Gothel couldn't tell if he was serious or baiting him, but he didn't have much else to grab on to. "Yes. I do."

A few seconds passed. Maybe years. In the glittering marble room, it felt like eternities.

"Let's do it!" Pepperjack boomed and clapped his hands, making Rosalind jump.

Gothel's eyebrows furrowed. "Sir?"

"There are three traits I value above all else." He held up fingers as he listed them off. "Loyalty, cleverness, and creativity. You showed loyalty to your debts, cleverness in trying to pay them, and creativity in your strategies. So I'll give you your chance. I will send your ransom letter with instructions on how to make payment to me. It will be delivered by sunrise. At that time, I will give you thirty-six hours for the money to come through. If it does, you will be cleared of your debts and released, and I'll arrange for Rosy's safe return."

Gothel's mind raced through the words, reviewing them again and again, searching for holes or threats or stipulations. As if he really had a choice. "And if it doesn't?"

Pepperjack gave a wolfish smile, fur rustling as he settled back into his chair. "Then you're both mine."

* * * * * * *

Once his men retrieved the letter, Pepperjack edited it with instructions and sent it with a messenger, then led Rosalind and Gothel into one of his 'sitting rooms.' It was half the size of the foyer, but still big enough to make Rosalind feel small, complete with three large golden couches, a connecting bathroom, a water fountain, and a table full of peeled food, with cheeses, of course. Thankfully, once he announced the thirty-six hour countdown had begun, Pepperjack left them alone. She knew he'd locked the door behind him, but at that moment she didn't care about anything but getting far, far away from him.

She sat next to Gothel on the couch. She didn't need to, not with so many seating options, but after being manhandled by those three barbarians, she needed a safe space. As safe as could be in this place, anyway.

To his credit, Gothel didn't complain when she curled into a ball next to him, though she made sure they weren't touching. Then they waited.

Gothel was terrible at waiting. He bounced his leg, drummed his fingers on his knee, pulled on his sleeve. He could not sit still. It almost made her smile in spite of everything—it reminded her of Zachary.

Rosalind sighed, resting her chin on her knees and feeling a few rogue hairs that had come loose from her braid tickle her neck. She knew they were thinking the same thing. It was a glaring thorn in her side, making it difficult to breathe.

Finally, she had to acknowledge it. "What if they don't pay?" she whispered, staring at nothing.

He came right back, voice blank. He was scared too. "You don't think they will?"

She didn't know what to think. That's why she asked.

"They love me," she said. It was the only truth she knew right now.

"Maybe." He allowed a bit of bitterness into his voice. "I'm just not sure how I feel about the fact that Sterling Corona holds both our fates in his hands—hands that locked up his own daughter."

"He didn't," she insisted. "He loves me."

"Enough to pay?"

Rosalind pursed her lips, eyes stinging. Gothel must've glanced at her face, because she saw him nod out of the corner of her eye, and he said, "He does. He will."

A second passed. Then two. Three. It took her five to breathe the question.

"How...how much were you asking for?"

"The amount of my debt alone, divided out from Boone's." He hesitated. "Do you really want to know the number?"

Rosalind squeezed her eyes shut. All she could see were her parents at the dining room table, discussing the letter, the amount, if they could pay. They had money, of course, as working for the crown was a profitable occupation. But a man like Pepperjack—a man with gold speckles in his floor and water fountains in his sitting room and countless nasty Lelands at his disposal—a man like that could drain anyone. Even her father.

"No," she whispered. "I don't."

She didn't want to open her eyes. She didn't want to see the skinned fruit on the table or the glitter of the chandelier. She wanted to sink into a hole in the earth and pop up somewhere else, anywhere else. Anywhere was better than here.

Her anxiety made her tired, and as the sluggish minutes turned to hours, plunging them deep into the night, she found herself dozing off. Her dreams were hazy, veiled and hard to follow. Knives glinted and someone screamed and there were grapes all over the floor and fur in her mouth, suffocating her.

When she blinked awake, her eyes were crusty, her stomach ached, and her head leaned against Gothel's shoulder.

"Sorry," she mumbled, wiping her eyes.

"You're okay," he answered, his voice soft enough that she believed him. Maybe he needed a safe space too. In her exhaustion, Rosalind almost snorted at that—the idea that she could ever be someone's safe space. Gothel was brave to sit next to her, even with the ring on.

That made her think of other brave things she'd heard, and after a yawn, her voice subdued and sleepy, she asked, "Tell me a story?"

Gothel snorted, an almost laugh. Had he ever laughed before? She was sure she'd never heard it. "A story? Now?"

"Yeah. I think we could use some magic about now."

She thought he might say no. Instead, he settled further in his seat and said, "Which one do you want to hear?"

Her mouth twitched upward. "I want a new one." She reached down and tapped the hard spot underneath his sleeve. "I want the story of your watch."

He fell silent for a moment, and Rosalind thought she had gone too far. But then Gothel cleared his throat and ducked his head down so he could talk quietly by her ear.

"Once upon a time," he started, and she almost laughed at hearing the phrase in his no-nonsense voice, "a little boy lived with his mother who had short, golden hair that was always tightly curled, every single day. She wasn't affectionate, really, but she wasn't cold, and she always smelled like cherries. The two of them had nothing, and the boy started helping with chores as soon as he could walk. He was very young and uneducated, but aware enough to know they had no money and that for him to be there, he had to have a father.

"Every time he asked his mother who his father was, she would brush him off or give some vague answer. In an effort to make ends meet, she had many suitors over, and each time any one of them came for however many weeks or months she could convince them to stay, the little boy would study him and wonder if this was his father.

"One man came several times for several months. He had the same dark hair as the little boy, an easy smile, and had a talent for convincing others to do what he wanted. His mother liked him most and he gave her the most attention, so the boy assumed this was his father. When his charms didn't work on the boy, the man grew distant and wary of him, and the boy often overheard him complaining to his mother about her strange, quiet son.

"The rejection stung, but it did not stop the little boy from watching him. And one night, he snuck into his mother's room to study the man while he slept—to see if he looked as nice as he did while awake—and the boy saw something on the windowsill: a watch. He didn't think before he took it. It was the first thing he ever stole. When the man awoke and hunted around the house for his missing watch in a frenzy, the boy felt a bit of pride for the secret that only he knew. It was the only time he felt grateful for or excited about his apparent invisibility."

Gothel paused for a moment. It was quick enough to miss, but Rosalind noticed.

"Then one day—the boy about seven or so now—his mother took him to a village he'd never been before, to a place he'd never seen, overrun with other children. She told him to wait there and play until she came to get him. Even then, somehow he knew she wasn't coming back. And she never did.

"She didn't know, however, that the boy still had the watch with him—he took it with him everywhere, despite having no magic, no way to power it. Years went by before he discovered what made the watch so special."

Then Gothel shifted his arm and pushed his sleeve back enough to see the clock face. At first, Rosalind didn't understand what she was looking for: it was an older style watch, with brown leather straps and a ring of dulled gold around the face. The hands were thin and black with a curve at the point, clearly set to the wrong time, and...they were moving.

Rosalind jerked her head up to get a better view, narrowing her eyes to catch the slight motion. "They're moving. It works. But how...but you're..."

"Because it doesn't run on magic," Gothel whispered to her, wiping the glass with his thumb. "I purposely keep it three hours ahead in case anybody happens to see it, so they'll just assume it's broken or I can't power it."

"But what does it run on?"

"I don't know. It has some kind of internal power source that turns the gears on its own. I never looked into it closely, because I didn't want Boone catching on, but over the years I've heard stories. Stories of illegal machinery that doesn't need magic."

Rosalind's mouth fell open, her heart beating faster in her chest as she considered the possibilities, suddenly aware of her throbbing ring finger. "That would be...that would change everything."

"I know." He sighed wistfully, sliding his sleeve back over the watch and dropping his arm in his lap. "There has to be more of it somewhere." For a moment, it seemed like he might say more, but he stopped himself.

"Did you ever try to find the man again?" she asked when he didn't continue. "Maybe he knows more about it."

"I tried. He didn't leave much of a trail, but eventually I found him a few years ago, buried in the dirt. Dead."

"Oh." Rosalind bit her lip. "I'm sorry."

Gothel shrugged, though she sensed he cared more than he let on. "I never really knew the guy."

"After...after the watch...then did the boy go to Donna's?"

"Ah, no." His face clouded over, and he dropped his eyes to his hand as he drummed his fingers against his leg. "Other places first."

"Bad places?" she murmured.

He nodded once. "Bad places. Then, finally, Donna's. I reunited with Calder there—we'd met once before at Wrothen's, but that place...that place you just had to survive. Flynnigan's was different. I was a scrawny kid, didn't talk, wouldn't look anyone in the eyes. He was the only one besides Donna and Levi that took to me rather than turned me away." He sighed again, his tone darkening with sarcasm. "Not much magic in that story."

She remembered Donna's face: harsh with hardship, for sure, but lined with fierce love. The kind of woman who would take in a quiet little boy after he'd been to so many terrible places. The kind who would ask anyone, even a stranger, to help him find his way, if she couldn't be the one to hold his hand.

"Why did you leave?" she asked, recalling the way Gothel had snapped at Donna before they'd left.

Gothel rubbed his eyes, chewing on the question for a second. "I—"

With a flourish, the door burst open, making both of them jump. Rosalind's heart leapt in her throat when Pepperjack swept in with his fur, eyes flaring bright orange, his aura crackling with power. His face was smooth and sharp, boyish and handsome, but had a timeless essence to it. As if he were both fifteen and fifty-five, the age changing every time you blinked despite having no wrinkles or blemishes. It was unsettling to look at him and be unable to figure out where he fit.

Rosalind's stomach dropped. She couldn't have slept for that long. Their time couldn't be up already.

"Six hours, forty-two minutes, and thirty-seven seconds," Pepperjack announced with extravagance. When Gothel and Rosalind just stared at him, waiting for their deaths, he smiled. "Dear old daddy paid your fine. In record time, too, I may add. You're sweet, Rosy, but, frankly, I wasn't sure you'd be worth that much to him."

Rosalind blinked, ignoring the familiar nickname in his horrid voice, her mind blank as she tried to process the news. Her father had paid. Her father had paid *for her*.

Gothel rose slowly to his feet, impassive mask on again as he studied the crime lord. "So I'm…"

"You're free." Pepperjack plucked a grape from the table and popped it in his mouth. "Clever young man you are. I will still be tracking down your old friends, though. It would be wise of you not to interfere with their deals now that yours has been separated. Understand?"

Gothel nodded, a flicker of disbelief lighting up his eyes. Pepperjack snapped his fingers and a piece of golden paper appeared on the table—Rosalind couldn't read the smaller print from the couch, but it looked like some sort of contract with Gothel's name printed on the bottom.

"All right, let's take care of the legal things and you can be on your way." He let out a roaring laugh, like the thought of him doing anything legal was hilarious.

Gothel sat back down and started studying the paper while those orange eyes flicked to Rosalind. She hated them.

"You may want to prepare for the trip home, Rosy," Pepperjack told her as he sat on the arm of the couch next to Gothel and ate another grape.

Buzzing with too many emotions to decipher and unable to put off her need any longer, Rosalind numbly got to her feet and went into the bathroom. For all his scary fruit and wolf fur and gaudy chandeliers, she found herself grateful that Pepperjack's expensive taste carried over to the bathroom as well.

After taking care of her business and washing up in the sink, Rosalind braved a look in the mirror. Her pale skin had a touch of color to it from time in the sun—mostly reddish pink—and her eyes looked bigger and more sunken than she wanted. By some miracle her braid had stayed largely intact with just a few stray hairs. Her lips were badly chapped.

Home, she thought. *I'm going home.* Her stomach still squelched. Even after everything, she wasn't sure how she could face it. Face her parents after their payment. Face Zachary after her accident. Face her lavish room after the orphanage. Stars knew there were so many other people who deserved it.

She didn't deserve any of it.

Gothel doesn't think so. The thought was sudden and intrusive, and it made her do a double take in the mirror. Yes, part of her felt different, yes, most of her stayed the same, and Gothel didn't seem to care either way. Of course, he'd been forced to stay with her the last few days, but he didn't have to bring her to the orphanage—a place difficult for him to both go back to and stay away from—and he didn't have to tell her about his mother, his watch, his past.

Maybe one person could accept her: a wanted criminal who hated her father, but maybe that still counted.

Of course, one person accepting her didn't change what she was.

With a sigh, Rosalind turned for the door, then paused. She knew she had come in from the left, but there wasn't a door there. Just a wall. Another glance in the mirror showed that the door was behind her.

Rosalind shook her head. This place was getting to her.

She went through the door and blinked, disoriented. Instead of coming back in across from the couches—like when she'd gone inside the bathroom—she entered the sitting room from the opposite side.

What *was* this place?

The nervous wonder evaporated from her mind and her spine straightened when she saw Pepperjack alone on the couch. He tucked a folded piece of paper into his fur coat, then beamed when he saw her.

"Ready?" he asked.

Her hands clenched into fists—her palms were so sore— and she took a step back so she could feel the wall. "Where's Gothel?" she mumbled.

"Gothel?" He said the name flippantly, already old news. "He left."

"He...left?"

"Well of course. Signed the paper and walked right out the door. He's free now. You know how those criminals are—only out to save their own skin." He laughed, stroking his fur. "I suppose he did a fine job of that."

Rosalind just stood there, blinking against the burning in her eyes. Gothel had left her.

Alone.

Here.

He wouldn't do that. They were...well, not friends, exactly, but not strangers. Not enemies. Sure, he was a criminal, sure, he had kidnapped her, but she'd seen past all that. They'd connected—or so she thought. Maybe she forgot what real connection felt like. Maybe he'd used her isolation as a means to gain the upper hand.

No, he wouldn't. She knew that. Gothel was just as lost as she was.

He's only out for himself, she thought, realizing the truth. *He's never been out for you.*

She tried not to feel the hurt, but something inside her still cracked. What had she expected anyway? That he could truly see past what she was and they could be friends forever? Had she really been that stupid?

He left.

You were wrong about Gothel, she snarled at herself, remembering her brief flicker of hope in the bathroom mirror. *And you were wrong about you.*

Smiling, Pepperjack waved his arm, gesturing toward the door. "Shall we, then?"

Aching all over, Rosalind hesitantly trailed behind him, back out into the foyer. Pepperjack stopped by the table to grab more fruit; she continued on toward the front door, feeling like a ghost in her limbs.

Suddenly, the air crackled behind her, sending a tingle down her spine. A whooshing sounded, a slash of wind in her ears, and her scalp sung with relief as a breeze kissed the back of her neck. She staggered, imbalanced. Her heart stuttered and somehow her soul knew what had happened before she reached up and felt the ends of her hair in her palm.

She whipped around and a half scream escaped her lips. There on the floor, lying like a fresh corpse, was her raven braid.

Crumbling to her knees, Rosalind snatched the heavy hair in her hand, a line of tears spilling over her right eye and trickling down her chin.

"What did...what...why?" she cried. "*Why?*"

Pepperjack kneeled across from her and pried the hair from her grip, setting it back on the floor. Then he took her face in his hands and forced her to look at him.

"Now, little Rosy," he said, his long fingernails scraping against her wet cheek, "I have plenty of thieves. But you..." He smiled, orange eyes twinkling. "I have other plans for you."

* * * * * * *

Nearly a week had passed since Gothel freed himself from his deal. A week without checking over his shoulder for Pepperjack's men. A week without the weight of his impending death on his shoulders. A week without Rosalind constantly at his heels.

Nearly a week had passed since Gothel freed himself from his deal, and it had taken that long for him to realize he didn't know what to do with that freedom.

Of course, he wasn't technically *free*, not really. He still had to duck his head every time someone looked at him too long or he thought he saw a royal guard. He still had to keep an eye out for Boone or Calder or Ulf or Tor, knowing they hadn't dropped their vendetta against him. He was still a poor, magicless, orphan nobody with nowhere to go.

He was aimless, wandering. And he *hated* that.

On day five of his newfound freedom, Gothel had actually considered going back to Flynnigan's for a moment—stars knew Donna could use the help, even from a grimy thief like him. But before he could really entertain the possibility, his head clouded with excuses. Like how he'd have to hide if any inspectors, royal or not, came knocking. Like how he didn't know the first thing about taking care of kids. Like how getting a job would limit his freedom anyway, and wasn't that just what he'd worked so hard for?

But deep down he knew that nobody had cared about the orphanages in a long time. He would be a better worker than many orphanage employees. Besides, he'd spent most of the previous day picking leaves off a tree because he had nothing else to do.

Underneath the excuses, though, he knew the rest of his soul would crumble if he ever went back indefinitely. He'd only briefly considered going back for a visit with his dark-haired shadow—even if he was still simmering over her senseless promise to get Prince Roman there.

She'd done something to him. All his life he'd been used to being alone, and now he found himself turning to say something to her, only to realize she wasn't there. And the only thing he hated more than that was the thought of her home again, locked away, reduced to a ghost under her father's reproachful gaze. Despite what she'd said earlier about not knowing where to go, he knew she'd gone back. Just as Gothel would always be running from a fragmented past, she would always be running back to the moment she felt defined her. Even if it meant running back to prison.

Even if it meant leaving him.

They were surprised at how fast the money came in—he'd seen the awe in her face. But despite her desperate insistence Sterling cared that much about her, Gothel suspected Pepperjack had been right about one thing: if anything got out about Rosalind, it could ruin Sterling's career. The entire family reputation. No wonder the man was so quick to hand over a mini fortune and plug up the hole in his pretenses before it leaked.

Gothel scowled at the ground as he walked through the neighboring village, Racine, fisted hands in his pockets. This used to be his home. He was just a short walk away from Boone's hideout, and it seemed like lifetimes rather than weeks ago he'd been sitting at the table, planning a kidnapping. The place was scarce and bare, like the very life and color had been leached out of it. Not quite as bad as the Jacklands, but still pretty dull. And the people were even bleaker. They watched each other with beady eyes and distrustful frowns, not acknowledging their neighbors as they shut themselves into their tiny shacks.

This was what people like Sterling did to people like Gothel. Reduced them to a dirty corner of the world to rot. It made him so angry Gothel almost couldn't see straight, and despite knowing that, despite seeing it firsthand, Rosalind had just gone right back to Sterling. Just got up and walked right out the door.

Once Gothel had finished taking care of Pepperjack's contract, he'd panicked, realizing she was gone, and ran out the door she'd gone through only to end up outside. He'd felt he'd been punched in the gut when he saw a carriage rattling away in the distance, taking her home. She had left, without a look, without a goodbye, without anything.

And to think he'd almost asked her to come with him. To think he'd told her his story—a story he had never once repeated in its entirety. He'd told her about his watch and considered asking her to help him find more of the technology. He'd have a purpose; she wouldn't have to go home.

But she had left.

Gothel didn't want to care. He was her *kidnapper* after all—of course she'd want to escape him as soon as possible. And Gothel didn't want her around, not really. He didn't do friends well, as Calder had proven. He didn't do *people*. So why did his neck itch at the thought of her running at the first chance she got? Why did it seem to sting just as much, or even more, than when Calder had abandoned him and let Boone slam the door between them?

He didn't know. He didn't know anything.

What's your play, Gothel? he wondered, but he had nothing. So he just kept walking, wandering aimlessly, feeling a bit like the hollow girl who had left him behind.

* * * * * * *

Eleven days. Eleven meals. Eleven afternoons agonizing over impossible work. Eleven nights curled against the wall in a cold sweat. There was a semi-comfortable cot available, but after realizing what it was made out of, the floor became the only option.

Sometimes, when it got really dark and everyone else fell asleep and Rosalind was really scared, she wondered whose skin made the cot against the wall. She wondered what they had done to make Pepperjack so angry at them, and how the people around her slept on them. She wondered if things would get even worse than they already had, and she'd end up as a cot rather than the person supposed to be sleeping in it.

Mackee had dragged Rosalind to another wing of Pepperjack's massive estate eleven days ago, depositing her on one of the empty cots that lined the far wall. She had counted twelve of them and eight people in the space. The room was a long, thin rectangle, one wall lined with cots and the chains holding the captives, the other side littered with heaps of assorted clutter, like yarn and silk and a ton of straw. Pepperjack had given her half her braid back, and she clutched it to her chest like an old stuffed animal, yearning for any sense of comfort.

"Prove your worth," he had admonished her, before letting Mackee take her away.

At the time, Rosalind had no idea what he meant—what job could she possibly be working in this place? But over time, as she watched the other people shackled there with her, she began to understand what kind of factory the crime lord had set up for himself.

Mozza, a bald woman at least ten years older than Rosalind, had the cot next to her. For the first couple days, Rosalind sat against the wall clutching her hair. Mozza had eyed her curiously, but that was all. Eventually, Rosalind started paying closer attention to what Mozza and the others were doing: they fought over the cluttered garbage, each marking and defending their territory as ruthlessly as if they were part of King Asher's military conquest. In between ensuring their belongings stayed protected, they used magic.

At first, the change was so slight, the magic so thorough, that Rosalind couldn't see what was happening. After a few days of watching Mozza, she realized they were each magically altering the yarn or straw or whatever else into something shiny. Gold. Gold they would then defend even more savagely than their straw. Rosalind had nearly burst into tears when she saw a teenage boy lash out at a man so viciously that he started bleeding.

Prove your worth, Pepperjack had said, handing over half her murdered hair, as though bestowing a gift. And after watching the bloodthirsty prisoners, she understood the significance.

He had thought desperation would force her hand, bring some magic out of her, but he did not know that Rosalind had met desperation a long time ago. It ran through her veins, tainted every feeling like the slight zing of lemon left in water. It would not make her break now. The thought of Pepperjack knowing the depth of her raw power made her want to shrivel up and blow away in the wind.

No. He couldn't know.

So Rosalind spent eleven days staring at the half braid, wondering how on earth she was supposed to make anything close to gold.

On day four, Mozza broke their silence to quietly explain some things to Rosalind. Like that, even if you could find a way to reach the top window that let them know what time of day it was, a strong magic barrier kept them inside and they were a hundred stories high. Apparently someone had managed to get through it, years ago, and jumped, but Mozza thought that was just a story. She had once been married, but had fallen into destitution after her husband suddenly died. Having nowhere else to turn to feed her children, she became entangled with Pepperjack, and now worked to pay off her debts.

"We are lucky he considers us valuable," she finished softly, running a palm over her shiny head. "If not, he would have taken our skin as payment."

Rosalind shuddered. Mozza put a comforting hand on her shoulder before climbing onto her own cot, apparently not bothered by the materials.

As the nightmare stretched on for four days, eight, eleven, Rosalind did not move from the wall except to relieve herself—she didn't dare join the merciless fray once the guards put food out, though after their one-sided conversation, Mozza started bringing Rosalind little scraps of bread and cups of water. Sometimes Rosalind got herself to eat or drink, in the dead of night while everyone slept (or at least pretended to), but she mostly just sat amid the humans without humanity and never once let go of her braid, a hollow ache in her gut every time the ends of her chopped hair tickled the skin under her jaw.

On day twelve, Rosalind couldn't see straight. Her stomach felt tied in strange knots, and it seemed a hammer pounded in her head, spreading through all her joints.

By day thirteen, she had to close her eyes.

When she woke up on day fourteen, her mind was muddy, eyes crusty, and skin cold. She roused to find her lap empty. The last vestige of her hair—and of herself—gone. Meanwhile, Mozza had a thick coil of gold strands and now looked through Rosalind as though she wasn't there.

So on day fifteen, when a woman with no front teeth came around to check quotas, Rosalind had nothing. Her tongue was a swollen piece of sludge in her dry mouth as the woman unshackled her and dragged her through the jail of barbarians and down a winding staircase. They rounded a corner and found Pepperjack, his back to them as he spoke with two other employees.

"I've reached a stalemate with Sterling and the crown—they won't pay more or agree to any of my terms. We'll use the rest of her hair as a bargaining chip for as long as we can, but she's just taking up space here. There are other ways into the castle, and there are plenty of Sterling's enemies who would pay a pretty price for his daughter."

Rosalind's eyes stung at the mention of her father. Where did he think she was? Could he ever guess the horrors she faced locked up in this place?

Would she ever see him again?

The woman holding Rosalind cleared her throat. Pepperjack turned at the sound, his gray eyes warm with glints of shiny copper.

"And here's our lady of the hour," he sneered. "Missed quota, did she Jeej?"

The woman—Jeej—nodded and bared what teeth she had when she spoke. "Take her to the underground, sir?"

Pepperjack gave Rosalind a predatory smile, and she shuddered in spite of herself. "Pretty little Corona girl has never worked a day in her life. Let's show her what happens when she misses quota in the real world, shall we? Just make sure to clean up any scars before you take her down—I want her all soft and shiny for the selling block."

Then he leaned down, arm outstretched. Rosalind cowered away from him, but Jeej jerked her forward with her hip, and Pepperjack roughly gripped her chin.

"Take notes during this lesson, Rosy," he said, the copper flecks in his eyes deepening, reddening. "For once you get out into the real world, you won't find people as merciful as I am. They will want you to suffer. But this?" His smile widened, exposing a line of perfect, blinding teeth. The wolf cornering his sheep. "This will be educational."

CHAPTER 8

THE TALLEST TOWER

When Rosalind was about seven or so, she would play on her family's grounds with Zachary and Roman. She and Roman would take turns being the knight—a word they had learned from old books in the castle—and they'd make Zachary be the dragon. He would always whine about it, but in the end he would accept his role if only so he could play with the older kids.

After Knight Rosalind had successfully defeated the dragon one day, she was on her way to save Prince Roman, who was 'stranded' on top of a rock wall overlooking part of her mother's garden. As Rosalind began to climb, she lost her footing and fell into a thick rose bush. The thorns tore open her skin, worsening every time she moved, though it was the sight of blood that really set her off. She screamed and Zachary started bawling and Roman dove off the wall, hurting his ankle in the process, but ran for help anyway. The limping little prince came back with Raf in tow, and the expert gardener helped cut Rosalind free. Despite being old and withered even back then, Raf carried Rosalind into the house, where her mom had tended to her and Roman's injuries. Of course, magic made them good as new, but for days, all she could think about were the lines of red running down her skin.

That was the memory that surfaced when Jeej delivered her punishment of choice.

"If you ever see your royal kissin' family again," Jeej had spat at her, words warped by her missing teeth, "ask them if they remember doing this to my Pap." Then she'd pulled out a long leather rope and hit Rosalind with it. A whipping, she'd called it. Fifteen lashes for fifteen days without work, and an extra five "'cause of your last name." But even as Jeej said that, Rosalind floated through the anguish, higher and higher, until something snapped. Suddenly everything was murky and distant, and with each lash of fire, she found she couldn't even remember what her last name *was*.

True to Pepperjack's instructions, once Jeej was finished with the malicious act, she erased all traces of it, healing her broken skin and leaving no indication it had ever been anything but perfect. Memories of thorn bushes scratched at her muddled brain as the gush of red was washed away.

It seemed her very skeleton was shaking inside her, every breath of movement a signal for a sharp spike of pain, as Jeej hauled her down a narrow staircase, so fast Rosalind nearly vomited. Then a stench assaulted her nose, and Rosalind had to swallow bile down. The space around her got darker, the air stuffier, and she immediately passed out the second Jeej dumped her on the ground.

When she woke up, she had to blink away tears that had formed in response to her smarting body. The world was hazy except for pain, and it took a minute for her senses to return and her sight to clear enough that she could see her surroundings.

It was dim. Her eyes worked to adjust to the faded light, aware of bodies all around her, and she wrinkled her nose against the stench stuck to the humid air. She was lying on her back on the hard ground, something firm underneath her head. Two pairs of eyes hovered over her, one grey, one green, and a set of whispered words found their way into Rosalind's ear over the continual collective groan echoing throughout the space.

A prayer. She recognized some of the words her grandmother used to cite on one of the rare occasions Mom would permit her own zealot mother to visit. Was Grammy here? Why would *she* be here?

Rosalind started to sit up and bit back a cry. The two pairs of eyes blinked, while a hand gently pushed her back down.

"Shh, stay down," a soft voice crooned, as though singing a lullaby with no melody. "It's all right. Take your time."

Panic bubbled on Rosalind's lips and she shuddered at the unfamiliar touch. The two girls hovering over her watched with subdued concern—one was about fifteen, the other no older than twelve, though there was a grave shadow to their expressions that made them seem years older despite their childish features.

Glancing helplessly between the two of them, Rosalind managed to ask in a raspy voice, "Where am I?"

But the answer came from the crooning voice above. "The underground."

"The underground?" Forcing herself through her dizziness, Rosalind pushed herself into a sitting position, her muscles whining with every movement. But the whines were quickly forgotten in her gasp of surprise when she got a look at where she was.

The place was indeed underground, evident by the dim lighting, stuffy air, and rock walls, but she didn't understand why it was called that. The place was a dungeon. Rusting rails divided up the space into five parts, one of which was occupied by six of Pepperjack's employees, loitering by a staircase. The other four squares of space were stuffed with people. There was barely enough room for everyone to sit, and many bodies were draped over each other, most of which were pale and dirty and groaning with pain. A dense wave of murkiness wafted from everywhere, and she realized the jail cells were made of the same metal around her finger.

The two girls watched her silently, as if anticipating something from her. She looked behind her to find a woman sitting cross-legged on the disgusting ground: the woman who had held Rosalind's head in her lap. Remembering Mozza just hours—or maybe days now—before, Rosalind eyed the strangers warily and curled into a ball, her eyes stinging with tears though she didn't know if they were in response to the awful scene, sickening stench, or overwhelming fact that she was stuck here.

"It's called the underground," the younger girl told her, "but some people call it the graveyard. Because once you go down, nobody you know ever sees you again."

The woman clicked her tongue disapprovingly, and the girl just shrugged.

"My name is Rashida," the woman told Rosalind, extending her hand in greeting. Rosalind stared at her hand warily until Rashida dropped it, though some old instincts were yelling at her to take the hand, if only to accommodate the etiquette she'd been taught as a child. It didn't matter. She was way past manners now.

Rashida didn't seem offended by the reaction. Instead, she nodded to the two girls. "That's Mela and Fern. Do you want to tell us your name?"

Rosalind licked her chapped lips, wincing as a boy in the cell next to them burst into hysterical sobs. She glanced at the girls. "You-your daughters?"

A cloud came over Rashida's warm face and she gave a sad smile. "They may as well be now." Her tone combined with the feeling in her words reminded Rosalind of Donna, and another new ache settled in her gut.

The connection drew truth from her mouth. "Rosalind. My-my name is Rosalind."

"Wonderful to meet you, Rosalind."

"What did you do, Rosalind?" the younger girl—Fern— asked, the freckles on her face like a map to her inquisitive green eyes.

Rashida clicked her tongue again. "Now, Fern, leave the girl be for a moment. Let her catch a breath."

But Rosalind didn't want to catch a breath of this stale air threaded with misery. She didn't want to be here, in this hole, drowning in sorrow.

"A...a graveyard?" The words trembled with her body. "What does...why? What is this place?"

This time, while Mela stayed quiet, Fern glanced to Rashida before speaking. Rashida nodded at her—more out of resignation than permission—and Fern leaned in close to talk over the grumble of suffering people.

"Three things can happen when Pepperjack owns you. First is what he's most known for: killing and skinning." She drew a line across her neck with her thumb, and Rosalind winced. "Second: you become a working slave for the rest of your miserable life. Third: he sells you for profit. We're in group three."

"Sell?" Rosalind gasped in disbelief. "But who would *buy* a person? That's so wrong."

Fern's mouth pressed into a hard line. "You'd be surprised."

Rosalind shuddered and held herself tighter, burying her head under her arms so she didn't have to look at the miserable scene any longer. But she could still smell the rancid stench. She could still hear the wails of suffering. She could still taste rotting death on her tongue.

Her eyes burned, but there wasn't any water in her to cry, so she dry sobbed into her arms.

She wanted Roman to come in, to speak to her softly and brush her hair without complaint.

She wanted Gothel next to her, with his quiet kind of calm and arsenal of stories to keep the loneliness and heartbreak and horror at bay.

She wanted to walk around to each prisoner in this hellish place and apologize that this awful crime against humanity had been going on while she'd been in her room, safely locked away.

Time lurched on, and with every unbearable second, she felt herself unravelling. When she couldn't take anymore, she jerked her head up to beg Gothel to tell her a story.

She saw him there for a second, sitting next to her with that same blank expression on his face. Then she blinked through her dizziness and the image vanished. Another sob got caught in her throat.

He was gone.

"Hey," Fern said, her forehead creasing as she looked over Rosalind. "You okay?"

Biting her trembling lip, Rosalind reached for something to grab onto. "A...a story?" she choked out. "Do you have a story?"

Fern raised her eyebrows, not doing anything to hide her skepticism. "Um, yeah, I guess." She glanced at Rashida and Mela as if to say 'is she going crazy?'

Rosalind didn't care. "Tell me."

"Tell you the story?"

"Yes. Please."

"Uh, okay." Clearing her throat, Fern launched into her personal history—not exactly the kind of story Rosalind had been asking for, but it worked all the same. She was an orphan too, like Gothel, after her parents succumbed to disease. Rather than consent to life in an orphanage, she found Pepperjack and squared a deal of survival.

"It worked for a few years," she said, "but now that I'm growing, Jack said I'm too pretty to be working and made for an 'economic advantage.'" She spat the words with disgust, and Rosalind marveled at the harsh edges on such a young girl.

Fern then turned to Rashida, who told her own, albeit much shorter story of desperation after her husband had left her. Rosalind was shocked to find out Rashida had once come from a noble family, and whether she recognized Rosalind was a Corona or not, she didn't say, which Rosalind was grateful for.

Last was Mela. The girl spoke calmly of her past despite obviously still bleeding from the wounds. She did not say who her uncle was or how he had come to be her sole caretaker, just that he was a brute and treated her savagely. When hard times came upon their household, her uncle sold her to Pepperjack without ceremony.

Rashida's face darkened and she called him a demon, though she must've heard the story before because she didn't seem surprised. Rosalind, on the other hand, was absolutely appalled. Roman had told her sworn secret instances of Asher hitting him, but even the prince's stories were nothing like Mela's nightmare.

But when Rosalind just stared with her mouth open and eyes teary, Mela put a hand over hers in comfort. As though *Rosalind* was the one that needed solace.

"It's okay," she said softly. "He always said he'd only give me what I deserve."

Fern just shrugged at that, but Rashida snapped something back—Rosalind didn't hear it over the roaring in her ears. Maybe it was the circumstances that had brought her here, being so far away from home—from her life—for so long, or the stark contrast of this prison to the sane world she had always known. Or maybe it was that Mela's grey eyes and despondent expression reminded Rosalind too much of herself, and suddenly she couldn't stand the fact that this sweet girl was tormented with so much suffering so young and actually believed it was justified.

"Nobody deserves this." Rosalind's voice cracked as she looked around again, at women attending to lonely children, men shedding tears with strangers as they quietly recounted the stories that nobody would get to hear again. People herded like sheep and sold like cattle.

The snake in her stomach knotted, and her chest felt tight and airless. She gasped for breath, the whole situation slamming into her with force, as though she had burrowed inside herself and finally looked up years later, only to realize how far away she had wandered from everyone else.

Rashida took her by the shoulders and told her to take deep breaths, but Rosalind barely heard her. She mumbled a string of incoherent thoughts, her vision darkening with the knowledge that she was in too deep and she was never getting out.

"Rosalind," Rashida whispered, her voice firm in her ear. "Breathe. Let me help you."

"I am Rosalind Corona." Her soft voice shook with dry tears. "I had a family that loved me and I tore them to pieces. I had everything in the world and I left it on the other side of the door." She shook her head miserably. "You don't want to help me."

She waited for the backlash, for one of the girls to insult her or spit at her or snarl that she had no right to complain about her spoiled life when they had scrambled for survival. She waited for them all to call her a monster and leave her to die in this place.

But none of that came.

Rashida's expression just softened. She kissed Rosalind's dirty forehead and met her eyes evenly. "Pain is pain, Rosalind. It will never discriminate, and you cannot weigh it against itself. In the end, we all bleed red. In the end, you are a survivor too." She took her hand, ignoring the swollen ring finger. "Nobody deserves this. Not me or Fern. Not Mela. And not you."

I don't deserve this.

Rosalind looked around at the prisoners again, but this time she saw the similarities: a group of people who had been forced onto a path they didn't want, who had made unbearable mistakes and were desperately trying to live with the consequences. People locked up—not only with physical weights, which always had a key, but with chains on the heart and mind, which were infinitely heavier and nearly impossible to unlock.

For the first time, she saw herself in the people around her. Their stories had woven together, and she knew what should come next for them.

She had to get home.

"This isn't our story," Rosalind muttered to herself before looking at Fern and Mela. "I used to read a lot. Stories of heroines and dragons and people that fought for things. I used to pretend to be them with my friends. To be treated like this, sold like...like animals only to wither and die..." She shook her head. "That isn't our story."

Fern's lips quirked to the side in a devious smile, while Mela cocked her head. "But if this isn't our story, what is?"

Rosalind glanced across the way at the employees laughing with each other as they watched over their prisoners, weapons and keys on their belts.

"Escape."

* * * * * * *

Gothel saw his shadow everywhere.

In the ripple of dark curls, the squealing of children, the smell of hazelnuts. It seemed she was always hiding in the corner of his eye, but when he turned toward her, she was gone.

Two weeks had passed since he'd seen her. Two whole weeks away, and he still couldn't escape her. It was driving him insane.

Why do you care? he demanded, though he never let himself answer. Caring got you nowhere. Caring got you lost when

Eugene takes off and Calder betrays you and you are left with nothing.

Caring about anything, especially a Corona, was a bad idea, and Gothel needed to stop.

He grumbled to himself as he entered the west market square. While many villages had their own trading posts, the east and west market squares were the hubs of commerce in Elaria—infinitely bigger and more crowded. The abundance of merchandise and people made them the perfect breeding grounds for Gothel's line of work, which was what he was seeking out.

It had been over a month since he'd gone to the forum where they'd planned the kidnapping, and he hadn't truly been back in the game since. His very being itched for the familiar thrill, and he was hoping that indulging would clear his irritated mind. The Corona scheme was over; it was time to go back to real life.

The midmorning crowd was ample and committed, full of driven people who had arrived early for the best merchandise to start their day. This kind of customer was harder to steal from during the process, as they were so focused on their tasks that they were more likely to catch on if something went missing. The prime time to slide under their noses was after their last stop, once they were done for the day and had successfully counted their wares before heading home, shoulders straight with pride for their haul.

Gothel passed three such people on his way into the square. From them he retrieved a peach, a small bottle of milk, and a heel of bread. He opened the package of bread and was assaulted by the scent of cinnamon. Gritting his teeth, he dumped the package and delved into the rest of his acquired breakfast.

As always, the square rattled with noise, a massive cacophony of mismatched sounds that wove together in tuneless music. The smell of so many bodies intermixed with aromas of warm pastries and fresh produce. Gothel breathed in the measured chaos as he tossed his peach pit aside. If anywhere, he only belonged when lost in a crowd.

Having finished his meal, he started forward, eager to ignore his restless thoughts and do the one thing he was good at. Just as he took a step, someone came from the other direction and bumped roughly into his shoulder.

"Excuse me, sir," the bumper said, straightening up. His eyes widened as Gothel's eyebrows shot up. "G?"

Gothel momentarily froze with indecision, but Calder wasted no time. Keeping a good natured—but fake—smile on his face, he steered Gothel away from the masses and behind a trading stall. Gothel shook off his hand the moment they were hidden.

Calder glanced warily around them before his eyes settled on Gothel. "Wow, G. I was starting to think you were dead." Gothel opened his mouth, but Calder held up a hand to stop him. "Boone is here. *Everyone* is here. Boone, Tor, Ulf—they all want a piece of you, and not in a nice way. Not to mention we're being tailed by Pepperjack's men, and they mean bad business. You need to get lost."

"I *was* lost," Gothel replied flatly. "I just came from the Jacklands."

Calder blinked. "You what? *Came* from the Jacklands? And survived?"

"Clearly."

"But how?"

"I paid up. I'm done."

Understanding dawned in Calder's face, and he chewed his lip as he regarded Gothel. They were older now, but it was the same expression Calder had when they first met, sizing Gothel up and deciding if he wanted him on his team.

"Well, G," he finally said, "that's an incredible feat. I always knew you were a smart one." He offered Gothel one of his winning smiles—smiles that had stolen goods and hearts and a sliver of Gothel's trust—but Gothel just clenched his fists and glared in response.

"Why did you do it?"

"Oh, come on, G." Calder looked up at the sky, as though the question of betrayal was so unreasonable. "Don't give me this."

"You *know* I didn't do it. Why did you leave me there, Calder? Why did you let Boone blame me?"

He ran a hand through his hair, exasperated. "It's not personal, G! It's life. Survival. You know that. You and I are the same—always have been. Orphan life teaches you to look out for yourself first, no matter what. I don't know who gave us up, and I don't care because I did what I had to do to survive. Don't pretend that if the roles had been reversed, you wouldn't have done the same to me."

Gothel rolled his eyes to hide the fact he wasn't sure Calder was wrong about that. "Your life is a con, Calder," he said, aiming the words so they sunk into Calder's swaggering bravado and hit the scared boy underneath. "And eventually you won't be able to cheat your way out anymore, and all your fraud will fall away, and you'll realize you have *nothing* real."

For the barest second, Gothel saw the wound in Calder's eyes, knew he had hit his mark. But then the second passed, the fastest blink, and the persona was back on again—the permanent mask he had fixed on himself years ago in order to survive.

"Fine, G," Calder said, giving him a derisive smile. "Go live your 'real life.' But if I were you, I'd stay out of Boone's way— he'll gut you if he has the chance, and I doubt I'll be there to hide you next time." With an arrogant tip of his head, Calder turned and strolled back into the square, allowing himself to get lost in the crowd.

Once he was gone, Gothel blew out a long breath and rubbed his eyes, wondering for the millionth time how he had gotten here. He tried to map the path he had unwittingly taken, the path that had led him from a quiet little boy doing chores with his mother to a wanted criminal without any kind of foundation.

Your life is a con. And eventually you'll realize you have nothing real.

The dig had been meant for Calder, but it had pierced Gothel too. He tried to blink the sting away, but every time he closed his eyes he saw the raven-haired girl staring back at him, easily seeing through the wall he'd spent his whole life building up.

"She's gone," he growled to himself. "She left and she's not coming back for you."

The words set off a flash of an image in his mind, a kind of daydream warped with memory: a child sitting on the steps of an orphanage, waiting for a mother who would never show up, for a girl who had left him behind.

You have nothing real.

Blowing a harsh breath through his teeth, Gothel stuffed his hands in his pockets and stalked out of the square, careful to watch his back in case one of his old friends tried to sneak up behind him and slit his throat.

He had never belonged with them. He'd never belonged in his own house, at Flynnigan's, or with Rosalind.

He was doing what he should've done years ago.

What's your play, Gothel?

He was leaving Elaria.

* * * * * * *

The plan was simple.

Rashida would fake some kind of heart attack. It would have to be big and cause a lot of racket, as the guards likely wouldn't care so much if just one of the prisoners didn't make it. It was Mela and Rosalind's job to scream and cry and spread panic like wildfire so the guards would be forced to come in if only to quiet everyone down. It was up to Fern to swipe the keys from the guard tending to Rashida. Once they had the keys, they would settle down and wait for the right time to use them.

It wasn't the best plan, but it was the best they could do given the time, place, and restrained magic. Based on the strong vibrations she could feel from the metal cages—which was likely why so many people were sick down here, now that she thought about it—Rosalind wasn't even sure her magic would work if she took off her ring. She also wasn't sure she wouldn't decimate the place and shred all the innocent people to bits.

"If something goes wrong," Fern whispered once the plan was set, "pretend that Rashida's scare is real and I just tried to take the opportunity. Jack likes me. He'll be nicer to me than any of you."

"I'll go down with you," Mela offered, but Rosalind shook her head.

"We have to believe it will work." She fingered the ends of her short hair, still not used to the new length, though, admittedly, it had been much easier to navigate without all the extra weight she'd carried for so long. With different hair, she could almost believe she was a different person, and she reached deep inside herself to pull out the remnants of the adventuring girl she used to be. The girl who would scale a wall to slay a dragon and save her best friend. "We can do it."

So they waited for what they thought was nighttime, when most prisoners were asleep and the guards were most relaxed. Rashida's spot was in the center of their cell, which meant anyone would have to come in deep in order to help her, and now she was faking sleep. All three girls sat quietly with their shoulders slumped and faces downcast, while their eyes tracked every movement and their hearts thumped with anticipation.

True to Fern's information, the guards did their routine switch. Rosalind clenched her fists as several of them disappeared up stone steps, leaving three to wait for the next guards to come. She heard Mela take a deep breath, then Fern nudged Rashida with her foot.

It was time.

To her credit, Rashida was an excellent actress. Rosalind didn't think she herself could pull this show off, but the second Rashida took a shuddering breath, Rosalind knew they had picked the right performer for this spectacle. All Rosalind had to do was be scared, and she wouldn't even have to pretend, really.

Rashida took her time, allowing it to build. Her breathing became harsh and labored, and she made low groaning sounds that turned the heads of a few people around her. It took a second—the prisoners here were used to the sounds of suffering—but Rashida was patient, and she had a little audience within a few minutes.

"Do you think she's okay?" Fern stage-whispered right on cue, with the perfect mix of indifference and fear for herself. This child was a force to be reckoned with.

"I don't know," Mela whispered back. Her eyes shifted around the crowded cell, and alarm started building in the atmosphere with every gaze she met. "What do we do?"

"I don't know," Rosalind answered, the panic in her hushed voice real. "Maybe—"

Then Rashida heaved and let out a painful cry, her entire body shaking and twitching. Rosalind winced in spite of herself.

Fern let out a gasp. "Something is wrong with her!" she cried, stabbing an incriminating finger at Rashida. If their audience had been small before, it grew now, more and more heads turning their direction as whispers flew.

And for the climax of her show, Rashida let out a blood curdling scream. It made Rosalind and Mela both jump and shriek, and the screaming spread like a raging disease, only intensifying when people looked toward the commotion and saw Rashida shuddering violently.

"Demon!" a lady shouted and pointed, crashing into people as she backed away. "She's possessed!"

The lady wasn't even part of the show, but her act sealed the deal. All at once people began throwing themselves out of Rashida's way, but there was little space in the first place, so they just crashed into each other, the small cell heightening the panic. A guard was yelling something; Rosalind couldn't hear the words over the chaos.

Suddenly, the havoc cut in half, a clean slice through the mayhem. Those on the outskirts of the cell quieted despite the commotion in the middle, and both Rosalind and Mela straightened up, though Fern didn't react.

"Quiet down!" a guard was shouting as he made his way through the throng. "Let me through!"

The prisoners obliged, having clearly learned to be on their best behavior for the guards. Rosalind's heart sunk into her gut when her fellow captives all kneeled on the floor, lifted their hands, and bowed their heads in surrender, and she could adequately see over them to find four guards in the cell. Three more were standing watch right outside.

As the shouting guard plowed through the crowd, the other three stopped at intervals to check on others or survey the space. The main man came all the way to Rashida and bent down to tend to her with more gentleness than Rosalind expected from him. The problem was he nearly stepped on Fern in the process, not caring about squashing her. Another woman sitting behind them grabbed Fern and yanked her out of the way just in time. Fern hissed and tried to break free, but the woman held fast, probably thinking she was helping to save her. The fiery girl bared her teeth in frustration, and the expression didn't match the sorrowful glint in her eyes as she mouthed 'sorry' to Rosalind.

Rosalind had been in between Fern and Mela. She was the closest to a guard now. Rashida was pretending to come to, nodding obediently in response to the man's questions.

They were going to lose their chance.

Remembering the heroines from her stories, wondering at Gothel's technique, Rosalind didn't leave time for reason or time for fear. Instead she swallowed herself down, waited until the man was sufficiently distracted, then reached for the keys attached to his belt.

For her, the moment happened in slow motion: her fingers looped around the metal just as someone snatched her wrist. She glanced up to see the female guard glaring, her grip like a vise.

All at once, time snapped, and everything happened so fast. Suddenly she was out of the cell, tripping on the stone stairs under her feet. Her shin hit against a stair once, hard, but Rosalind choked on her cry of pain as she was dragged along.

Then they were in a different room—one Rosalind vaguely recognized—and the female guard was gone. In her place, smiling down at her like a cat cornering her mouse, was Jeej.

She claimed she gave thirty lashes this time, though Rosalind couldn't remember past the nineteenth.

When she came to, she was clean of blood and back in the cell, her head resting in Rashida's lap. The others were speaking quieter than before, but she could still hear them. Pepperjack's people had been talking while she was gone: the transports were coming tomorrow to take the prisoners to the selling block.

Terror crashed through her, disappointment bubbling in her gut like acid. She stared up at the kind woman holding her.

"I'm so sorry," she whispered. "I'm so so *sorry*."

Rashida brushed hair from Rosalind's forehead, her voice a soft melody compared to Rosalind's cracked tone laced with despair. "No, Rosalind, shh. Don't apologize. It's okay. You tried."

"I failed."

"We knew it was a risk. You did everything you could."

Tears leaked down Rosalind's cheeks. "I'm not smart or strong or fast. I can't fight them and I can't run. I actually tried and I failed and now we are all going to be sold to awful people that can't see *us* as people." She took a shuddering breath and closed her eyes. "Why did I try...why did I...I did everything I could do and it was not enough."

Rashida let Rosalind cry herself out, only interrupting to offer comforting words. She appreciated the woman so much, but at the same time, it made her ache for her own mother. It made her ache to sit on the chair in her mother's art gallery and watch her paint; to hear the door open and run down to give her father a hug after his long day of work; to go exploring with Zachary in the summer and build snowmen in the winter and listen to all the funny things he had to say.

For the first time in as long as she could remember, Rosalind wanted to go back. For the first time in forever she did not care that she'd have to face the storm she had left behind if it meant she could go home.

Stinging inside and out, Rosalind pushed herself up to see Fern and Mela. The sight of them watching over her, still stuck here, still hurtling toward a horrible fate, made her start sobbing again. Mela cocked her head, as though she couldn't understand her tears, and Fern jerked her chin defiantly, letting Rosalind know she would not be bullied by whatever circumstances she found herself in.

The desperation was so thick inside her, the heartbreak so absolute, the pain so vivid, that Rosalind curled into a ball and prayed for some kind of comfort. She had never prayed before—she couldn't even remember one of the goddesses' names—as her mother had never taught her after being raised by a religious extremist. Her mother had been conditioned to fear the goddesses, but Rosalind hoped that they weren't like that. She hoped they were kind. Or, at the very least, understood pain.

When she opened her eyes again and saw Fern, Mela, and Rashida still there in the cramped cell, somehow it reminded her of the orphanage. Of Gothel. For the millionth time, she wished he were here with her.

"I knew someone who climbed Mount Brenne once." Rosalind wasn't sure exactly where that had come from, but she said it and couldn't take it back.

Mela and Rashida's eyebrows shot up in surprise, but Fern narrowed her eyes. "What? Nobody has ever survived that climb. Not since King Rowan."

Rosalind just shrugged. The movement hurt so badly. "My friend did."

"What was at the top?" a woman next to her asked, her face alight with curiosity.

"Nothing," a man answered. "It's just a legend."

A boy puffed out his chest. "I heard there's a magic stone at the top. It was the stone that helped King Rowan defeat the rebels in the Great War."

"No." The man shook his head firmly. "There was no stone. That's just a legend too. King Rowan squashed the rebels with his own strength."

They continued to argue about it, and someone tapped on Rosalind's shoulder. She turned to find a girl a few years older than her—maybe twenty or so.

"So what happened?" she asked, a spark lighting up her face haggard with hopelessness. "How did your friend get to the top?"

Rosalind told her. She recounted the tale Gothel had told the orphans, and even though she was sure most of the people listening knew it was fake, they were all enraptured by what she had to say.

So she kept talking. Spewing Gothel's stories, then blending the ones she used to read with the games she used to play. She kept going, even when the entire cell turned to listen and the guards leveled glares. Even when her mouth dried up, her lips cracked, and her throat ached.

She kept telling the stories, the words a meager distraction from their grave reality. It was all she could do.

* * * * * * *

He didn't know how he ended up here.

Gothel had been planning on heading for the northern port. Elaria's borders were closed, locked up tight after the Great War for reasons either nobody knew or understood. It was nearly impossible to travel out of the kingdom, but the best avenue was the northern port: it was easiest to barter passage on a ship without anyone asking questions. The hard part wasn't getting on a boat—it was surviving once the boat got out to sea. But Gothel had planned on dealing with possible siren attacks later, when he finally got to the port.

He was nowhere near his destination. He looked up from his feet and recognized the wealthy street, worlds different from the villages he'd been wandering through for weeks.

The Coronas lived just four households down.

This was crazy. It was crazy and Gothel knew it. What was *wrong* with him? He should turn around right now and get far away from this place. He certainly didn't belong here.

But *she* was here. She'd echoed behind every thought, stood as a silent observer in his head at every decision. No matter how far he went, how hard he tried, he could not shake his raven-haired shadow from his mind.

What was she doing now? He'd nearly driven himself insane with the question. How had her family received her? Was she ripped from her life and thrown into danger only to go back to a prison cell?

The thought made his blood boil. Gothel tried not to care, told himself it wasn't his business, but as he stared down the street toward her house, he knew that he couldn't live with himself if he didn't know she was okay.

One look. Just one. To make sure she hadn't been completely locked away again. To check that Sterling hadn't extinguished the tiny little flame that Gothel had seen light in her once or twice.

Just a confirmation. Then he was gone for good.

The Corona estate looked different than the last time he'd seen it, though nothing seemed to have changed. But it was emptier. Still. As if the house itself were holding its breath.

All the servants and workers he'd seen milling around the last time he was here were gone. The flowers looked good, but the rest of the grounds were in disarray—a far cry from the pristine near-castle he remembered.

A bad feeling settled in his gut. He shook it off and headed toward the back, prepared to use the same servant entry he had when he and Calder had posed as employees here. But when he got to the backside of the house, he found that the door was now locked.

It took about fifteen minutes for him to inspect the house since *every* door was locked and he kept having to duck if he thought he heard someone passing. It was still early afternoon, after all, and with one glance his way, anyone could see he wasn't supposed to be there.

Finally, he managed to find a low window that he could wedge open and slide through. With a quiet thud, he landed in a dark cellar lined with shelves of supplies. A storage area. Gothel stumbled through the place, accidentally kicking a shelf once or twice, before he found a door to a hallway that led to some stairs. He climbed them to find another door, and paused to listen to the voices speaking on the other side.

"King Asher ordered us to hold off," Sterling was saying, a kind of defeat to his poise that surprised Gothel. "He won't even entertain a conversation about negotiating anymore."

"He's wrong!" a younger voice shouted back with vehemence. "This is Rosalind. We can't just sit here. It's already been too long." He spoke so differently, without arrogance or a title, that it took Gothel a moment to recognize Prince Roman's voice.

"I know. I know." Sterling sighed. "I don't know what to do." It was quiet for a few seconds before he spoke again. "Asher is right about one thing, though. This criminal will drain us, and the crown, of everything. He'll turn Elaria into his playground."

"Then let him!" Prince Roman snapped. "It's *Rosalind.*"

More silence. So thick and heavy, Gothel nearly retreated back down to the cellar just to escape the truth that was hiding in the tense quiet. It couldn't be real. He'd heard wrong.

Rosalind was upstairs in her room, staring blankly at the ceiling. She had to be.

Gothel willed Prince Roman and Sterling to *do* something, either keep talking and disprove his speculation or move so he could go check on her himself.

Finally, the prince spoke. "I have to go. Send me any updates as soon as you have them."

"I will," Sterling promised. "You know, I haven't seen Griffin lately. Is he okay?"

Gothel frowned. Griffin was the prince's advisor, right? Everyone in the kingdom knew they were almost always together, and it sparked all kinds of crazy rumors.

Prince Roman's response was late and unconvincing. "Yeah, he...he's fine."

"Are you guys okay? Stuck in an argument? It's not like you two to fight."

"No, it's..." The prince sighed. "It's complicated. He just...he lost someone he cared about, and we can't lose anyone else right now. Especially not her."

"You know I will do everything I can."

"I know." With that, footsteps sounded, passing in front of Gothel, then a distant door opened and shut. Sterling sighed and papers shuffled before another set of footsteps disappeared.

Breathing through the panic prickling the back of his neck, Gothel silently opened the door and stepped over the threshold, making sure to close the door behind him. As he had sensed, the hallway was empty now. An open door was across the hall to his right, displaying what looked like Sterling's office. The urge to go through his enemy's belongings was fierce, but he buried it and forged ahead.

He had to think to remember the layout he had once memorized. It seemed it was lifetimes ago when he and Calder had stolen through these hallways, exacting a plot of both preservation and revenge. Now that all felt ridiculous—

childish, even—compared to the desperation coursing through his veins.

The hallways were empty. As was the living room. Rather than go up the back way—the safe way—he took one of the front staircases two at a time, barreling over the plush carpet toward her room.

He skidded to a stop in the open doorway. The curtains were drawn, blacking out most of the afternoon sun. The desk was broken, the books dusty, and the floor a mess of garbage, dishes, and old clothes. A path had been made through the clutter, a worn strip of carpet that led from the entrance to the bed.

Gothel sagged against the doorframe like he'd been punched in the gut.

She wasn't here.

Suddenly, the door slammed shut in his face. Gothel jumped back, his heart leaping into his throat, and he nearly tripped over something behind him. Steadying himself against the banister, he froze when he realized that something was a chair. And that chair held a person.

Rosalind's little brother—Zachary, he remembered—stared up at him, eyes narrowed and lips pursed, his expression somehow displaying disapproval despite his severe disfigurements. Gothel felt guilty for having to blink and do a double take.

"That's my sister's room," Zachary stated, clearly distrustful. "You aren't allowed to look in it."

Gothel just glanced from the boy to the magically shut door, wondering how long he'd been watching. "She isn't back yet?"

Zachary's one good eyebrow crashed into his half one.

"Does it *look* like she's back yet?"

"Zachary?" The voice echoed from downstairs, and even though Gothel hadn't heard it more than once or twice in his life, he caught the strain in it. The loss. "Zachary, who are you talking to?"

But the boy ignored his mother's questions and studied Gothel. "Who are you? I know I've seen you here before, but not since the party. Not since she went missing." Apparently, the kid was just as perceptive as his sister.

She's not here.

"Zachary?" the voice called again, worry showing through. "Zachary!"

She appeared at the top of the staircase, took one look at her son talking to a stranger who had somehow materialized in her house, and ran toward them. Even before she got close, Gothel could see the suffering etched out in her expression. One of the greatest women in Elaria and she was wrapped in a wrinkled robe with a frizzy knot of hair on her head, sharp cheekbones cutting across her sunken face.

Genevieve looked nothing like herself. In fact, she looked more like her daughter.

She put herself in between Gothel and Zachary, just as they heard Sterling run into the living room downstairs. "Gen?" he called, frantic. "Was that you? Are you okay?"

"Sterling!" she called back. Then came the sound of footsteps pounding on the other staircase, and soon Sterling was standing on Gothel's other side, demanding to know who he was and telling Zachary to get downstairs. Of course, the boy didn't budge.

Cornered by the Coronas. For once, Gothel didn't care.

Instead, he looked from the door, to Zachary, to the lifeless mother, his shoulders slumping as he allowed the weight of the truth to crash into him. Pepperjack's trick. Rosalind's sentence.

Of course she wouldn't have just left. How could he have not seen it?

"She isn't back yet?" He knew the answer, but he asked again anyway, as though there was some chance he just misunderstood everything.

Sterling clenched his jaw and started advancing, but Genevieve held up her delicate hands, stopping him. Gothel felt hypnotized by her brown eyes as she took a step toward him. Then another. Those deep eyes—as deep as Rosalind's—paralyzed him until she was right in front of him. She reached a bony arm out, as if to touch him, then thought better of it and retracted. Gothel was afraid if he breathed too hard, she would crumble into dust.

"You...you know where she is," she murmured. It wasn't a question puffed up with hope. Just a soft statement, as fragile as she was.

Instantly, his mind started racing. He pored over the details in his head, counting the time they'd been separated, the plays he could make, the danger he'd put himself in. The plan was to leave Elaria, as difficult as that was with the closed borders, and never look back. The plan never even involved coming here. Not only was he considering endangering his future, but his life, and that was something he'd never once done for anyone.

He could just give the Coronas the information and run. They would save her; he'd save himself. Everyone would get what they wanted.

But with one blink, one glimpse of her permanently etched behind his eyelids, he knew the worth of the risk. Within a few moments, the plans that had seemed so crucial earlier all melted away when compared with Rosalind's fate.

Finally, Gothel nodded at Genevieve. "I do," he answered quietly, "but we have to hurry. She doesn't have much time."

CHAPTER 9

THE CLIMB AND THE FALL

The Jacklands didn't look much better during the day—maybe less sinister without the shadows hiding all kinds of deeds and threats. But the sun filtering through the foggy air only highlighted how foul the place was.

Gothel could taste decaying fruit on his tongue as he walked on, head down and shoulders straight. Here, you wanted to stay out of everyone else's business while looking capable enough that nobody messed with yours. He counted the people he passed but didn't acknowledge them. The last thing he needed was the locals discovering he was bringing a councilman and fairy into their territory. He didn't know exactly where the two of them were at the moment, but he hoped they were capable enough to have entered the Jacklands undetected.

Sterling didn't know who or what Irina was, and he decided not to question when Gothel wouldn't offer up those details.

He was desperate to leave *right then*, rather than waste time trying to assemble a guard, and Gothel agreed. Irina, to her credit, didn't hesitate to find Gothel after he signaled to ask for her help despite the danger it put her in. Genevieve had gone straight to the palace with Zachary in tow in an effort to ask King Asher for help in retrieving her daughter.

Help hadn't come yet. Gothel was sure it wouldn't. He wasn't even sure he trusted Sterling's motivations in saving his daughter, but they couldn't pull off Rosalind's rescue without him. Assuming she was still alive.

Gritting his teeth, Gothel clenched his fists in his pockets and sped up slightly. He couldn't think like that.

There weren't roads here, just worn paths overgrown with weeds. Gothel maneuvered them smoothly, eager not to draw attention to himself. Irina was supposed to meet him just outside Pepperjack's hideout. Her task was to get Gothel information, help him sneak inside if necessary, then get herself out of here. Pepperjack was notorious for playing on fairies' desperation when running from royal hunters, and Irina wasn't about to get cozy with a councilman either. Truthfully, it was a miracle she had agreed to help at all.

Gothel didn't believe in miracles, but if they all survived today, he might have to start.

He came upon a stretch of ransacked buildings, their eerie silence broken up by echoes of scratchy scurrying. He refused to look directly at the vermin he could feel scuttling around his feet.

There were more people around, leaning up against walls while drinking, smoking, or talking quietly to someone close to them. They all seemed angled somehow. Aligned in a near circle, as though their beings were tethered to something outside themselves, and they couldn't drift any further. Puppets on a master string.

Gothel's mouth pressed into a hard line as he recognized the front of a structure. One nobody was loitering around. One he'd been to before.

He was here.

As Irina had instructed him, Gothel continued on past the structure, though the hope of meeting her almost wasn't enough to keep going. What if Rosalind was inside? What was happening to her right now?

Stop it, he commanded himself. He had a play. A shaky one maybe, but he had to stick to it.

A silent sigh of relief escaped him when he rounded the corner of the third building and saw a hooded figure waiting for him.

"I found your friend Leland," Irina started quietly before Gothel could ask.

"We aren't friends," he muttered.

"Nonetheless, he remembered you. According to his knowledge, the girl has been here since the day she was brought. He isn't sure where she was kept for the entirety of her imprisonment, but, for at least the last few days, she's been in the graveyard. Her group is being transferred today."

The graveyard. Gothel did not like the sound of that. "Leland just told you all this?"

Irina's head lifted slightly so he could see one side of her mouth pull up, a sharp cut across her marred face. "He had to be persuaded."

"I see." Good thing he didn't care what happened to Leland. "Where are they being transferred?"

The grin disappeared as disgust sparked a dangerous flame in her eyes. "Evidently, Pepperjack makes quite a profit on people."

Gothel blinked. "On *people*?"

"He has a regular selling block, and she's the jewel of this crop. The fortune gained for a Corona girl will be monumental."

"That's…"

Irina nodded, a harsh bop of her head. "I know."

"Where's the graveyard?"

"Somewhere behind his palace. He calls it his garden."

His garden? For the thousandth time, Gothel cursed Boone for entangling them in such a web. "This guy is insane."

"As I tried to tell you from the beginning." Irina glanced behind her, cat-like eyes taking in every detail, before turning back. "If they get her to that block and auction her off, it's likely she'll never be seen again."

"Get her before she's gone. Got it." He took a breath, then nodded. "Now it's best for you to get out while you can."

He half expected her to make some kind of quip before a sudden exit—Irina's humor was as keen as a slashing blade, and just as unpredictable—but instead her face hardened into a stone riddled with jarring lines. She stared through him for so long, he wondered if she hadn't heard him.

Finally her grave voice came through. "Much is at stake here, Gothel. For everyone. You all *must* be careful."

Gothel inwardly winced, careful to not let it show on his face. He already had Rosalind's life on his shoulders. He didn't want to think about the repercussions of his decisions any more than he had to.

Instead of addressing it, he grunted, trying to find the right words to say. "It was…it was good of you to come, Irina."

A commotion sounded a ways off: the rattling of chains and barking of orders. The transfer.

Irina and Gothel's eyes locked for a moment. He nodded at her; she nodded back. Then Gothel surged ahead toward the noise, and Irina turned and disappeared.

Going as fast as he dared, Gothel made his way back to Pepperjack's estate, still marveling at how something so gaudy and huge could be made to fit in such a tiny shack. Hugging the wall, he poked his head around the corner. The weeds had been cleared back here, the ground just an expanse of soft dirt. Half buried rocks the color of the moon dotted the earth in what was surely some kind of artistic pattern. Gothel nearly tripped on one of them, ripping it halfway out of the ground. His throat closed up when he realized it wasn't a rock at all. It was a skull.

He forced himself to take a breath. *You have a play, Gothel. Get Rosalind. Get out. Stay focused.*

Taking all his willpower, he tore his gaze from the skulls and surveyed the space ahead of him. Two large, boxy carriages were parked with their back doors open, showcasing space that was usually reserved for trading goods. Gothel had robbed many of them in his time. But instead of crates filled with silk or berries, people were being loaded inside, packed in like animals. The sight made Gothel's stomach knot.

There were roughly ten to fifteen guards, some with weapons and others likely relying on magic. They watched the procession as a line of chained prisoners were forced out of what looked like a cellar and into the transports.

Steeling himself, Gothel crept silently around the edge of the property toward the transports. When he was close enough, he dropped to the ground and rolled underneath the nearest one. From there, he could hear some of the guards and actually see the prisoners' expressions. They were all gaunt and miserable, pale and lifeless, already dead in some ways as they shuffled toward their fate. Gothel searched every face for one he recognized, scoured every inch of the procession for a glimpse of her hair. Nothing.

He stiffened when two guards approached the side of the transport he hid under.

"No way." The voice came from a man who couldn't have been much older than Gothel. "You serious?"

"It's her," a woman responded. "I saw with my own eyes. Corona through and through. I heard there's already a buyer lined up for her. Jack's gonna make a fortune."

"I heard the Coronas never left their mansion. Except Sterling, obviously."

The woman snickered. "Yeah, well she picked the wrong day to leave home, didn't she?"

Gothel gritted his teeth as he listened to the exchange, still watching the line of prisoners. He was so focused on what the guards were saying, that it took him a moment to notice the girl in line nearly upon his hiding place. She watched the two guards, her face white and gaunt, stained with whispers of death, and framed by a shorn bob of raven hair.

He blinked, his mouth falling open into the dirt.

Her *hair*. It was gone. The inky black cloud that used to nearly touch her ankles now barely brushed the base of her shoulder.

But she was here. Out in the open. Sterling had better have found his position by now, or they were going to lose their chance—lose *her*—forever.

A moment went by. Then another. Rosalind moved up in line. No sign of Sterling. Gothel bit the inside of his cheek so hard he tasted blood. As Rosalind came next to be loaded, he resisted the urge to act. Revealing himself without Sterling would only get Gothel killed too.

But she was *right* there.

And they were going to lose her.

Gothel cursed under his breath as he watched her bare and dirty feet step up to the transport, then rise and disappear. She was inside.

Where was Sterling?

Suddenly, the earth lurched underneath him, a distant explosion tearing through the air. Guards cursed or shouted in surprise, and a couple prisoners screamed as they tried to shield themselves with shackled hands. Then another explosion sounded closer to Pepperjack's estate. Then another. A ripple of chaotic confusion ripped through the crowd as the guards yelled for everyone to stay put, and they advanced on the threat.

It was about time.

Once all the guards' feet faced away from him, Gothel dug a skull out of the dirt, rolled out from under the transport, and glanced inside. About fifteen prisoners were chained to the walls, and one guard was in the middle of doing the same to Rosalind.

Her eyes found Gothel and she blinked once, twice, her face pinching with dread and lighting up with elation at the same time.

He didn't tell her what to do. She just used her one chained arm as leverage to kick the guard with all the force she had— not a lot, but enough to surprise him and knock him off balance. Gothel jumped inside and lurched forward, then slammed the skull into the guard's. It cracked in his hand, and the guard went down.

As quietly as he could, even with the cover of another Sterling explosion, Gothel wrenched the keys from the guard's grip and threw them at Rosalind. She unlocked herself before tossing the keys to the prisoner next to her. Together, she and Gothel jumped out of the transport.

Gothel wasn't sure what he expected from her. Maybe confusion. An outbreak of anger. A timid thank you. But she didn't do any of those things.

Instead, she looked at him a moment, her eyes a heavy storm of raging emotions, before turning around and running right back into the graveyard.

For a split second, Gothel could do nothing but gape as she disappeared under the earth. Then he rushed to follow.

* * * * * * * *

Rosalind dodged shiny rocks, scared prisoners, and bewildered guards as she ran back into the graveyard, nearly losing her balance as the earth rocked under her again. She forced herself to swallow the panic that came from diving back down into the crypt after she'd only just escaped its dark grasp.

"What are you doing?" Gothel shouted after her, but she kept running, taking the stairs two at a time. She couldn't think about the fact that he was here yet. She had things to do first.

There were only two guards left in the graveyard—all the rest had gone to defend against whatever attack now rained down on them. Rosalind used the brief moment of surprise to go at them head on. Knowing Gothel followed right behind her, she sidestepped the first man and shoved the woman into the wall. A resounding crack sounded behind her as the woman dragged Rosalind to the floor and climbed on top of her with a raised fist, but then she slumped forward onto the ground. Rosalind sat up to see Gothel standing over both unconscious guards, a wild glint in his eyes.

"What are you *doing?*" he demanded again, the desperation in his voice making his words sharp.

Rosalind ignored him. Climbing over the limp bodies, she yanked the keys from their belts and threw a set at Gothel. He caught them reflexively.

"Rosalind?" a voice whispered.

She looked up to see Rashida in their cell, her protective arms over Mela and Fern. By now, not only did she have their attention, but every prisoner in the cells was either watching her or Gothel, their eyes on the keys in their hands. The air stilled, as though the entire room held its breath.

Rosalind met Rashida's eyes. "This isn't our story, remember?" Then she slammed the keys into the keyhole and wrenched the door open. It lit a fuse that exploded through the people. Everyone burst to life. "Be careful!" she warned the prisoners as they swarmed out, clogging up the narrow staircase. In the chaos, Rashida caught her by the arms and gave her a tight squeeze. Then she was gone in the crowd.

Gothel stood there frozen, staring at the prison, then at Rosalind, with wide eyes.

"We can't pick our story," she told him, "but maybe we can help write it, if we're brave enough." Then she nodded at the precious keys in his hand. "Don't just stand there. Help me."

Together, they unlocked the rest of the cells and set everyone free. Rosalind winced against the sounds of conflict she could hear up the stairs, but hoped that the sheer number of unchained prisoners with their magic back and freedom on the line would be enough to liberate them.

Only once all the prisoners were free and the staircase was congested again did Rosalind turn to Gothel. "Why did you come back?"

He pocketed the keys before looking up to meet her eyes. "I only left because I thought you did."

Her eyebrows furrowed as her mind went back to Pepperjack's sitting room. It seemed like years ago. "I went to the bathroom. I came back and you were gone."

Gothel winced. "I know that *now*. But Pepperjack tricked us both—it looked like you walked *out*. As in outside. Into the carriage. Gone."

"And if you had known?"

"That you were still there?"

"Yeah."

He dropped his eyes and shrugged. "Well I'm here again, aren't I?"

He came back. He came back for me.

A riot of clamor came from above, and Gothel pushed her toward the emptying staircase. "Time to get out of here, princess."

Rosalind climbed the stairs as fast as she could despite the ache in her legs, prepared to ask Gothel how they were going to get away. Just run and hope nobody caught up to them? Maybe with all the prisoners out and fighting, that was feasible, but it seemed like Gothel hadn't been thrilled with her impromptu liberation.

They broke out of the graveyard, and Rosalind's soul sang when she tasted freedom, even though the air here was hazy and foul. And smoky, she realized, recognizing the smell as well as the zing of magic in the atmosphere. Sections of the weeds across the road had caught on fire, and the grounds were utter pandemonium as prisoners and guards alike fought and ran. And in the center of it all, dark hair matted and face harsh with concentration…

"Daddy!" she screamed and plowed ahead. He somehow heard her over the mayhem and turned around. Her entire being swelled when she saw the relief crash into his expression just before she crashed into him, and his arms engulfed her in a hug that held so many lost years.

"Oh Rosy, my Rosy," he whispered as he crushed her against him and kissed her head. Then he pushed her back and cupped his hand against her cheek, his blue crystal eyes filling with tears while they roamed over her again and again. "Oh Rosy."

She found tears falling down her own face as she sniffed and blurted, "Sorry I've been gone for so long, Daddy. I missed you so much."

He must've understood that she meant more than just the last month, because he shook his head and hugged her again. "Thank you for coming back. I missed my Rosy."

Just then, Gothel shouted something, his words lost in a new swell of voices. Her father broke away from her just in time for them to see a mini army gathering from the mansion, each of them glaring as the last of the living prisoners disappeared in the distance. And prowling in front, teeth bared and hair swept up in pointy spikes, was Pepperjack.

Icy fear coursed through Rosalind's veins, but somewhere in her stomach she felt a warm glow of satisfaction. The prisoners were gone and free. Rashida, Mela, Fern, and the rest of them would get their lives back—get another chance to tell another story.

That was worth everything.

"Sterling Corona," Pepperjack growled. "I'd say it's an honor to have you here, but your daughter is causing so many problems for me." He flicked his wrist, and the earth fractured underneath him, the fault line cracking like lightning. Rosalind had to lurch to the side to keep her balance, and the ground split between her and her father.

"I'm only here for my daughter," Sterling responded, as calm as ever despite the hard set of hatred in his jaw. "This is not official business. We can leave without an issue."

Pepperjack flicked his other wrist, hurling a blast of magic. Sterling lifted his arms just in time to shield himself, though he stepped back and shuddered against the blow. At the same time, Rosalind saw Gothel running toward her, but Mackee intercepted him, and threw him to the ground. Pepperjack sent a harsher attack at Sterling; he managed to block it.

"Diplomacy suits you, Sterling," Pepperjack sneered, "but it has no place in *my* kingdom. Your daughter just multiplied her charges, and she knows how I feel about settling debts." Then he nodded, and a swarm of his people descended on them, the stale air instantly heating with the buzz of so much magic. Within seconds, she couldn't see her father anymore.

Panic lurched in her gut, and she prepared to fight through the horde to reach him. She'd *just* gotten him back and wasn't about to give him up again. But as she stepped forward, a root shot out from the ground and wrapped around her wrist, yanking her down. She yelped in surprise, and another one came for her ankle, and two more for her left arm and foot, until she was pinned down against the dirt.

Gritting her teeth, she struggled against the roots, but they only bit into her skin, and in her desperation, she didn't realize her ring was slipping until it slid right off her finger.

Magic coursed through her so forcefully that she gasped. Power hummed in each nerve ending as she watched her ring float above her face before a shadow appeared above her, blocking out the sunshine.

Rosalind swallowed a shriek. Pepperjack's eyes were scarlet.

"Fun trick," he growled. The ring hovered for a second longer before dropping into the dirt next to her head. She heard the soft impact by her ear. "You lied to me Rosy. Now I can sense you." He inhaled deeply as though breathing her in, and she cringed away, pushing herself into the dirt.

Then he smiled at her. Hateful and manic, as deranged as his crimson eyes. "Do you want to see *my* trick now?"

She started to shake her head—something about this man demanded a response—but then his fingers twitched and suddenly Rosalind was on fire.

A scream tore through her throat, but it sounded like a low buzz compared to the roaring in her ears. Every bone snapped, every muscle contorted, every inch of her skin ripping itself into bits. She was made and remade again and again with a kind of torture that shattered her entire being. The seconds turned to years as she burned and burned and burned.

Then it was gone. She choked on another scream and a steady stream of tears, bile bubbling up her throat and spilling over her lips. Her darkening vision cleared enough to see Pepperjack scowling down at her. She couldn't even find the words to beg, though she would've given him anything— *anything*—to keep that anguish at bay. Instead, she could only gasp and sob in between the incensed shouts of her father calling her name.

"Do you know how long it took me to master that, Rosy?" Pepperjack asked over her crying. "It's so delicate, taking hold of a person's power and forcing it back into them. The stronger they are, the more it hurts. Clever, isn't it?"

Rosalind saw the moment the bloodlust took over his expression again. Terror seized her gut, and she threw up a little more as she shook her head over and over, a blubbered plea on her grimy lips.

"Please," she sobbed, the roots tight on her wrists. "Please, please, please."

"Do you know how much money you just cost me?" he demanded. "Can you even guess what profit I lost when you set all my pets free?"

He twisted his fingers again and the agony dragged Rosalind under. She screamed and writhed as images flashed in her mind. Thorns slashing at her skin. Boone's slap across her face. Gothel forcing the ring on her finger. The river yanking her below the surface. Jeej and her whip. The lashes were feather dusters in comparison to the torment racking her now, and she found herself wishing for it instead. She would take a whipping with a smile and a thank you.

Forevers came and went, and Rosalind ran out of screams. Somewhere she could hear Gothel hurling curses at Pepperjack with a kind of rage she didn't know he could possess, and she wondered if they were all dead. Was this the afterlife? Was this punishment for what she'd done to Zachary and her family?

It finally ended, and she vomited again, the bile scalding her raw throat, as Pepperjack shouted over the roaring in her ears.

"You think you saved them?" he snarled. "You think you can let them all out and be the hero of the hour? Guess again."

Wheezing and shuddering, her eyelids fluttered open to see him kneeling over her. His hand wrapped around her jaw, and he forced her head back to expose her throat.

"You think I won't track down every single soul I had down there? I will. I remember all my debtors, all their faces, all their names. There is no crevice they can hide in, no lost corner of earth far enough away. I will find them and I will skin each one alive, just because of you."

He reached for his belt, and Rosalind winced as something sharp bit into her neck, a trickle of warm blood running down her skin. "After I finish with you, I'll start on Gothel. I'll retrieve every one of my prisoners and punish them for going along with your scheme, beginning with Mela and Fern. I'll display your father's decapitated head on a pike in my castle. I'll find your mother, your brother, your prince. I'll show them your bloody coat wrapped around my shoulders before I slide my blade under their skin."

The grisly scenes appeared in Rosalind's head as he painted them, and she couldn't stand the sight. She squirmed, then gasped when the knife dug deeper into her neck. Blood soaked her shirt, her hair, and she felt like she was drowning in it.

Pepperjack's crimson eyes glinted with hostile anticipation. "Stay conscious for me, okay Rosy? I want to savor this, and I'm going to make sure you feel every second."

Rosalind had only a moment to close her eyes and send up a plea to the stars to keep Zachary safe; to hear Gothel and her father yell, "No!" She sensed a heightened level of magic in the air, her awareness of it sharper than it had been in weeks. All at once, she felt the blade start to delve into her neck just as a force blew Pepperjack off of her.

Instantly, the roots released their hold on her, and she curled onto her side to spit out the last remains of bile. Then a soft hand on her cheek.

Daddy. She'd recognize his touch anywhere.

"Get her out of here," he ordered, then his hand was gone. She cracked her eyes open to see Pepperjack's small army waging a battle against a lone warrior. Irina's hood had fallen back, and her scarred face was fierce with concentrated rage as she took on the force alone. Across the field, Sterling was closing in on a fuming Pepperjack.

A shadow leaned over her, and something brushed the wound on her neck. Rosalind flinched automatically, a hoarse cry caught in her throat. "Please," she gasped, expecting the crimson agony again.

"It's just me, princess," Gothel said quietly. His left eye was turning purple and his bottom lip had split open, but he gaped at her injuries, seemingly unaware of his own. "We have to go. Now."

Whimpering in answer, she struggled to sit up. Gothel nudged her softly with his shoulder, letting her use him for support as needed while still giving her space as she staggered to her feet, knees shaking. One step. Another. They broke into a wobbly run. She was so focused on staying upright that she didn't see the incoming threat until it was too late.

Mackee appeared out of nowhere, slugging an arm around Gothel's neck and yanking him off his feet. Gothel slammed against the ground, the air rushing out of him, and Mackee wound up his fist for a blow.

"Stop!" Rosalind rasped. Her limbs were twigs in comparison to Mackee's thick trunks, but she grabbed his arm anyway and pulled back with whatever strength she had left.

Mackee just grinned at her and turned, punching her hard across the jaw. Stars flew across her vision. An echo of Gothel's voice sounded in her ears as she slumped to the ground.

Rosalind was slow to get up; her brain rattled in her skull. She forced herself through the pain, forced herself to her feet, just as a cry sounded.

She glanced over to see Pepperjack's people finally overwhelming Irina, and several of them abandoned the fight with the fairy to attack Sterling from behind. As Mackee closed in on Gothel behind her, her father fell to his knees in front of her, and Irina visibly trembled in the distance as she held on to any strength she had left, a wave of despair surged over Rosalind.

The three people who had come for her. The three people she would lose.

It all happened so fast: Gothel shouted in pain, Pepperjack went for her father's killing blow, and somehow Irina sensed something through the madness. Her vivid green eyes found Rosalind's across the battlefield just as the taste of metal laced the girl's vomit-coated tongue. The being inside her awoke with a vengeance, and electricity sparked through her veins before she could think fast enough to stop it.

The raging beast inside her roared, and the burst of magic that followed shattered through everything.

It was such a powerful surge, streaked with frenzied desperation after being coiled up for so long, that Rosalind collapsed as soon as the energy exploded from her core. Her limbs went limp; her vision went black. When she came to, she thought she might've been out for hours.

What she saw suggested otherwise.

Irina's knees had buckled. Her pale face shone with sweat, her arms still held up in a defensive position. Gothel lay on his back in the dirt, blinking up at the sky, while Sterling had dragged himself up from the ground, wide eyes taking in the scene.

The three of them were unharmed. Irina dropped her arms, and a buzz in the air subsided. She had saved them.

Rosalind's body started convulsing, and she didn't have any voice left to scream, so she just mouthed 'no' over and over again instead.

The three of them were unharmed. Nobody else was so lucky.

The battlefield had turned into a massacred pit. Bodies ruthlessly fighting for the crime lord moments ago were now strewn every which way, limbs twitching as moans of suffering survivors rose louder and louder. Red rivers ran through the dirt and stained the white rocks. The moldy air reeked of blood and death.

The worst of it all was Pepperjack: his face was lacerated, right arm bent the wrong way, with his carving knife lodged into his chest. The color had leached from his eyes, leaving his entire being in a chalky whiteness.

Except for the blood.

It was a nightmare. It was *her* nightmare, again, but different. Bloodier. Laced with enough of her own physical pain that she knew she wasn't dreaming.

She opened her mouth to scream again. Only a mangled gasp came out. Irina barked something at Gothel before yanking her hood back over her head and running the other direction.

Rosalind didn't care where she was going. All she knew was the massacre in front of her. The beast inside of her. The nightmare behind her. She knew what happened now. She knew she would turn around and see the monster just like she had every night for years.

But she couldn't. If she turned around, she'd see the mirror from their living room suspended in the air. If she turned around, she'd see who the monster was, and she couldn't face her reflection. Not now. Not again.

"No," she breathed. "No." She sagged, and her skin heated, a mass of power mounting just below the surface, wanting to burn through something. Using the rest of her willpower, she trapped it there. If it detonated under her skin this time, maybe it would just shred through her instead. Melt her from the inside out.

Then arms were around her, holding her too tight against a lanky body. "Stop it, princess," Gothel said in her ear. "If you go down again, you take me with you."

Rosalind winced as his skin singed audibly where it met hers, and it gave her momentary clarity until she caught another glimpse of Pepperjack's body. He looked younger dead. Just a boy.

"I didn't..." she rasped. "I didn't mean to. I didn't...I didn't want...I..."

Gothel hissed as her temperature continued to climb, higher and higher.

She was a *monster*.

She should have to die here too.

"I know you didn't," he told her. "Get in control. You can do it."

She squirmed, but he wouldn't let her move an inch, and she realized he was serious. He wasn't going to move, and despite how badly she wanted to let her magic scald herself to ash, she *could not* hurt him.

"Get...get away. Away. Get away from me."

"No."

Hanging onto any threads of control she could find, Rosalind clenched her fists and let out a grating sob. "I didn't mean to, I didn't...I didn't mean to."

Zachary.

Pepperjack.

Sterling.

What did you do Rosalind? What did you do?

"You saved them," Gothel ground out, his teeth clenched in pain though he only tightened his grip on her. "We came back just for you and you saved them all."

Mela.

Fern.

Rashida.

Nobody deserves this. This isn't our story.

"This isn't how this ends," he muttered. "Not after everything. Not like this."

Not after everything.

Not after she'd shredded her brother's life, blasted her family to bits, and locked herself away.

Not after she'd been kidnapped, imprisoned, and tortured until she shattered.

Not after she'd brought herself through nightmare after nightmare despite the odds stacked against her.

Not after Gothel and Irina risked their lives to save her, after her parents had put her damning mistakes aside and given a huge sum of money just for her safe return.

We came back just for you.

"Why?"

"Because," Gothel answered, "you were right: they love you."

She wanted to argue, to use the grisly scene around them as her evidence. But Sterling had swallowed the sight and ran up to them, stumbling to a stop a foot away once he read the situation. She could see the truth of Gothel's words in her father's terrified eyes, see the same fear in his expression that laced Gothel's limbs around her sickly frame. Both of them waited for her to implode on herself.

Not after everything, they silently begged her. *Not like this.*

Gothel's arms shone an angry red where they pressed against hers. "You said you were writing it. You said it. Is this really the end?"

We know how it ends, Gothel, she'd told him once as firelight danced across the night. *The hero saves the day, the princess is rescued, and the monsters are slain. Nothing else really matters, does it?*

"Nothing else matters," she echoed. She heard her father's breath catch.

Gothel's voice strained with desperation. "It does. The stories always matter. The stories are all we have."

They have the story wrong, she'd said. *I'm not the princess. I'm the monster.*

Raging grief wracked through her soul and a dangerous wave of flame rippled across her skin. Another hiss went through his teeth, and he swore. "Stars, Rosalind, this is it? You survived this hellhole and *this is it?*"

Self-hatred clawed up her throat, taking the last of her breath, and she was ready to succumb to the heat. End the story.

"We came back for you," Gothel raged on. "*I* came back for you. I've never come back for anyone. Calder. The orphans. Donna. *Anyone.*" His voice struck through the searing wall between them. "I know you hurt your brother and your family and these people and you think it's all over. You think you're the monster. Maybe you are. But you aren't just that. You're

Elyse's princess and you're those prisoners' hero and you're Roman's most trusted friend. That counts too. *Every* part of the story counts."

A sob shook her body as she met the frozen fear in her father's gaze, and images flashed across her mind.

Zachary, beaming at her after they finished building their snowman.

Roman, laughing in her ear as he twirled her around the living room.

Sterling, ruffling her hair and chuckling at her incessant questioning.

Genevieve, calling her down for her favorite dinner of hazelnut soup.

Irina, telling her painful truths and listening to what she had to say.

Elyse, giggling and shyly volunteering to braid her hair.

Gothel, giving up everything just for a shot to save her life.

Rosalind, staring at her reflection in the bathroom mirror and wondering what might lay ahead.

Is this really the end? they all asked her.

Maybe it should be, she cried back.

But above the clamor of questions in her head and cries of agony in the field, Rashida's voice broke through.

In the end, we all bleed red. In the end, you are a survivor too.

Corona.

Monster.

Princess.

Survivor.

"Please." Gothel choked on the word. "*Please.*"

Rosalind trembled and surrendered. Her skin slowly started to cool as she fought to reign the beast of her magic in. Once he sensed the shift, Gothel let his breath out in a rush, his shoulders caving in over her. His touch was cautious and gentle as he used his hands to slowly open one of her fists and push the ring onto her swollen finger.

Instantly, the wall of heat evaporated, leaving a deep cold that seeped into her bones. When her father saw the ring—and likely guessed it held her power at bay—he crumpled to his knees in relief. She couldn't help but look past him to scan the massacre again and find Pepperjack's colorless corpse.

"I never...I never meant to hurt anyone," she whispered. "Never."

Sterling met her gaze, a single line of tears falling down his face. "I know, Rosy," he said softly. "I know."

Overwhelmed, Rosalind collapsed fully into Gothel, fresh tears streaming down her cheeks. Everywhere she looked, she only saw carnage.

And now she had to live with it.

Her body shook with sobs as she buried her face into Gothel's shoulder so she wouldn't have to see the monster's destruction anymore.

CHAPTER 10

LET DOWN YOUR HAIR

She knew the monster was with her.

Rosalind's breath stuttered as she stood frozen in the inky dark, every muscle stiff
and sore from being rigid so long.

How long *had* it been? She didn't know. She never knew.

It always felt like years.

Electricity shot through the stagnant air around her, and it smelled like something had burned. The tightly coiled dread in her stomach unfurled, spreading through her veins like slow rolling magma that scorched her from the inside out.

All at once, the darkness lifted, and she found a different scene before her, though a part of her had expected that.

A sea of people. A mountain of bodies. Limbs bent wrong and skin stained red. And right before her feet, spread out on a blanket of wolf fur, was the luminous crime lord, pale lips parted in shock, even in death, at his own knife in his chest.

Hyperventilating, Rosalind looked from him to the pile of people. She searched for a face she recognized and hoped she'd come up empty.

Dad, Mom, Gothel, Irina, Roman. None of them were there.

Zachary. Where was Zachary? He couldn't be here. He couldn't.

A hand snatched Rosalind's ankle. She looked down to see Pepperjack's red eyes on her, his cut mouth spreading into a vicious smile as he dragged her down, and she screamed.

Rosalind woke with a start. The ends of her hair were plastered to her sweaty neck, the sheets tangled in her legs. Her eyebrows furrowed as she gazed at the ceiling, heart hammering in her chest. She had to blink a few times to understand the familiar image.

Wincing, she pushed herself up on her elbows to confirm. She was in her room.

She was home.

Thick curtains guarded her against the early morning sun poking through their seams. Her mom had curled up on the window bench facing Rosalind. She had wrapped the curtains around her like a blanket, and a streak of sunlight shone on her honey hair. Gothel was a healthy distance away from her mother, slumped on the floor against the wall by the closet also facing Rosalind. Both were asleep.

Footsteps sounded down the hallway. Rosalind quickly huddled back under her blankets and closed her eyes just as her door opened. It was her father; she could tell by his breathing. Silence lasted for a moment as he checked on them, then the door shut again. She heard him open and shut Zachary's door down the hall, then his footsteps disappeared.

Mom, Gothel, Dad. They were all okay.

Where was Zachary?

Logic reasoned he was somewhere, shielded as much as possible from the chaos Rosalind had brought into their house. But she didn't feel like relying on logic right now. It had been so long since she'd really looked at him, touched him, held his hand. In the last few years, every time she'd been forced out of her room for one reason or another, she'd tried her hardest not to acknowledge him.

At the time, she'd been swallowed up by guilt and shame and so much anguish. Now, that all seemed minimal in comparison.

She had to see him with her own eyes. She had to take his hand and ruffle his hair and make sure he knew what he was to her. She would never ask his forgiveness, but she owed him truth. After that, he could decide what to do with it, and she would live with that decision. But she couldn't sit here and hide from him anymore. Even if he said he never wanted to see her again, even if he hated her for leaving him to face his struggles alone, she had to tell him the story she had kept buried for so long.

The purpose gave her something to hold on to instead of drowning in memories she wasn't ready to face. Silently, she untangled herself from her blankets and gently stood on her sore feet. Her body felt like it had been trampled on, and the clothes Gothel had stolen for her were disgusting. But the ring was back on her finger, and that was all Rosalind cared about. She couldn't allow herself to think of anything else.

Zachary was likely either on the grounds or in his room, but after the craziness that had transpired, she bet their father had kept him inside. Going out her own door would bring attention to her, and she wasn't ready for that yet. She just needed a minute with Zachary.

Holding her breath, Rosalind kneeled on the floor by her bed and slowly cleared the clutter around her nightstand. The nightstand used to be on the other side of her bed; she'd moved it after the accident to cover up the little door despite the fact he probably couldn't use it anymore anyway.

It had been Zachary's idea. Their father wasn't thrilled with it, but their mother loved that Rosalind and Zachary were close enough to share a secret tunnel between their rooms, and said she wished she'd been close enough with her brother to do the same. She'd even helped them paint it in a blue stain that was spelled with little golden stars to light the path. Rosalind ached at the memory of the three of them playing hide and seek, laughing so hard their stomachs hurt.

Finally, she managed to scoot the nightstand over enough that she could wedge the door open. A wave of stale air hit her, and she had to hold back a cough. Nobody had gone in here in a long time.

She bit her lip, then, taking a breath, she got on all fours and forged ahead. She eased the little door shut behind her and the glowing stars greeted her like old friends showing her the way despite the dusty floor and muted paint that cried of abandonment.

Halfway through, Rosalind's knee brushed against something. She stopped to pick it up and had to squint to recognize what it was: the special notepad Griffin had given her, so she could write to Roman. Her mouth twitched with a fond grin as she shoved the pad in her pocket. She couldn't wait to see him.

As she got closer to the end, a sharp stone settled in her stomach. What if Zachary had barred his door too? What if it was too late?

Rosalind felt sick as she approached his door, and she stopped. This was a terrible idea. Zachary didn't want to see her.

But then the familiar nightmare flashed across her mind—the nightmare she'd had for years. Maybe he didn't want to see her, but she had to see him. She had to know he was okay.

So, for the first time in her life, Rosalind knocked softly on Zachary's door. When nothing happened, she slowly, painfully, turned the knob. The door opened with ease, and she held it cracked.

"Zachary?" Rosalind whispered through the gap. "It's just me. I just...are you there?"

"Rosy?" a squeaky whisper sounded back. "No, Rosy, no."

She winced, feeling like she would cave in on herself, but she opened the door the rest of the way and climbed through anyway.

The room was dark, the curtains drawn. Zachary's empty chair was on the other side of his bed, and he lay sprawled on the floor in the corner, a good ten feet away. His shriveled legs were curled in and he trembled with wide eyes.

"Zachary?" Rosalind pushed herself into the room, forgetting her own throbbing body. Had he fallen out of his chair? "Are you okay?"

His hushed voice broke as he shook harder. "No, Rosy. Please no."

Sharp spokes of panic poked her stomach as she slid on her knees to him. She had been absent from his life; she didn't know how to care for him. Should she call for help? Surely at least her father would hear.

Unless...unless Zachary didn't want her near. Unless he was afraid of her.

The thought nearly froze her forever, but Rosalind was within reach now, and Zachary snatched her hand, holding it tight enough to hurt.

"Zach, what's wrong? Do you need me to…" She trailed off, noticing his eyes weren't trained on her but on something above her head. Slowly, she turned around to see two figures standing there in the dark, blocking the door.

Rosalind's sore throat closed up. Boone and Ulf.

Ulf remained as impassive as ever, but Boone scowled at her. "Make a sound," he warned quietly, "and you're both dead. Understand?"

A soft whimper escaped Zachary and he clutched her hand tighter. Rosalind nodded.

Ulf made some kind of hand gesture at Boone, and Boone watched it as if reading a book before giving a curt nod. Then they both looked at Zachary.

"He's dead," Rosalind blurted, her voice still raspy, and she stuttered over the name. "Ja-ack, he's…he's dead. You don't need the money anymore."

Boone actually laughed once, but it wasn't a friendly sound. "You really expect me to believe that?"

"It's true," she insisted. The words scalded her tongue.

"Stupid girl." He stepped toward Zachary as Ulf moved closer to her, and she saw their plan before they could enact it.

It didn't matter what she said. Just like in her nightmare, she couldn't stop it.

She would lose him again.

"Take me instead," Rosalind said. Zachary shuddered and whimpered, "No." Ulf blinked. Boone glared at her and opened his mouth, but she cut him off. "Ja-jack was going to sell me. He said he already had an interested buyer, and he would make a fortune off of me. Leave Zachary alone, and you can take the deal for yourself. Jack doesn't need to know where you got the money. You never have to deal with my family again—just go straight to his buyer."

She didn't know if he'd believe her, or how soon news of the Jacklands massacre would get out. She didn't know what Boone would do with her if one of his own sources confirmed Pepperjack's death before he could sell her for the money. She didn't even know what day it was.

She only knew that she hadn't been able to save Zachary before, but she could do it now.

"Besides," she continued despite Zachary's tightening grasp telling her to stop, "Zachary is too hard to travel with. Why do you think we always stay here? Nobody will want to buy him with all his extra liabilities, if you even get that far—he'll likely die an hour into your journey, and you'll have nothing to show for yourselves. Again."

Boone glowered at her, and for a second, she wondered if he would kill her right then. But Ulf did another set of hand gestures—longer than before—and Boone let out a small sigh of acceptance. Evidently, Ulf either made a convincing case or Boone had a soft spot for him.

"Fine, little mouse," Boone growled at her. Then he turned his glare on Zachary, and Rosalind felt the boy tremble harder. "If you make one sound, let out one warning, or lift a finger to stop us, I will slit your sister's throat and bring you back her head. Do you understand me?"

Zachary went white as a sheet and nodded. Rosalind found herself glaring at Boone despite the ice cold jab of fear in her stomach.

Boone went to the window and started to pull it up, careful not to make any noise. Keeping one mental tab on Ulf, who could take down either of them with magic, Rosalind turned to her brother and held his hand in both of hers.

"You can't go, Rosy," he gasped, eyes filling with tears. "You can't, you just—"

"Zachary, listen to me. Please." Then her voice cracked, and her eyes filled with tears too, and she found years' worth of words spilling from her mouth like a waterfall. "I'm so sorry. For everything. For what happened, how it happened, what it did to all of us. I know being sorry doesn't make a difference, but I am, and you need to know that I didn't stay away because I didn't love you anymore or couldn't imagine you as my brother. I stayed away because it hurt so much to look at you knowing that it was my fault. It hurt so much to see everyone's pain, especially yours, and know it was brought on by me. I felt guilty and ashamed and so afraid it would happen again, and it was too much to face, so I ran. I ran away from all of you and never came back.

"But it wasn't because I couldn't stand you broken—it was because I still loved you so much it nearly killed me every day. And the longer I stayed away the harder it was to come back, because I thought you must hate me after I hid from my problems while you were forced to face much harder ones."

The window was almost all the way open, and Zachary was quietly crying. "I never blamed you, Rosy. I didn't. I only wanted you to come back."

I only wanted you to come back.

The words lodged into the wall of guilt that had trapped her for years, chinking at it. Never in her wildest dreams did she imagine she would ever, ever hear them.

Rosalind's tears spilled over, and she found herself at a loss, feeling relieved and grateful and desolate at the same time.

I only wanted you to come back.

"I don't...I don't know how you can say that. You are such an amazing person, Zach. You are. You deserve so much more than this, and I...I'd do anything to give it to you."

"But not this."

"It has to be this."

"No, it...let me come with you then. So you aren't too scared."

Rosalind smiled through her tears in spite of herself. "No, Zach, this is something I have to do alone."

"*Nobody* should be alone," he retorted, and for a second Rosalind could see the haunting isolation in his eyes. He'd been so alone. How could she leave him again?

"I...Zachary, I—"

He grasped her hands as tight as he could, staring into her eyes. "You don't have to make up for anything, Rosy. You don't. You can stay. We can play games again. We can read together and explore together and build snowmen in the winter. We can. You can."

Having finished with the window, Boone growled under his breath and reached for Rosalind. She ducked out of his way and stood up on her own despite the pain in her limbs. Then she forced herself to put on her bravest face and pried her hands out of Zachary's grip.

"Rosy, please," he cried softly.

All this time she wondered if she had lost her heart, which used to beat so freely, but now she realized she'd had it all along, hiding under overgrown roots and crusted layers of rock. It was this moment that she found it, and this moment that she felt it break.

"Love you," she whispered, then went to the window. Like the first time, they'd brought a rope to scale the wall, which

Boone had already attached to the windowsill with a hook. He reached for her. Instead, she grabbed the rope, swung her legs over the ledge, and lowered herself down. It wasn't a long trip, but it hurt her arms and yanked on her sore muscles. She could barely feel it over the pounding of her heart.

This is for Zachary, she told herself. *For Zachary.*

Boone came next. He dropped so fast, Rosalind barely scrambled out of the way to avoid getting clomped by his boots. This time, he gripped her arm and dragged her along, leaving Ulf to climb down by himself.

They rounded the side of the house and ran into Tor wrapped in a cloak. The woman hissed when she saw Rosalind, her bared white teeth a milky contrast against her dark skin.

"What's this?" she demanded. "I thought she was dead."

"Change of plans," Boone snapped back. "Let's go."

Giving Rosalind a look that could kill if allowed, Tor pulled off her cloak and forcefully wrapped Rosalind into it before yanking the hood over her head. Ulf joined them, crouching down on the ground with his back to the group, and Tor started leading Rosalind toward the street. One house down, Calder stood next to a parked carriage, looking all the part of a dashing nobleman enjoying the day.

Rosalind's heart stuttered, and she fought the urge to vomit.

As Tor pulled her toward the carriage, Rosalind dared a look back at her home. Boone had also stopped and turned back—to watch Ulf, she realized. Her eyebrows furrowed. He was still kneeling on the ground at the corner of her house, moving his hands against the wall. What was he doing?

Then she saw it: a spark. But he didn't have a match or anything to make fire…

The color drained from her face. It wasn't just some little blaze that could be put out with a splash of water. It was inferno: fire conjured by magic that was difficult to produce and nearly impossible to control. Ulf went pale and nearly passed out with the effort of creating a single lick of flame.

But a single flame was enough. It caught on the corner of the house and instantly started a steady climb up. Toward Zachary's room.

A hand clapped over Rosalind's mouth just as she opened it to scream. She thrashed violently and gave muffled shrieks as Tor and Boone picked her up, rushed to the carriage, and threw her inside. All at once, the crew was in their seats with Rosalind shoved on the floor between them, and they were moving.

"What did you do?" Rosalind screeched, her dying voice as gravelly as Irina's. She scrambled for the carriage door, but Boone kicked her back in place before picking up a shackle attached to the floor and locking it around her ankle. The effects of the metal suppressant coursed through her, as if a heavy weight now laced the blood in her veins.

Her magic was gone. Even taking off her ring wouldn't bring it back.

"I made a distraction," Boone snapped. "Necessary to make sure this plan works."

Rosalind gaped. "A distraction? You'll *kill* them all if they don't get out in time!"

"Not my problem." He glowered at her. "But if you don't shut up and sit still then I will *make* it a problem."

Still reeling, Rosalind did as he said, her mind numb with panic and shock she desperately tried to placate.

Her father would get them out. If he couldn't stop the inferno, he would get everyone out. They would be okay.

But what if Zachary couldn't get to his chair? What if he couldn't get out of his room, and the blaze became too thick to get through? If her dad caught it in time, he could find Zachary, but...

Her mother and Gothel had been asleep when she left. Were they still asleep? Would they pass out from smoke and burn before they could wake again?

Desperate and infuriated, Rosalind jerked her chin up and looked at Calder. He'd been closest to Gothel, after all, and she wanted to get back at them somehow, in some small way.

She leveled her stare at him. "He didn't turn you in."

Calder raised his eyebrows and gave her the most arrogantly patronizing look. "Excuse me?"

"He didn't turn you in," she repeated.

"Who didn't, sweetheart?"

Rosalind glared at his slick expression. "Gothel."

Calder's face twitched. The carriage went silent. Tor waved her hand and looked out the window, pretending to be bored. Calder did his best to not look uncomfortable while Boone and Ulf exchanged a meaningful glance despite Ulf being nearly unconscious.

"He didn't do it," Rosalind said again. "And I think you all know that."

The statement settled in the air, making it thick and heavy, and suddenly nobody would look at each other.

She yanked on her ankle chain, but one glare from Boone made her stop. It was useless anyway. There was nothing she could do.

Desperate to not think the worst about her family, she pulled the hood further over her head to let a few tears fall, stuffed her clenched fists in her pockets, and tried to remember how to breathe.

Travelling on the carriage floor wasn't comfortable for anyone, but the arrangement wreaked havoc on Rosalind's already battered body. Add the metal band around her ankle, possible death of her family, and her own uncertain future, and she wanted nothing more than to raise the white flag of surrender with every bump on the road.

But she wasn't ready to surrender. Not yet.

Her neck cramped from craning it to watch out the window, and her arm ached from being bent so her hand could be in her pocket. Her mind hadn't stopped racing, and she was sure she was just a few heartbeats away from a heart attack.

But she kept her face impassive and stayed still and quiet, knowing the story would continue.

She'd already been the monster, the fiend that gushed blood and left scars.

She'd tried being the hero, the one brave enough to step forward alone on behalf of someone else.

And she'd long since been the princess locked up in her tower, awaiting a rescue she was sure would never come.

Now she found herself hurtling toward a climax, the story building into a crescendo, and it seemed the world around her held its breath while it waited for her to choose what little she could. For her fate to be sealed. Her story written.

But for the first time in her life, she knew what her role was. She knew what to write.

In the end, you are a survivor too.

Eventually, they came to a stop, and Rosalind willed herself to stay calm as her captors exited the carriage. Then Boone reached back in to unlock her ankle. Tor muttered something, stopping him, and they both disappeared from view of the open door.

Once again, Rosalind yanked on the metal chain. If only she could run.

She stopped squirming when she heard Boone's voice echo from outside.

"Who are you?"

Rosalind went still. Someone else was out there.

Was this it?

A new voice, male and gruff, sounded. "I heard you have the Corona girl."

Boone didn't back down at the dominance in the stranger's voice. "Maybe you heard wrong."

There was a pause, as if the two men were sizing each other up. "Jack had promised her to me," the stranger said. "If you give her over, I'll double the payment for your effort."

Rosalind's stomach lurched.

Another, longer pause. "I need assurance of your payment."

"I need assurance of your cargo," the voice replied coolly.

Someone snapped their fingers, and suddenly Tor appeared and unlocked her ankle, then yanked her out of the carriage. Rosalind gasped when she saw Boone, Ulf, and Calder, standing opposite twelve figures on horseback. They wore all black and were led by two others with dark hoods covering their faces.

A chill ran down Rosalind's spine. It was an effort not to collapse on the spot. Not for the first time since she'd been kidnapped, she found herself praying.

I know I don't deserve to ask for anything, she begged, *but please help me.*

Tor hauled her up to Boone, and he ripped the cloak off her, exposing her tattered and soiled clothes and the bruised and bloody skeleton of her body. "There," he said tightly. "It's her."

The hooded leader went silent for a moment. "Her hair is different."

Rosalind's heart skipped a beat, fingertips tingling. Tor shifted on her feet while Calder held his cocky smile and Ulf looked on.

Boone cleared his throat. "We have the girl. Do you have payment or not?"

"I do." He waved a hand and several of his attendants trotted forward on their horses. For a moment, it seemed they were coming to exact the trade, but then they passed by Boone's group altogether and stopped behind them, fanning out in a circle.

Now they were surrounded. The corner of Rosalind's mouth pulled up.

"Boone, Tor, Ulf, and Calder," the leader announced, abandoning the fake gruff voice he'd been using. "Your payment will be imprisonment for your crimes and justice for your offenses."

"What?" Calder gasped, floored for once in his life while Tor and Ulf tried to make a run for it. All four of them were quickly apprehended, leaving Rosalind free.

"You can't arrest us!" Boone bucked against his captors like an irate horse. "On whose authority?"

"Just mine," he answered, his cheeky tone matching the one in all her childhood memories.

The two pulled their ridiculous hoods off their heads and Rosalind nearly sang with relief to see Roman and Griffin.

Ulf and Calder's jaws dropped at the sight of the prince, and they went still. Tor's eyes widened as she was forced to her knees, but Boone spat at the ground with all the hatred he could muster.

Roman didn't pay them any attention, letting his little army deal with the arrests. Instead, he reached into his saddle and pulled out a small notepad—the match to the one in Rosalind's pant pocket.

"It's been a while since you wrote me on this," he told her, sliding off his horse. "I checked often just to see, but—"

Rosalind slammed into him with all the force she had, throwing her arms around his shoulders. It had been ages since she'd hugged him—he was so much bigger now, she almost couldn't reach—and Roman staggered in surprise before hugging her back.

"It's so good to see you, Rose," he said softly in her ear. His arms tensed and relaxed repeatedly around her, as if he could feel how fragile her body was and didn't want to break her, though he refused to let her go. "You look…" His voice cracked and he started over. "I'm…*extremely* glad you're okay."

"I missed you," she croaked back. It hurt to talk, and her voice hurt to hear.

"I missed you too." He made an effort to keep his tone light. "And I'm very curious about your hair."

"It's quite the story."

"I'm sure."

Finally, she made herself pull away from him so she could meet his eyes. "Thank you for coming." She glanced at Griffin, Roman's advisor and best friend, who she'd never once seen smile, and she wondered how much that had to do with the scars on his face. Somehow, he looked even worse than his usual stoic self.

They'd always been kind of friends through Roman, but now she felt a true connection bonding them together. He had come for her too.

Hesitantly, she offered him her hand. Griffin's eyebrow twitched, and he was a moment late, but he shook it.

"And you. Thank you both." Then she paused, wondering how much they knew about what had happened. If she thought too much about it now, she'd unravel. "How did...how did you know he—Ja-ack had a buyer? For me, I mean."

Roman's lips quirked to the side, obviously proud of himself. "Because it was me."

"It was *you?*"

"Everyone had different ideas on how to get you back," he said, his tone hardening a little. "But nothing 'acceptable' was going to get us there. I knew we would have to go deeper than politics, so Griffin and I got our hands dirty in case we couldn't get you out in time." He paused. "I have no regrets, Rose, at all, but if you wouldn't tell my father about—"

Rosalind nodded with a smile. "I would never. I just...I can't believe you pulled it off."

Roman grinned, elbowing Griffin playfully. She hadn't seen him grin like that in months. "We put on a good show, didn't we?"

She rolled her eyes, though she couldn't stop smiling. "A little dramatic, maybe, but you always have been."

"You wound me, Rose." He smiled back at her. "I haven't had fun like that in a long time. Reminds me of the good old days."

"Yeah, me too." The good old days when the monsters were only pretend and the stakes were only as high as the garden walls. When the craziest things that happened were those she read about in her books while tucked safely in bed.

The guards threw their new prisoners into the stolen carriage and arranged for their transport. Rosalind caught a last glare from Boone before he was shoved inside.

"Have you heard anything from my family?" she asked.

Roman slid his notepad back in his saddle. "No, but I'm sure they'll be thrilled to have you back. You wouldn't believe how much they missed you. I didn't have time to tell them I was coming for you, so they're probably worried sick."

Rosalind blinked. "You haven't heard anything? Did you send someone to the house?"

"Send someone? I was coming for you."

A slow, steady roll of terror took hold in her stomach. "I know, but I wrote another message. To send someone to the house."

Roman's eyebrows furrowed and he shook his head. "No, you said they were 'in front' of your house. I assumed you meant the criminals."

One knee buckled. She wrapped an arm around her waist in an effort to keep herself standing as her eyes widened in horror. "I said they started *inferno* at my house."

Both Roman and Griffin stiffened, a line of panic creasing Roman's forehead. "What?"

Rosalind felt sick. Her hand had been so shaky trying to scrawl out messages blindly in her pocket without her captors noticing. The letters must've slurred together.

Griffin reached behind him and grabbed the reins of his horse, then leapt forward and pressed them into her palm. "Go," he told her, a slight edge of urgency to his voice. "Now."

It had been forever since she'd ridden a horse, but she didn't stop to think about it now. Instead, she let Roman help her up, and he squeezed her hand.

"We'll catch up," he promised.

Rosalind squeezed his hand back once for comfort, then urged the horse on and raced for home.

✳ ✳ ✳ ✳ ✳ ✳ ✳

Smoke was everywhere.

It clogged Gothel's throat, and he woke up coughing. Sweat plastered his skin as everything crackled around him, and he heard Genevieve gasping somewhere nearby.

"Rosalind?" she shouted through the fumes. "Rosalind!"

The name snapped Gothel to total alertness. He cracked his burning eyes open to see the curtains on fire, the room filled with smoke, and Genevieve peeking under the bed.

"Rosalind!" she cried before glancing at Gothel coughing on the floor. He checked the closet, under the desk, by the bookcase. She opened a tiny door by the bed and shouted her daughter's name.

Rosalind wasn't here.

The fire from the curtains spread to the wall, then the ceiling. In a matter of moments, their exit was almost sealed off. Both of them did a last desperate look around the room, but ran for the door when they came up fruitless.

For an awful second, Gothel remembered Rosalind crying in the field, ready to burn through herself and leave the ashes behind.

Had she done this?

No, that was wrong. She would never endanger her family like that. At least, not on purpose.

She got out, Gothel told himself. *Of course she did.* Not that Rosalind would leave them sleeping if she found her house was on fire.

She got out. He had to believe that.

The hallway was a little clearer than her room, but both smoke and flame barreled through. Genevieve automatically went to go left, and Gothel barely grabbed her arm and yanked her back before the blaze swallowed her too. Her eyes widened in desperation—for a moment Gothel wondered if she was crazy enough to jump into it anyway—but he pulled on her arm again and she followed him to the right. They managed to jump down the first few stairs on the staircase before it caught too, reaching the ground floor just in time.

There they found Sterling, using his magic to brace up part of the caving ceiling while three battered servants ran out from the kitchen and through the front door to safety.

"Zach?" Genevieve shouted at her husband as their house collapsed around them. Sterling's gaze darted upstairs, his mouth pressed into a hard line. He hadn't been able to get up there yet. Genevieve hadn't been able to get through.

Sterling. Genevieve.

No Zachary. No Rosalind.

She went back for him.

Without pausing to think, Gothel turned on his heel and ran up the blistering right staircase.

He'd only been downstairs for a few moments, but the fire had already expanded up here. He coughed into his arm, his sweaty clothes stuck to him, as he dashed through the flames devouring the walls and trying to lick at his skin.

"Rosalind!" he yelled as he bolted up what was left of the staircase. "Zachary! Can anyone hear me?"

A scream sounded through the crackling, making Gothel jump. "Help! Help! I'm in here!"

Gothel barreled ahead, following the terrified voice to the door down from Rosalind's. His palm burned as he turned the doorknob; it didn't budge.

"*Help!*" the voice screeched from behind.

Gritting his teeth, Gothel slammed his shoulder into the door once, twice, three times, until it broke open.

A solid wall of heat and smoke hit him so hard and thick that he staggered back. The floor was hot, but he got down on his stomach and crawled forward, his hands blindly searching through the haze.

"Hello?" he coughed.

"Over here!"

Gothel ignored his screaming instincts to flee and forced himself toward the voice. He crossed the room where Zachary lay curled into a ball on the floor, his hair stuck to his forehead and tears streaming down his red face.

Gothel motioned for the kid to wait a second, then scoured the rest of the room. Besides the furniture and his chair, it was empty. Panic clung to every smoky breath, but Gothel ordered himself to keep going.

The ceiling cracked—the place was coming down. They were out of time.

In a frenzy, Gothel made his way back to Zachary and threw the kid's arm around his neck, then scooped him up and ran out the door. He winced when the kid coughed violently, and the flames singed his arms as he used them to protect the lump of a person he carried.

The stairs crumbled underneath them, and he would've had to jump if it weren't for Sterling and Genevieve: each plastered with sweat and soot, they stood facing each other a few feet apart, their brows furrowed in concentration. Sterling focused on the ceiling, Genevieve the stairs, paving the way for Gothel to run for the exit. The kid yelled something, but it was impossible to understand amidst his hacking.

They made it through the front door just as the frame fell. Gothel collapsed onto the grass, and he and Zachary sprawled on the ground, coughing their lungs up. Genevieve followed close behind, with Sterling at her heels. When Gothel pushed himself up on his elbows, he found her at her son's side, hands flitting over him in a practiced way as tears streamed down her face. Within a few moments, the kid was breathing a little easier—enough to scream coherently.

"She's gone! She's gone, she's gone, she's gone!"

Gothel closed his eyes against the blow of his words, unable to accept the truth. When he opened them, she'd be there. She'd be alive, she'd be okay, she'd be safe.

Something snatched his hand, and his eyes snapped open. Rosalind was nowhere in sight. Instead, several neighbors had gathered and were trying to help Sterling get the blaze under control before it spread. Zachary leaned toward Gothel and clutched his hand tightly. When Genevieve's eyes narrowed and she tried to pull her son away, Zachary howled, and she let him go.

"She's gone!" Zachary cried to Gothel. "She's gone!"

Noting the wary—and powerful—mother who had watched his every breath since he arrived, Gothel coughed again and looked at the kid. He thought of Rosalind's harrowing battle with herself, but he couldn't bring himself to voice the awful possibility that she had simply stayed behind.

"She's stronger than people think," he muttered.

Zachary shuddered with a miserable sob. "I know, I've always known that, but...but this time...I don't think they'll let her come back."

Both Gothel and Genevieve froze, exchanging glances with each other—which was strange. Rather than dwell on her stare, he turned back to the kid.

"You mean, she wasn't in the house?" he asked.

Zachary wiped snot from his nose and nodded.

"Are you sure?" Genevieve pressed, desperate hope clinging to her voice. "Are you absolutely sure?"

"Yes. There were these...these two...they were men. One big and one small. They came for me, but she...she…" His frail body shuddered with another sob.

Gothel cleared his smoky throat and sat up. Zachary clutched his hand tighter. "Was the big one bald?" Gothel asked. "With a beard?"

Genevieve's gaze snapped up to him, accusatory, while Zachary nodded again.

"Do you know where they took her?" she demanded, her eyes going from soft brown to harsh stone in an instant. For the first time, Gothel could see why someone would be afraid of her. "What did you do to her?"

"It wasn't his fault!" Zachary screamed, making them both jump. "He wasn't even there!" The outburst caused Genevieve to go still and quiet.

Gothel waited a moment, testing the waters, but it seemed the kid was willing to talk to him. "The big bald man—did she know him?"

Zachary sniffed and struggled to catch his breath. "Yes, I— I think so. He called her 'little mouse.'"

Gothel pursed his lips and tried to keep the alarm out of his face. Genevieve stared at him like the stranger he was.

"Did they say what they wanted?" Gothel asked. A million ideas ran through his mind, a thousand different ways Boone could use Rosalind for leverage or power or revenge.

"Something about money. Rosy said a man named Jack was going to get a lot of money for her, and the bald man could do it instead." His voice broke, and he slouched miserably. "They had come for me first because they thought she was dead already. But then she came in and...and...and she *traded* herself for me!" With that, the kid descended into another fit of sobs.

"Who is he?" Genevieve asked quietly, but her glare was still sharp enough to cut. "Who has my daughter *now?*"

Gothel's hand was going numb. He glanced from Rosalind's mother to her brother, desperately wishing he had something better for them—for her. "His name is Boone. He wants to sell her for profit. He probably started your house on fire."

"Where would they take her?" she asked the same time Zachary cried, "Can you save her?"

His tongue felt scratchy and everything inside him ached. "I...I don't know. She could be anywhere by now."

Genevieve rubbed her face as a few fresh tears fell free. Zachary squeezed Gothel's hand again and stared into his eyes in a way that reminded him of Rosalind.

"What can we do?" the kid asked. "There has to be something. You found her before."

"Talk to your father," Gothel answered automatically, surprising even himself. Somehow Rosalind had become worth more than his prejudice against Sterling. "Assemble a search party—as many people as possible. If we catch them before the transaction, we can bring her home."

Genevieve wasted no time. As Sterling worked with his powerful friends to control the inferno, she gathered the closest servants and neighbors watching the burning house in horror. As she ushered the first group over, she ordered Gothel to tell them what he knew. So he did.

There were four of them, three men and one woman, two with magical capabilities and two without. He guessed they travelled in a stolen carriage meant for prisoners, so they could use the metal shackles to suppress Rosalind's magic. They lived in a hideout on the edge of the Racine village, but he doubted they would go back there since royal guards had found it weeks earlier. According to the kid, Boone was planning on selling her to a buyer, but Gothel had no idea who that could be or where the meeting would take place.

It didn't take long, since he didn't know very much, but he found it ironic that Boone had accused him of giving them up. He hadn't then, but he did now, and it wasn't to save his own skin but to save Sterling Corona's daughter.

Not for the first time since this insane disaster began, Gothel wondered how he got here.

As he finished explaining three different times to the three different groups Genevieve assembled, he was itching to *get out there*. Even though he had no idea where Rosalind was, it killed him to sit here. Too much could happen too fast. But when Genevieve sent off the search parties, she glared at him, as if sensing he wanted to go too, and told him to stay put. Gothel gritted his teeth but did what she said, only so she didn't feel the need to use any magic on him. Once she got distracted, he'd be gone.

What are they doing to you? Where are you now?

Zachary stayed next to him, still clutching his hand. Gothel's arms stung; his chest hurt. They sat in silence, the thought of Rosalind's fate a heavy weight on their shoulders.

He could only think of his shadow, shoved in a carriage, berated by Boone while Calder played with her and Tor itched to settle her score. And all he could hear was the sound of her screaming when Pepperjack tortured her.

How could he have let this happen?

Time passed too fast as day plunged into night. By the time Sterling managed to smother the flame, the house was gone. Spent, he collapsed in a pile of ash, and Genevieve went to him to explain the situation. Gothel watched, waiting for the moment she turned her back to him.

"You're going to sneak away, huh?" Zachary whispered. "To look for her."

Gothel glanced from Genevieve still watching him to the sniffling kid next to him. He doubted the kid would believe him if he lied, but he didn't want him giving Gothel away. Slowly, he nodded once.

"Can I come with you?" he asked, concern and desperation lined into his young face. "I want to help."

He thought of trying to carry Zachary as they went after people who wanted to kill Gothel—not to mention Genevieve, who would certainly think he was taking her child, and he really didn't need to get charged with kidnapping twice.

"No," he said quietly. "I don't think that's a good idea."

Zachary pursed his lips, not surprised. "I can distract them, so you can go. I'll keep the secret."

Gothel looked from his determined expression to the little hand still clutching his own. When, exactly, did Gothel get this new partner?

He debated with himself for a second, but thoughts of his shadow urged him forward. He nodded at Zachary, who nodded back as if this were the most important mission of his life. Maybe it was.

Five people stood on the grounds, not counting Zachary and Gothel. He watched them talk with the Coronas, waiting for the right moment to get up and slip away.

Just as he prepared to make a run for it, a horse thundered down the street, screeching to a stop at what used to be the Corona's house.

Gothel gaped when he recognized the rider: a frazzled and exhausted-looking girl with short raven hair. Relief crashed into him like the current of the river, and he had to take a breath.

She was okay.

Her eyes found her house first, or what embers were left of it, and her strangled gasp tore through the cloudy air. Then Zachary shouted, "Rosy!" and started dragging himself across the grass toward her. Genevieve collapsed into tears, and Sterling ran up to the horse, practically yanking his daughter off and crushing her against him. When Zachary finally reached them, sobbing, Rosalind pushed herself out of her father's arms, fell to her knees, and pulled her brother into a hug.

Numb with relief, the back of Gothel's neck started prickling in warning. Now that he knew she was safe, now that he was on the edge of the scene rather than right in the middle of it, he remembered that he did not belong here. That it was dangerous.

Slowly, to not draw attention to himself, he got to his feet and glanced around, wondering how he was going to get past the family's notice. He'd have to scale the back garden wall and hope for the best.

He started backing away just as another horse raced down the street like Rosalind's had minutes before. Prince Roman and his advisor, Griffin, dismounted. Rosalind and Zachary called out to them, and while Griffin's scarred face remained as impassive as ever, the prince broke into a wide grin of relief.

No, Gothel did not belong here.

Two steps closer to the garden wall. Three. He truly wished Rosalind the best, and something in his chest ached at the thought of never seeing her ever again.

But if he didn't leave now, he'd never see anything besides the inside of a prison cell ever again.

Four steps. Five. One of the men that had helped Sterling pulled the prince aside, and Gothel froze when he stabbed an incriminating finger in Gothel's direction.

The prince's glare zeroed in on Gothel, and even from across the grounds he could feel the burning accusation.

Gothel's stomach dropped as he realized this was it.

He'd been caught.

Prince Roman quietly beckoned Griffin, and the two of them started for him, the prince emanating hostility, and Gothel knew he wouldn't get any leniency in his sentence. For a moment, his feet wanted him to run, but his mind knew better: the prince alone could down him with magic in less than a second, and he would probably make it hurt.

It was over.

Griffin took the lead, coming around to circle Gothel from behind while the prince cut him off at the front. Gothel turned to keep them both in his sight.

What's your play, Gothel? His mind whirled in a frenzy, desperately trying to find a way out. As the prince and his advisor closed in, the movement caught Rosalind's eye from across the grounds. She looked up over Zachary's shoulder. Her eyes widened, and she gasped as she read the situation.

Time stilled for a moment: Gothel's heart pounded in his chest as every eye turned from him to Rosalind.

"No!" The scratchy shout burst from her lungs, and she staggered to her feet. Both Sterling and Genevieve said something to her, but they were both drowned out. "No!"

She ran for Gothel, but the prince caught her around the waist as she passed him and held her back. An awful, raspy scream tore from her throat as she kicked violently against his hold, and everyone froze as Griffin's eyes slid from Gothel to the prince.

"Rosalind, calm down," Prince Roman said as he struggled to keep a hold on her, a lilt of panic seeping in. "He can't hurt you anymore. It's okay."

She just hysterically screamed, "No!" over and over again, making Gothel flinch and Zachary start crying. Rosalind slipped out of the prince's hold just as Genevieve shouted at Sterling, and Griffin took a step toward the prince.

"Rosalind, stop!" Prince Roman yelled, both he and Sterling running after her while Genevieve threw herself in front of sobbing Zachary and told the neighbors to leave. Gothel realized their fear just as Griffin held up his hands and Rosalind crashed into nothing. It startled him to see her fall to her knees right in front of him.

Eyes wide, Rosalind threw her fists in front of her, only to have them meet an invisible wall. Griffin had put a magical barrier around her.

"Let me in there," the prince demanded. Gothel was shocked when Griffin pursed his marred lips and shook his head. Prince Roman glared at him.

Griffin didn't back down against the royal order, even though Gothel thought obeying was his job. "If she loses control," he said, his voice like chilling gravel, "I can't guarantee your safety."

"I don't care!" Frustrated, Roman tried to talk her down from outside again, but Gothel could see she was too far gone for that. Only one word reflected in her haunted eyes:

Trapped.

The panic in her expression exploded, and she started hitting the wall and screaming in a frenzy.

The sound grated on Gothel; he couldn't stand it. He surged toward her, though he didn't know what he could do, and Griffin's gaze snapped back to him. It was an effort to not run away from that heated gaze—especially with Sterling and Prince Roman to back him up—but Gothel stood his ground.

"She has the metal ring on," he growled. "She can't hurt anyone. Let her out."

"Get away from her," Roman snapped back.

Still screaming, Rosalind lurched to her feet only to shudder, lean over, and throw up. It looked like she might actually snap in half.

"Let her out!" Gothel shouted. "She has the ring on!"

Sterling nodded at Griffin, and the advisor lowered his hands. Before the prince could grab her again, Rosalind launched herself at Gothel. He caught her before she fell, and she latched onto him, and he found it alarmingly easy to support her slight weight.

"You aren't taking him!" She shook so hard. "You can't. You can't." A cry of pain went through her teeth, and her nails bit into his burnt arms. He suddenly felt a lot of sympathy for her scarred palms.

Griffin's gaze was locked on the silver ring. His fingers twitched uneasily when the prince stepped closer to Rosalind, as if he didn't believe the metal was really a suppressant. What lengths would he go to in order to protect his prince?

He had to get Rosalind out of here. She didn't need to be a part of this.

"It's okay," Gothel told her quietly, even though it was anything but okay. His eyes darted between the three powerful men circling around them—men that wanted to lock him up for life, at best. Kill him at worst. "You can go home now. It's okay."

"No." Her voice cracked, and she pressed her back against his chest as the men around them advanced. As if she could protect him. "No, no, no, no. It's wrong. Please no."

Sterling's eyebrows furrowed as he looked between the two of them, but the prince and his advisor didn't look like they cared about anything but burying Gothel deep in the ground.

"It's okay," he said again. He didn't know how he kept his voice even. "I'll be fine."

She finally seemed to get a handle on herself, enough to speak coherently. Even if she did sound mildly crazy. "I know what you think, what it looks like, but please let me explain. I can. I can explain. You can't arrest him. You can't."

"Listen to her!" Zachary shouted from behind as he clung to his mother. Genevieve glanced between her daughter and her husband, as if holding her breath.

Prince Roman's voice softened, though his eyes still shot daggers at Gothel. "Rose, you're really hurt, okay? Let us help you. You can tell us everything tomorrow."

She shook her head. "Then he stays with us tonight."

The prince scowled. "Absolutely not. Griffin will take him—"

"No!" she screamed again. Gothel couldn't stop himself from flinching, and that caught the attention of both Roman and Sterling. "No, you can't! You—"

"Okay, Rosy," Sterling said, taking a cautious step forward. "Take a breath. I will listen to what you have to say, okay? Just take a breath."

Rosalind wasted no time on breathing. "It was at the party. We were at the party and then—"

"Hang on." Sterling's gaze flicked to Gothel for a second. "I'd like to go somewhere private." He gestured to the gardener's cottage on the edge of the property, which looked untouched by the fire. "I don't think Raf would mind if we used his place for a bit to rest and catch up. Is that okay with you?"

Her shoulders shook as she tried to catch her breath. Several heavy seconds passed. "But…" The whispered words trembled and her grip on his arms tightened. "But once I leave you'll take him away. I'll come back and he…he'll be gone."

He'll be gone. Gothel's stomach lurched. Because the last time that had happened…

Sterling's face fell. He took another step forward. "No, of course not. I would never do that to you. Do you know that? You're safe now. You're safe." He waited a few moments until she slowly nodded. "Why don't we have Gothel stay while we talk? Just stay right out here. Would that be all right with you?"

A couple beats of silence. Then she whispered, "Yes."

Sterling reached out his hand. Keeping her grip on his arms, Rosalind twisted around to look at Gothel.

"I'll come back for you," she rasped. "I will."

Memories of tight blonde curls and the scent of cherries assaulted him, pummeling him with the harsh truth.

Nobody had ever come back for him.

Gothel could barely make himself nod, if only for her sake. She took a wobbly step away from him, and he didn't let go of her until Sterling had picked her up.

"Do you mind watching our guest for a bit while we talk some things through?" Sterling asked Griffin.

Gothel tensed. Out of everyone here, the scarred advisor, with his permanent scowl and nearly bared teeth, scared him the most.

"Not at all, sir," Griffin responded.

"Thank you. We'll be back." He carried Rosalind to the rest of her family and said something quietly to Genevieve. She pursed her lips and nodded once, then pulled her daughter's head against her chest and kissed her hair. When she finally let her go, Genevieve picked up Zachary and carried him to a neighbor's house. The kid waved at Gothel as he disappeared.

Then Sterling took Rosalind to the gardener's cottage, and Prince Roman shot Gothel one last dirty glare before he turned and followed. Rosalind's hollow gaze stayed trained on Gothel until Sterling took her inside. Even from across the grounds, Gothel heard the door click shut, and he felt the sound reverberate in his bones: the sound of a jail cell closing.

Griffin turned all his focus on Gothel, like a predator scrutinizing its prey, and Gothel tried not to shudder. He half expected Griffin to haul him to an execution right then. When that didn't happen, he found a clear spot to sit down and drink in the stillness of the night. His last dredges of freedom.

He was going to prison for a long time.

They were gone for hours. Despite Griffin's watchful eye, Gothel found himself dozing against the garden wall when he heard the door to the gardener's house open. His spine straightened when only Sterling exited.

"You can go home Griffin," Sterling called to the advisor, who had barely blinked during his post. "Thank you for your help."

Griffin nodded curtly before turning and disappearing into the night—was he *walking* back to the palace? Sterling watched him go for a moment before he headed for Gothel.

He held his breath as the Corona approached. Here it was: after all these years, he was going to be taken down by the man he had hated the most.

Surprise jolted through him when Sterling came right over and sat down on the ground next to him, face pale and posture bent with exhaustion. "Nice night, isn't it? Nicer if all the smoke would clear, of course."

Gothel sat stone still, unsure what to do. Was this some kind of trick or power trip? Going to prison was bad enough; Sterling didn't need to gloat about it.

"I'm assuming you took the gardening job to learn our house," Sterling said, staring straight ahead, just like Gothel. "Then took the opportunity of the party to sneak her out unnoticed. Am I right on that?"

Gothel swallowed hard. "Yes, sir," he managed.

"Hm. And you did all this to pay off a debt that you had to Pepperjack? That was how she got there in the first place."

He wanted to explain himself, let Sterling know that he didn't mean for Rosalind to end up there—in his plan, she always came back home and she never got hurt. But then he realized that Sterling was a Corona and Gothel was a nobody, and nothing he said would matter. So he settled with another, "Yes, sir."

"Hm." Sterling paused for a moment. "And then your friends came back for her—well, for Zachary, but then for her. To finish the job you all started."

Gothel couldn't talk anymore. He just nodded.

"They're all in prison now, where they'll be for a while. That Boone, especially, has quite the criminal record to pay for."

Something inside him winced at the news. He waited, brushing a burnt part of his arm with his fingers. This was it. All these years of running and surviving, all gone. For some reason, instead of mourning his freedom, all he could think was how disappointed Donna would be.

Sterling took a breath and shifted so his arm was resting on his knee. "I know what she said. What some of those criminals have said. But I want to hear it from you."

"Sir?"

"I want to hear your side of the story, Gothel. How did it happen?"

Never in his life did he think his side of the story would matter, but Gothel was so caught off guard, so tired, that he told Sterling everything, from the moment he came up with the plan at the forum to pulling Zachary out of the burning house.

Sterling listened with perfect attention, only interrupting once or twice to clarify a detail.

"I know you have no reason to believe me," he finished, his hoarse voice growing quieter. "But I never meant for this to happen. I never wanted her to get hurt."

"Hm." Sterling nodded thoughtfully, taking a few moments to mull it all over. "I understand where things might have spiraled out of control. Things can get messy, though I don't know that as well as others. I did once go a few months without using magic, just to get a better understanding of things. Helped me get appointed to the council, actually."

"You went without magic to get appointed to the council?" He didn't mean for the words to sound so accusatory.

"Not for that reason, no. It was for me. Once I realized the people around me thought I was crazy for even suggesting the idea, I decided to keep my project a secret. I pretended to go off travelling while really I was living under different names in different villages, doing different jobs without magic. Asher and I went to academy together—he was prince at the time, of course—and one day he came to Genevieve to ask where I really was. At his prodding, she let him in on my secret. When I returned, the prince appointed me his advisor, which ultimately led to the royal council." Sterling gave a wry grin. "Of course, the old guys didn't like us coming in and causing all this change, but that's what new generations are for."

There was a moment of silence as Gothel took that in. It was a lot to chew on, nearly too much to swallow.

Finally, Sterling took a deep breath. "My point is, I believe everyone deserves the chance to make a living for themselves, whether they were born with magic or not. But that's beside the point. I'll be honest with you, Gothel: nobody here is your biggest fan. I *will* say that you saved both of my children's lives, and that's not something I look over or forget. Rosalind says she wouldn't be alive without you, and after what I saw...what...what you pulled her through..." His voice cracked, so he cleared his throat and started over. "I might be the only one besides Rosalind and Zachary at this point, but I'm willing to give you the benefit of the doubt."

Gothel's eyebrows furrowed. He was afraid to see where this was headed.

"Rosalind told me the whole story—or, she told me the parts she wanted me to know. I'm sure there are many details she left out, likely to spare me. She..." He cleared his throat again. "Her story matches up with yours. She argued with everything she had left against you going to prison. She says she won't stand for it, and both Roman and I are having a hard time saying no to her right now, as you can imagine. She sees you as a friend, and, as you may have noticed, she doesn't have many of those. She's a very guarded person, oftentimes too distant to reach. But it seems you have.

"That being said, here's my proposition: instead of going straight to prison, how about we start you off on probation? I'll give you a job to begin working off your debts. If, after three months things are still good, we can start working with Roman on getting you pardoned and back to a real life."

The world froze for a second. Gothel went rigid, sure he hadn't heard right. How far would Sterling go just for a cruel joke? The man didn't seem to be joking. But he had to be.

"Um, sir?"

Sterling gave a faint smile. "I hope we can be friends someday, Gothel, but, for now, I'm going to have to keep a sharp eye on you—and make no mistake, if you do threaten her or my family, I won't hesitate to give you over to the law. But Rosalind wants you here, and I'd like to give you a chance. If you're okay with it, I believe it's the best situation for all of us. What do you think?"

What do you think?

"Uh, I...honestly I don't know what to think, sir."

"You expected to be going to prison?"

Numbly, Gothel nodded.

"But you came back for her anyway. Can I ask why?"

"I..." A dozen answers ran through his head before the truth came out. "I just thought she deserved a better ending than that."

Sterling's blue eyes glistened, and for the first time, Gothel saw him as a regular person—as a father. "Well, thank you for that."

Then Sterling brushed off his pants and stood, so Gothel did too, though he wasn't sure what was supposed to happen next.

"She wants to see you," he said with a gesture to the gardener's cottage. "Proof that nobody locked you up while she wasn't looking." He paused for a second, swallowing a lump in his throat. "It was bad there, wasn't it?"

It was an effort not to shudder, and he didn't even see everything she had. "Yes, sir. It was."

"Hm." He nodded and collected himself once again. "Would you be willing to come see her? I imagine she doesn't have much longer before she passes out."

"Yes, sir."

The door to the gardener's cottage opened just as they reached it, and Roman stepped out.

"I got her to drink a little bit more," he told Sterling with a glance behind his shoulder. Gothel had never seen him so tired and...human. Like a mask had been peeled off. "She's managed to keep it down so far. I nearly had to tie her to the bed just to keep her there." His eyes flicked to Gothel, the aversion in his expression now battling with begrudging gratitude. "She's asking for you. Made me swear about six times I wouldn't arrest you, even after I told her I accepted her terms. Are you taking that probation deal?"

It was a struggle to keep his composure; Gothel's mouth fell open for a second. Sterling hadn't been lying after all. "Um, yes, sir. Your Highness."

The prince nodded to himself, then took a breath. "Look, I don't like you, but Rosalind would probably be dead without you. I owe you for that. And I...I understand starting out thinking you're doing something right and then it turns out to be wrong. Regardless, thank you for bringing her back."

"Yes, Your Highness."

"Please," the prince said, "call me Roman. Any friend of Rosalind's, however misguided, is a friend of mine. Also, thanks to her advice, I'm assembling a new council to represent orphaned children. Their first task will be to investigate the current system and ensure everyone is being treated fairly and humanely. If you have any ideas on how to improve the system, I'd like to hear them. I have time next week for a trip to Flynnigan's, but I could also wait and go next month if she needs the time. She said you have to come as well, so just let me know when you're available."

Gothel blinked in disbelief. "Uh, that's...you don't have to—"

"Oh, sure I do." Roman waved his hand. "I'm not doing it for you, anyway. Visiting orphans is a princely duty I would actually enjoy. It's too bad I haven't thought to do it before. Plus, Rosalind is really excited about it." His face fell, and he glanced at Sterling. "It's good to give her good things to look forward to. I imagine the next few months are going to be rough. I hope you all can heal."

"They will be." Sterling shook his hand and squeezed his shoulder. "Thank you, Roman. We owe you a debt."

"No, of course not. Rosalind is my family too."

"And I thank you for that too. I know you'll always be there for her, no matter the personal cost to you."

"No matter the cost," Roman echoed as if dazed. Then he gave a soft, sad smile before nodding at them and turning to head home.

"That boy has gone through a lot," Sterling muttered with all the affection of a concerned father. "It's a miracle he hasn't cracked under the weight on his shoulders."

He opened the door and gestured for Gothel to go in. They walked through a small kitchen before entering the bedroom in the back. Rosalind lay curled in the tiniest ball on the bed. Her pale skin nearly blended into the sheets, and her bones protruded underneath, but despite the crevices of pain lining her face, she smiled in relief when Gothel walked in. He'd never really seen her smile before, and between the expression and new haircut, she was a far cry from the girl he'd first taken.

"You're still here," she murmured. "No more tricks."

Gothel nodded. "No more tricks."

She glanced at Sterling standing in the doorway behind him. "Daddy can you give us a minute?"

A second of awkward tension passed, and Gothel could feel Sterling debate if it was a stupid idea to leave her alone with a criminal, especially after everything that had happened.

But looking at her wide eyes, shorn hair, haggard face...who could say no to her now?

Sterling's eyes softened into an expression so loving Gothel had to avert his gaze. "Five minutes, okay?" Then he squeezed Gothel's shoulder before turning and leaving. The gesture was so foreign, and his skin almost burned where he'd been touched. "I won't be far."

Silence settled between them, heavy and awkward. It hit Gothel now that they truly were just strangers. Without ransom plans and escape routes, they didn't really have anything to talk about.

Or maybe they had too much. But how were they supposed to talk about what had almost happened in the Jacklands? Or what had really happened to her after they'd separated—the parts she'd left out for her father or maybe couldn't even think of herself?

His gaze wandered over her skin stained with blood and bruises to the two thick wounds around her wrists from the roots that had held her down. Again, he tried to block out the sound of her screaming.

"They told me what you did," she finally said. Her gaze had settled on his burnt arms. "You should hear Zachary tell the story—I think you'll be his hero for the rest of his life."

Gothel shrugged. Rosalind studied him for a second. It seemed she'd been the only person that had ever really *seen* him, and Gothel still wasn't sure what to do with that.

"I'm sorry I told them about the orphanage," she let out in a rush. "It was just an important part of the story. And I wanted to help Donna."

Gothel blinked in surprise.

"I didn't tell them about your mom, though. That's just yours." Her forehead creased. She looked like she might break. "Should I not have?"

Finally, Gothel regained himself. "Ah, no," he told her. "Or yes. It's okay."

She deflated in relief. "Okay. I didn't want to make you upset." A fleeting grin appeared on her face. "I told you Roman would come. Elyse is going to be so excited."

His stomach turned to lead at the thought of returning to the orphanage—as it always did—but the corner of his mouth pulled up at the thought of going back with her. "Elyse is going to lose her mind."

Rosalind let out a breathy laugh that turned into a hacking cough. Her shoulders shuddered violently as she pushed herself up on her elbows just in time to spit up all over her pillow. Gothel managed to fall to his knees and catch her by the shoulders before she face planted into it. She moaned through her teeth and clenched her hands into fists. Sweat broke out on the back of his neck as he saw her wrist wounds and remembered her scream. Would he ever be able to forget it?

"What's wrong?" he demanded, ready to shout for Sterling to come back. It was a stupid question: she looked days away from death.

"No." She swallowed hard and tried to sit up. "Don't...don't get them. I didn't want to show this much...I already hurt them enough. I'm okay. I'll be okay."

Her body was skin and bone, and even with the little bit of healing magic Genevieve had used when Rosalind was unconscious, his shadow was a wreck.

"What did he *do* to you?" Gothel growled through his teeth. The question was supposed to be banned from his mind, but it snuck through.

A dozen different nightmares flickered in Rosalind's eyes, crushing the rest of the resolve that had kept her calm so far. She started hyperventilating, her frail form trembling violently, and her gaze flicked everywhere in a frenzy, as if the walls were closing in on her.

He read the panic in her eyes again: trapped.

Without thinking, Gothel scooped her up, and she clung to him with her broken fingernails like she expected someone to rip her away. A muffled sob escaped her as he walked as carefully as he could outside.

He set her down on the grass and sat next to her. She scrambled back into his shoulder, shaking, and he kept a protective arm around her.

"See?" he told her, watching closely for any sign she was about to lose it. "Stars. Sky. You're free."

"Stars." Her voice wobbled as she repeated it. She took a deep breath and tipped her head back to look at the sky, and that seemed to help ground her a bit. "The stars. I missed them."

Gothel sat stiff and tense, unsure how stable she really was.

"Do you believe in the goddesses?" Rosalind asked softly, as if afraid of her own voice.

"No," Gothel answered, surprised. Not many people believed in the goddesses or even really talked about them as more than some old story. Donna had tried to teach him, but he hadn't been interested. If they did exist, what had they ever done for him? "Do you?"

"I didn't. But...but I think I might now."

"Why?"

"I think they helped save me."

"Why do you think that?" He could only half concentrate on the conversation. His free hand tapped anxiously against his leg.

"Because I..." Her voice caught for a second. "I was in the deepest, darkest, scariest place. Underground. Lost. I was all the way down there, so far from the sky, but I prayed anyway. And they heard me."

A few moments of silence passed. Rosalind dropped her head, so she looked at the ground now.

"I think...I think my father...I think he's afraid of me...hurting myself."

Gothel stiffened. His heart started pounding.

"You're afraid of it too," she whispered. "I can tell."

He could've lied, but he knew she would know that too. So he asked the only question he'd been able to think since he'd walked into that cottage. "Will you?"

More silence. Gothel thought his heart would pound out of his chest.

"It's complicated," she finally answered. "But when I...when I can think clearly, I don't think I really want to. It's when I get caught up in...when I...um…" She shuddered again with another sob, and Gothel found he was grateful when she buried her face in his shoulder, if only because it made him feel like he could keep her safe.

"About Peppe—" She choked, like the name physically hurt her to say, and she had to start over. "About *him*. I...I don't know what to say."

Gothel's skin crawled at the memory of Pepperjack's body, but his bones also sighed in relief. He could never come after Gothel or hurt Rosalind ever again. "You don't need to say anything."

Her voice shrunk with her shoulders. "I'm...I'm sorry. I don't know what else to do or say or...Roman and my father are working to cover it all up, so nobody knows what I did, or that I was there—and I'm grateful for that, I am, really, but...it still feels...wrong." The words cracked as they left her mouth, and he had a feeling that these were some of the words she'd held back from her father and her prince. "I hurt all those people...*killed* all those people...and I...I just go home?"

"They didn't deserve it?" Gothel asked darkly.

She raised her head and her wide, wet eyes darted to his. "Would *you*? You could have been in that crowd. In different circumstances, the slightest change in chance, it would've been you. And you don't deserve that. A lot of them were monsters, maybe, but most were just trying to survive. You can't blame them for that, just like I don't blame you for anything that happened."

Gothel blinked, the jolt of surprise overtaking her perceptive observations. He'd heard her wrong. "You...you don't blame me?" Just repeating the words, seeing the genuine confirmation in her eyes, made a heavy weight slide off his shoulders and fall to the ground.

"No." She stiffened, as if suddenly realizing she was touching him. "You aren't afraid of me?"

"No."

She took a shuddering breath. It sounded painful. "Okay then."

"You've been through enough," he said quietly. For the first time in his life, he adamantly agreed with Sterling trying to cover something up. "Living with it is punishment on its own."

He froze the second the words were out of his mouth. Of all the *stupidest* things to say when she was in such a fragile state...

Thankfully, she didn't notice. She took another breath and leaned her head against him again. "I finally talked to Zachary," she said. "*Really* talked to him. For the first time in years. He told me...he told me he doesn't blame me for what happened."

Her tone went airy, as if she couldn't believe it. "He said he never did."

Gothel didn't realize he'd gained any respect for the kid, but it grew even more now. "Maybe you shouldn't either."

"Maybe." She gave a half shrug, then went quiet for a second. "Did they tell you...well they probably did. About Boone and Ulf and the rest of them?"

Tensing, Gothel's jaw worked at the thought of them. "What about them?"

"They're in prison now. Roman arrested them. They'll have a trial and all, and I...I'll probably have to testify." Her voice grew smaller. "I'm sorry."

"You're *sorry?*" he snapped, harsher than he meant. "Why?"

"Because they...weren't they like your only friends?"

"Oh. I...I don't know. I guess." He couldn't say he'd be very friendly if he saw them again.

"I told them you didn't turn them in." She said it like a victory and Gothel almost smiled. "I'm pretty sure they knew too. But it felt good to throw it at them. You deserve better."

You deserve better. Never in his pathetic life had he heard those words.

Rosalind tilted her head up again to look at him. "Thank you."

He was so surprised that he snorted. "Thank you? For what? Kidnapping you?"

She grinned faintly. "No. But if you were like Calder or Boone things would've gone very differently. Very badly. And not just for me—Zachary would've died if you hadn't gone back for him. I guess...thank you for being...you."

Gothel blinked, stunned to silence. After a long moment, he managed to clear his throat. "Don't mention it, Princess."

"Rosalind," she corrected.

The corner of Gothel's mouth twitched up. "Right. Rosalind."

Dropping her head against his shoulder, she curled herself in a ball and leaned more on him as if she would fall asleep. Stars knew she needed it. But then that got Gothel thinking about where *he* would be sleeping—not in a prison cell, apparently, but as part of the house that once represented everything he loathed. And he had the daughter of that house tucked underneath his arm, the person he had once conspired against but would now risk his own life for.

How did he get here again?

"Did my father tell you about the job?" Rosalind asked softly. Not asleep after all.

Gothel grunted. If she hadn't brought it up, he wouldn't believe it had actually happened, and now he wondered how hard she had to fight for it. "Yes."

"What do you think?"

"I think it's crazy. And I can't...I can't believe it's real."

"You came back for me," she said. "So I came back for you."

So I came back for you. She had, in more ways than one.

"How did you get them to agree?" he asked her.

"I just told them what I really thought. The truth."

"Which is?"

"That you could be so much more than this. If you had the chance. And I think if they can truly give me another chance after what...what I...what I've done, then...they can give you one too."

He didn't have anything to say to that. Who *was* this girl?

Several seconds of quiet passed. "You'll stay, though, won't you?" she asked.

Pursing his lips, he really considered the offer. It wasn't anything like his usual plays—more like the exact opposite of what he'd decided to do. All his life he'd been running from everything and chasing nothing, wandering without purpose and refusing to let anything try to fill up the empty void. His mother, the orphanages, Boone and his crew, all the stealing to hide the fact that he couldn't take what he truly wanted...it was all smoke in the air. Water in his palms. Nothing real to hang onto.

But Sterling's clap on his shoulder, Zachary's hand clutching his, Rosalind's form tucked under his arm—those were the realest things he'd felt in a long time.

What's your play, Gothel?

Taking a breath, he looked up at the hazy stars. "Yeah," he answered. "I think I'll stay for a little while."

* * * * * * * *

The transport rattled along the rocky road, the wood shuddering against the rough terrain. Eight people filled the rows of seating, each clad in dark, armored suits and carrying their weapons of choice. Some were talking quietly with each other. Marshall had his eyes closed in prayer while Moyra mouthed the plan to herself as if she hadn't memorized it in the last week—each rituals for the two of them. From her seat, Rosalind watched the world pass by through the window. After what seemed like a lifetime locked away, she still marveled every time she got the chance to see someplace new. The explorer in her hadn't completely died off.

But also, secretly, she had claimed the window seat as hers because she needed something to look at, an assurance she wasn't trapped, a distraction to keep her eyes open. Every time she closed them, she saw another nightmare.

Zachary in a puddle of red. Boone climbing into her room. Strangers piled up around her. Pepperjack's crimson eyes.

All monsters she had to live with.

But living with her monsters had led to discovering others. Turned out, the graveyard wasn't the only place Pepperjack had kept his human pets, and he wasn't the only criminal that traded in people. And the only thing that could get Rosalind through her nightmares was knowing she did something about them.

Roman had given Rosalind a team of six of his best trained, specialized guards—he'd wanted to give more, but she insisted six was fine—and they had become her task force. In the last eight months, they'd raided five prisons and liberated nearly a hundred people.

Roman had tagged along the first time, just to see what it was like. Sometimes her father came too, but he couldn't always with work. She brought Zachary once (on an extremely safe case), and he hadn't stopped talking about it since. Often they found people who no longer had a home; Rosalind brought them back to her house and her mother took care of them for a while.

Rosalind had missed her family. 'The ordeal', as it was known in her house, had made her realize that she needed people—she needed *her* people—and they meant more to her than anything else.

Many of the prisoners she saved kept in contact, and her circle of family had only grown with the amazing people she met during her missions. And the foundation of that was Gothel: he came with her everywhere, whether a dangerous raid or just a strategy meeting. Out of everyone, he was the one she trusted the most, and as he had worked the last few months to help rebuild their house, he had earned trust from Zachary, her parents, and her team. And after a few awkward interactions, an orphanage visit, and an alliance made to pull Rosalind through her kidnappers' trials, he and Roman had become unlikely friends.

Even though she and Gothel had carved places for themselves in the family, there were things they kept to themselves. Like the few details she'd managed to tell him of her imprisonment with Pepperjack. Or details about Gothel's mother, father, his past. His watch. Magicless technology was illegal, so they kept their interest to themselves and waited for the right opportunity to come their way.

Rosalind glanced at him, as she often did, just to make sure he was still there. He caught her eye and gave an encouraging nod.

Yes, despite the awful circumstances that had brought them together, she thanked the goddesses in the sky that she had him.

As the world passed by out the window, Rosalind had to stifle a yawn. She hardly slept anymore. She hadn't been able to sleep in her room at all since she'd gotten home, so she usually slept on one of the couches in the living room, or on the floor of Gothel's or her parent's room. If she were out on a sofa, Gothel would always sleep on the other one, and stars knew how many times she'd woken him up in the night after hearing a strange noise only to find it was the wind or a creaky stair or her imagination. She didn't sleep much, and because of that, Gothel didn't really either. But he never complained, even if her nightmares and fears woke him up several times in one night.

The transport slowed to a stop, and everyone rose from their seats. Rosalind touched her finger absently, ensuring the ring was still there, as she found herself doing more often. The metal still made her sick, but sick was better than the alternative.

When she had free time, she met up with Irina for training. Her father knew she was training with *somebody*, and probably guessed it was the strange woman that had shown up to fight Pepperjack only to disappear, but Rosalind kept Irina's origins a secret, and her father didn't press it. Training helped a little, made her feel like she could gain a semblance of control, or at least release the buildup of power inside her. But it was a hard battle. Her 'magic muscle,' as Irina called it, just wasn't strong enough to handle so much raw power. Even the fairy admitted a few months ago that Rosalind would likely never attain a completely safe level of mastery. There was always hope, of course, but she had to face the real possibility that without the ring, magic may always be a danger to her. Another monster to live with.

Some days, her monsters overwhelmed her, and she could barely breathe. She would lock herself in her room and drown in her bed sheets like nothing had changed. Other days, she painted with her mother, played with Zachary, visited Roman, strategized with her task force, read a book, or even worked with Gothel. She found purposes. She didn't have everything figured out, but she had found ways to live.

Maybe life wasn't about figuring it all out. Maybe it was just about growing a pile of good things and living off of it. Isn't that what Irina had said? Balance of all things. Good and bad. Joy and pain. Light and dark. No one was complete without the other.

That day in the Molds, she had thought her story was over, that it should be. And even now, on her really bad days, she had doubts. In all the stories she read, once the princess went on her adventure, she came back better, fixed, and she lived happily ever after.

Rosalind had found it wasn't that easy. She found it took bravery and strength and a kind of desperation to keep her pages turning.

Maybe she was the monster in her story, but she'd started to understand that wasn't her only role. She could be the hero too, the one that saved everyone else—and the one that sometimes had to ask for help to save herself.

She had never been able to choose her story, but she was writing the parts she could. And she lived with that; she had to.

Marshall and his group exited the transport first. They were the muscle, the ones that got the rest of them in and out safely, no matter what. Nobody moved without Marshall's consent, which made Rosalind feel better. Marshall was a good man.

On her left, Gothel stretched out his legs and bounced on his feet, bursting with unused energy after being cooped up in the transport. She would have smiled if she didn't feel wound so tight. Missions, while the only things that made her feel true peace, also unraveled her. She always had to breathe deeply and focus, to highlight her surroundings and make sure she didn't get memory confused with reality. Yes, this was a prison, but she was no longer a prisoner.

On her right, Moyra, the team leader, waited for Marshall's command, her body leaning toward Rosalind as though she were ready to jump in front. And she was. Roman had specifically given Moyra the job of keeping Rosalind alive and safe. It only took one trip with Roman, Sterling, and Gothel for them all to be convinced that Moyra would do just fine, and they let Rosalind continue with her task force vision.

Honestly, Rosalind had been surprised. Everyone had treated her so softly since the ordeal, and they rarely left her alone anymore, which wasn't as scary as it used to be now that she had the ring. Sometimes it was suffocating and a bit annoying, but Rosalind managed, for her family's sake. She couldn't complain about having people who cared about her.

Marshall's whistle of safety echoed through the air. As usual, Moyra motioned for her to wait a second, but, as usual, Rosalind surged ahead, out of the transport, knowing her team had her back. After all, nothing was scarier out there than what she had already faced.

The sky was swathed in a blanket of clouds after having sprinkled a spring rain on the world. The air smelled clean and refreshed, the earth ready to be revived after a harsh winter.

Six scruffy-looking guards were bound on the wet ground with Lark and Sven watching over them. Riz and Delle were flanking the dungeon entrance, a cave-like slab of rock with an opening that led underground.

Rosalind had to stop for a moment, caught between past and present. Jeej and Moyra. Jack and Marshall. Memory and reality.

Gothel nudged her softly with his shoulder, a word of comfort in the language they had developed between them. Taking a breath, Rosalind blinked her nightmares away and focused on her task, focused on the people, and soon her feet were moving forward again.

The dungeon air was thick with dust and the stench of human neglect. Rosalind breathed through her mouth as she made her way through a downhill tunnel, careful not to trip.

Gothel had to duck his head to follow her, and Moyra never let Rosalind get more than three steps ahead.

Eventually, the tunnel opened up to a cavern lit with candles. A sea of eyes glinted in the light, and a rustle of murmurs rolled through the echoing air.

Rosalind's breath caught, and her eyes stung. Two cells, barely the size of her room combined, stuffed with at least thirty people. Most were caked in dirt and dried blood, and several looked to be knocking on death's door.

Memory and reality. Two different things.

A woman jammed against the bars took one look at Rosalind and gasped, her eyes widening with terror as she rattled off a desperate plea under her breath.

Rosalind nearly tripped over her own feet as she rushed forward. Dropping to her knees, she put her arms through the bar and took the woman's hands in her own.

"You don't have to be afraid anymore," she said softly, meeting the woman's eyes. "My name is Rosalind. And I'm here to save you."

Emilee King is the author of the Arie's Story survival series and the Elarian Chronicles. She loves fairy tales, superheroes, and murder mysteries, and is constantly on the hunt for good stories. When she's not writing, you can find her reorganizing her bookshelves, eating food, beating the high score on Galaga, or spending time with her family.

@emtheauthor

www.emileeking.com